THE

SILENT ORDER

THE
SILENT ORDER

MELANIE DOBSON

summerside
PRESS™

Summerside Press™
Minneapolis 55438
www.summersidepress.com
The Silent Order
© 2010 by Melanie Dobson

ISBN 978-1-60936-019-1

Scripture references are from the following sources:
The Holy Bible, King James Version (KJV).

All characters are fictional. Any resemblances to
actual people are purely coincidental.

Cover design by Chris Gilbert | www.studiogearbox.com.

Cover images: iStock Photo and Amana/Corbis

Interior design by Müllerhaus Publishing Group |
www.mullerhaus.net.

*Summerside Press™ is an inspirational publisher offering fresh,
irresistible books to uplift the heart and engage the mind.*

Printed in USA.

PROLOGUE

"Let's go home," Nikki whispered, her lips quivering. Even her toes, squashed into the sharp points of her strapped Mary Janes, wouldn't stop shaking. "Liz..."

"Hush," her sister hissed as she swung open the side door of Mangiamo's. Nikki held up the small battery-powered lantern, and the shiny countertops in the kitchen glowed.

Nikki's knees knocked under her navy blue skirt and she pressed them together. Her father's employees left the restaurant hours ago, around midnight or so. Everything inside was still except her heart, which had been hammering in her chest since she and Liz snuck out of the house. Somehow Liz had secured the key to the side door of Mangiamo's, but she wouldn't tell Nikki why they needed to get inside.

"No one knows," she whispered as the door creaked closed behind them. No one would find out she and Liz were here.

Their parents and older brother were asleep in their large home, a few blocks up Murray Hill. As she and Liz snuck down to Mayfield Road, the usually bustling streets in Cleveland's Little Italy were draped with an eerie fog. The silence unnerved her—even the alley cats had stopped howling for the night.

As Nikki followed her sister across the kitchen, Liz pulled a second key out of her purse.

Nikki gasped. "Where did you get—"

"I told you to shut up," Liz barked as she pushed the key into the lock of another door—a door that kept the kitchen staff out of their father's private lounge.

Nikki leaned closer. "Papa's going to kill you."

"He'll have to catch me first." Liz laughed, sounding more like she was twelve than twenty-one.

Her sister teetered daily between the frivolities of her youth and the weight of adulthood. The shiny red barrette in her bobbed black hair matched the red bow on her scalloped dress. Even in the dull light, she exuded glamour.

Until this moment, Nikki never thought to ask why Liz was dressed to the nines—she was still trying to wake up after her sister shoved her out of bed in the middle of the night, saying she needed help. She hadn't told Nikki why they needed to come here, but it didn't matter. Nikki always seemed to be on call for her older sister, and Liz knew it. She covered for Liz whenever her sister slipped away to visit one of Cleveland's many nightclubs.

But never before had Liz tried anything as daring as breaking into Mangiamo's back room. Their father's sanctuary.

Their brother was allowed inside this room when invited—and he bragged about it often—but Salvatore never talked to either of his daughters about the place. Didn't really talk to Nikki at all. She knew the extent of his fury, though, and she feared him almost as much as the spineless henchmen who bowed to him like he was God on earth. She'd never bowed, but she usually cowered when he was around, hoping he wouldn't notice her. He rarely did.

Her sister wasn't afraid of anything, including their father. She had the gift of being able to charm almost any man. If their father discovered them trespassing in his den, though, no charm would work. Discipline would be swift. And painful.

The knob turned in her sister's hands, and as she cracked open the door, the stench of cigar smoke mingled with the lingering smells of spicy sausage and cheese from the kitchen behind them.

"Liz—" she repeated.

Liz grabbed the lantern from Nikki's hands. "Tell me if someone comes to the front door."

Light illuminated the gray stone that lined the narrow staircase below them. Her sister stepped down and slowly descended into the dungeon.

Nikki propped the door open with her heel, waiting in the darkness. She had thought there was a small room in the back of the restaurant, not a basement, but she wasn't surprised. Secrets bound their family together like the tangled silk threads layering the web of a black widow.

The girls at Nikki's school envied these seemingly luxurious threads, but she knew that the Cardano money only covered the secrets with a blinding sheen that most people couldn't see past. She and Liz knew the truth, and they were trapped in their family's web for the rest of their lives.

Her mother refused to talk about their family's secret life, and her father usually refused to talk to her, period. Silence stopped even the walls of the Cardano mansion from sharing their secrets, but the walls knew. They knew about her father's mistress over on Woodland Avenue. They knew about the bitter tears her mother shed. And they knew about the dirty money that surged through her family like water from a fire hose, money that never seemed to extinguish the smoldering inside her father for more.

Nikki watched the light in her sister's hands turn the corner at the bottom of the steps, and she rested her back against the post, praying Liz would hurry.

Light from the city lamps trickled in through two small windows at the side of the room, illuminating the shiny tops of the kitchen ovens and the draped tables that filled the dining room. Instead of windows by the imposing front door there was a wall filled with paintings of Italy.

The restaurant couldn't possibly support the Cardano family lifestyle, nor could the factory where her uncles refined sugar, but there was always plenty of money. Some mornings she walked down the stairs and the dining room table was hidden under silvery green mounds of cash. Someone supplied her father with thousands and thousands of dollars at least once a week, but she didn't know who paid him, nor did she want to know. She just wanted to rush out the door each morning before the others woke up to join her friends at Saint Anthony's.

Their mother liked to pretend that her husband's business ventures were perfectly legitimate as she tried to induct her daughters into the high society circles like they were members of Cleveland's elite. Two years ago, Liz began rebelling against the dog-and-pony show and decided to flaunt herself in circles not so pleasing to their mother. The more their mother and father disapproved, the happier Liz seemed to be.

Salvatore ignored Liz's exploits for a long time, but everything changed in July. For the past three months, her father had kept Liz home around the clock, under surveillance. On the rare occasion that her father let Liz go outside the estate, she was escorted by two of his bodyguards.

Tonight, however, the man who was supposed to be standing guard outside Liz's door was sleeping beside it instead. Nikki assumed Liz, with her smooth words and alluring smile, offered him a couple of drinks from the stash she snuck into her room under her longer dresses.

The lantern light blinked below her.

"Liz?" she called in a hushed voice.

When her sister didn't answer, her gaze wandered back toward the six rows of tables that separated the kitchen and the front door. The chairs and table settings appeared to be in their proper place; there was no hint of the loud patrons who had departed four hours ago and no bloodstains left from the man shot inside the parlor back in March.

Nikki shivered. Did the man's ghost stay behind to haunt those who'd murdered him?

She glanced back down the staircase, at the light bobbing on the wall below. She should have asked Liz why they needed to come here in the middle of the night, but it was much safer to play along than ask questions.

A sharp click sounded in the dining room, and her heart leapt. Turning, she squinted in the dull light, but nothing moved. No one was in the restaurant at this hour, she told herself. No one but her and Liz.

She whispered her sister's name one more time, but Liz didn't respond.

Holding her breath, she pressed her hands against the doorframe and pretended to be one of the Sicilian statues in her father's pictures. If the murdered man had come back for vengeance, perhaps he wouldn't see her. Surely he would know she didn't have it within her to hurt a soul.

She peeked around a column as the front door crept open and a man walked inside, built thin as a rail and a good head taller than she was. The evening was warm, yet he wore a dark overcoat and hat, the uniform of a Cleveland Mafioso.

And he looked very much alive.

She stepped down into the stairwell. If anyone except their father caught her and her sister, they might bump them off, and there were no guarantees with their father.

She and Liz had to get out of here.

Nikki locked the door behind her, and as she rushed down the stairs, she struggled to catch her breath. Air didn't come until she reached the bottom, but even then, her breathing was shallow. The room in front of her seemed to spin.

Steadying herself against the wall, she took a deep breath and hiccupped.

The basement was one room, a dank space fortified with cold stone and a solitary brown hat rack that hovered in the corner. An old table stood in the middle of the room, surrounded by folding chairs, where the men probably dealt business ventures along with their cards. At the side of the room, a much shorter set of steps led up to a storm door.

Liz swiveled around by an open closet door, a narrow metal box clutched in her hands. "I told you to stay upstairs."

"But someone's—" Nikki didn't finish her sentence. The door above her swung open, banging into the wall. Apparently her father wasn't the only one with a key to this place.

Liz shoved the lantern into Nikki's hands and tucked the metal box under her arm. Then she stepped toward the second set of stairs. Nikki followed her lead, but at that moment, the storm door began to shake. Someone else was outside.

Liz swore and grabbed Nikki's arm, shoving her into the closet. Liz squeezed into the tight space beside her and yanked the door closed, the lantern shining like a beacon until Liz punched the button on top. The closet turned black.

On the other side of the door, Nikki heard muffled voices as several men greeted each other. At this time of night, surely this meeting wouldn't last long. They'd finish whatever deal they'd come to resolve and disappear back into the night. She and Liz would escape minutes later, going home to the safety of their beds before daylight. No one would be the wiser.

Her ear pressed against the door, Nikki strained to listen to the men's words. Rough talk about the Puglisi family, interfering coppers, and the blessed Volstead Act floated under the thin crack beside her feet and burned her ears. They were making a pact to work together under the nose of the government.

A hiccup swelled in her throat again, and she swallowed hard, holding her breath for a good minute. When she finally released her breath, her hand raced to her mouth to squelch another hiccup, but in her panic, her fingers knocked the lantern in Liz's hands. She groped for the lantern in the darkness, trying to stop its fall.

Liz reached out to catch the lantern, but when she did, the metal box in her arms fell to the floor, and the crash echoed around them.

Nikki froze.

Liz swung open the door to the closet, pushing Nikki in front of her, and Nikki stumbled forward. Chairs slid back, and the men at the table opened their coats. She saw her father's face first. The anger etched in his eyes. And there was another emotion she'd never seen before.

Fear.

Her brother sat there, stunned. And all three of her uncles.

There was another man beside them. A man with bushy blond hair.

Nikki watched in horror as the blond man reached for his gun.

"Stop, Heyward," her brother yelled, but she could see the malice in Heyward's eyes. He wasn't going to stop.

"Blast it, Nikki." Liz shoved her toward the storm door, her eyes still focused on the blond man. "Run."

Heyward shouted, commanding the others to shoot. Nikki snapped out of her stupor when she saw the gleam of his gun. Racing up the stairs, she slammed open the storm door and burst outside.

Cool air flooded over her as a gunshot echoed down the alleyway. Lifting her skirt, Nikki ran into the billows of the fog, but with every step, her sister's face trailed her. The faces of the men haunted her soul.

Another thread for their family's web of secrets. A thread she could never escape no matter where she fled.

CHAPTER 1

August 1929

Shadows danced along the sculpted wings of an angel trumpeting from the tombstone's spire. In the starlight, the angel looked like she was about to take flight over the columned mausoleums on the hillside and the placid lake below, over the shady alleyways along Mayfield Road and the sugar refineries and stills that supplied Cleveland with the hooch that had turned their beautiful city into a bloody battleground.

Only an angel could see and hear what went on behind locked doors in Little Italy, but Detective Rollin Wells and the rest of the police force were supposed to find out who was supplying the goods to make liquor. And they were supposed to stop it.

Leaning against the trunk of a red maple, Rollin lifted his fedora and raked his fingers through his thick hair. Tree limbs brushed over the angel and the other tombstones in front of him, the warm breeze dusting the engraved heads of lambs, eagles, and lions. Everyone on the hillside was resting in peace except him and his partner. They'd been waiting more than two hours in the old cemetery, but it was long past midnight now and no one else had joined them.

Lance Dawson flicked a match to light a cigarette, and the orange glow between his fingers flickered like a firefly in the darkness. He took a long drag and then held out his silver case. "You wanna smoke?"

Rollin shook his head. "No, I don't want to smoke."

"It'd calm you down."

"Calm?" His voice climbed a notch. "This is not the time to be calm."

Lance slid the case into his front pocket and shrugged. "I just thought it might do you some good."

Sweat pooled under Rollin's starched white collar, and he loosened the striped tie that felt like a noose strangling his neck. At twenty-two, his new partner didn't know a thing about the liquor industry—he barely knew a thing about life. Rollin had nine years—and a heck of a lot more experience—on the kid.

When the captain assigned Lance to work with Rollin, Malloy said Lance's idealism might rub off on him, but Rollin didn't need idealism, nor did he need some naïve kid backing him up. Naïveté was a death wish along Mayfield Road. And downright annoying.

Lance took another draw on the cigarette and smoke filtered out of his lips. "I hate to tell ya, boss, but they ain't comin' tonight."

Rollin's nerves chilled like steel. "Yes, they are."

"Nah." He took another drag of his cigarette. "They're out gambling or raising Cain down on Woodland."

"My contact told me they'd be here tonight."

Lance tapped his cigarette against a branch and ashes sprayed over the bark. "Your little contact has been wrong before."

Rollin brushed his hands together. "One of these days, our canary is going to sing big, and you and I will be ready."

"Sing 'Mine, All Mine' maybe," Lance muttered.

Rollin loosened the knot in his tie another inch. His contact better sing a whole lot more than a silly jazz tune. His little bird promised him to help bring down the powerful Cardano family's hold on the East

Side, but promises were cheap in the underground world where black and white smeared into gray.

The angel in front of them might be able to look inside a man or woman, see the motives behind their actions, and perhaps even see if they were being lured over by the bribes or the power. But he and the other overworked police officers had to rely on bad guys who were willing to trade information for immunity. Bad guys who often pointed fingers at the ones who were supposed to be good.

The business got bloodier by the year. In the past seven months alone, eight criminals and three bystanders had been shot. The criminals didn't seem to care who they killed, as long as they kept their power. And most of their cash.

A big chunk of their blood money went directly into the pockets of corrupt cops and politicians who pretended they couldn't smell the telltale creosote and burnt sugar odors that emanated from attics and basements and shops boarded up long ago. But Rollin wasn't getting kickbacks, nor would he take one if offered.

Everyone knew the Cardano family's refinery was the chief supplier of sugar to Cleveland bootleggers, who used the sugar to make and sell liquor, and now he was close to proving their business was a racket. He needed to bring them down soon. There had been rumors in the underworld that powerful racketeering families like the Cardanos and Puglisis might unite and form a powerful alliance that would make it almost impossible for him and the other detectives to disband.

Before the local gangs united, he would unravel the Cardano family enterprises and put Salvatore "Club" Cardano and his squalid band of nephews behind bars.

Lance threw his cigarette on the grass and ground it with his toe. "I'm getting hungry."

"You're always hungry."

"I'd like a decent dinner for once." Lance leaned back against the tree and closed his eyes. "Onion soup, maybe. A nice whitefish."

"I hate fish."

"And Crêpe Suzette."

Rollin's stomach growled, but it wasn't like there was a restaurant open at this hour. Even if there were, it wouldn't deter him. "So go find yourself some fancy place to eat—tomorrow night."

Lance reached up and plucked his jacket off a branch. "I'm going home."

"No, you're not."

"I think you're crazy, boss," he said as he pushed his arms through his jacket.

"Get in line."

"We should have told the captain we were staking out this place tonight."

"Malloy doesn't care a bit about surveillance. He wants proof."

It was a lie, but he hadn't wanted to tell Malloy or anyone else except his partner about what might happen tonight. All it took was one person to overhear, a person with loose lips, and they'd never find out what was going to transpire on this hill above Mayfield Road.

Right now, he wished he hadn't even told his partner.

Lance shoved his hands in his pockets. "We all want proof, but we ain't gettin' any tonight."

"We'll wait here all night if we have to."

"You'll wait here." Lance stepped out from behind the tree, and

Rollin wanted to slug him. "I've got to get my beauty sleep before spending another ten hours with you."

"No amount of sleep is going to make you beautiful."

Lance laughed. "I like you, Wells."

"I might like you if you'd stick this out."

"No can do." Lance punched his shoulder. "We'll get 'em tomorrow."

The kid was grinning tonight, even as he was tossing in the towel. What kind of person smiled as he admitted defeat? This wasn't idealism. It was insanity, and he was pushing Rollin over the brink as well.

Lance took another step. "You comin'?"

"Nope."

"You need your beauty sleep even more than I do."

Rollin fingered the pistol in his holster. He'd never been tempted before to use it on a fellow cop. "I'll take you to get some fish this weekend. Over at Marie's or the Hotel Cleveland."

Lance spun around to face him. "What'd you say?"

"You stick with me for one more hour, and I'll buy you a decent meal."

Lance crossed his arms. "I don't want to go to dinner with you."

"Feeling's mutual," he muttered.

"But if you pay for a ritzy dinner for a dame and me," he said, "I'll take her out on the town in my new machine."

"Fine," Rollin said. He was tired of Lance talking about his new Chevy. Tired of hearing Lance talk, period. "But you have to clamp that trap of yours shut for an entire hour."

"A half hour…"

The churning sound of an engine cut off his words. Lance's head whirled toward the sound, but his feet didn't move.

"Get back," Rollin hissed.

Lance sprang toward the tree, ducking behind branches, as an automobile crept up the hill. Rollin watched a black Cadillac as it parked under a willow tree about thirty feet in front of them, beside the tombstone with the angel. The tree dangled limbs over the front window like it was trying to lure its occupants out of the car, but none of the four doors opened.

Rollin saw the second vehicle before he heard it. A tan coupe, it was moving even slower than the Cadillac as it rounded a bend and parked on the other side of the road, closer to a cliff above the lake.

Rollin's fingers brushed over the leather holster again, and he felt his Colt 45 strapped to his hip.

Two more automobiles worked their way up the hill, but both of them stopped short of the hilltop, parking in the shadows of the mausoleum. Rollin squinted, trying to see the models of the cars, but he couldn't tell in the darkness.

Which of the men had brought reinforcements—and why?

The front doors of the Cadillac snapped open and four shoes hit the dirt and grass with a soft padded sound. The tan coupe's door creaked open as well, and he watched Antonio Cardano step out into the night air. A twig cracked as Antonio crossed the narrow lane, toward the two men who stood like soldiers beside the towering angel and the grave she guarded.

In spite of the warm summer night, the three men were dressed in dark overcoats. Even with a pistol at his side, Rollin suddenly felt naked. There was no telling what kind of arsenal each of those men hid under his coat. Probably enough to take down half of Cleveland's police force.

The men faced each other, and Rollin held his breath, listening.

Lance had one foot behind him like he was preparing to run down the other side of the hill, and Rollin placed his hand on Lance's shoulder with a quick shake of his head. If Lance ran, the men would pop them off before sunrise.

His last partner never left him, not for a good night's sleep or because he was afraid. And no matter how scared he was, Lance wasn't going to leave him tonight. This job wasn't made for those who were scared of their shadow or the shadows of men like Club Cardano and his family.

"You're a smart man for coming alone, Junior." Rollin recognized the raspy voice of Leone Puglisi, the boss of the Puglisi family.

Antonio shrugged, his voice strong. "You didn't give me much choice."

Leone's laugh sent a chill down Rollin's stiff spine. "Sergio and I want to talk about a little deal with you and your family."

Rollin watched Antonio step back. "We're not looking for a deal."

"It's not about looking for a deal, my friend." Leone brushed his hand across the front of his coat, leaning toward Antonio. "It's about needing one."

"We don't need your assistance."

Leone clapped the younger man on the shoulder. "You've lost three people in the past month alone. Profits are down."

Antonio shrugged again. "It's only a hiccup."

"Hiccups can be fatal." Leone rolled his thick neck. "All we want to do is offer you a little protection, a brother helping a brother."

"Protection?" Antonio's laugh sounded weak. "At what cost?"

"The cost would be minimal, and I can guarantee your distribution will increase, along with your profits. We could call it a partnership."

"We're not looking for a partner either," Antonio said, and Rollin almost smiled. He could relate.

"Maybe I'm not making myself as clear as I should." Leone took a step closer. "This is an offer you can't refuse."

"You mess with me, Leone, and you'll start a war."

"Where have you been, Junior?" Leone's voice chilled. "The war's been raging for a year."

At one time locals called Leone Puglisi the Sugar Baron of Cleveland, but there was nothing noble about him. Rollin had heard rumors for years of plots to kill Leone. Last year, Captain Malloy gathered enough evidence to put the man behind bars, but he wasn't in prison for long. The Puglisi family figured the Cardanos assisted the cops with the evidence against their leader. The Cardano family figured the Puglisis were trying to take over their share of the sugar business.

Rollin figured both families were right.

Leone walked out the prison doors in June, and the tension between the Cardanos and Puglisis was even worse than before he went to the pen.

Rollin watched a man quietly climb out of one of the vehicles beside the mausoleum, followed by another six or so men. The men left their car doors open as they swarmed the tombstones and trees along the edge of the hill. For an instant, Rollin considered running away, but instead of retreating, he hugged the tree even closer.

Leone stepped forward. "We need your answer."

Antonio turned and started walking away. "I'll think about it."

Leone's bodyguard reached out and grabbed Antonio's arm, stopping the man. Across the hillside, Rollin watched the darkly cloaked men step out from behind the tombstones, their weapons poised.

"You better think fast," Leone said.

Antonio didn't turn. Shrugging off the hand, he kept walking toward his coupe, but when Antonio opened the door, Leone reached into his coat. Rollin never saw his gun.

A deafening blast rocked the hill as gunshots splayed across the tombstones. Rollin ducked behind the tree, his mind racing, but his feet didn't move. He and Lance were no match for a mob of armed Sicilians.

When Rollin separated the leaves again, he saw the powerful head of the Puglisi family and his bodyguard on the ground.

"Who'd they get?" Lance whispered.

Rollin hushed him.

Seconds later, the men surrounded Antonio, and the group marched like a regimented troop toward the bodies. Antonio kicked Leone, and his body rolled over.

"Good work, fellas." He thrust his hands into his pockets, sarcasm weighing his tongue. "Now, let's get rid of them."

In a flutter of arms and legs, the men gathered around the large bodies, struggling to lift them. The retribution from the Puglisi family would be brutal...or at least Rollin thought it would. With Leone dead, the entire organization along Mayfield Road would change. And perhaps change was exactly what Antonio and his gang wanted.

The regiment dragged the dead men to the side of the hill, and one of the dark coats kneeled down by the men's feet, tying something around them. The mob heaved both bodies over the edge, and a splash echoed across the hillside.

The men stepped back.

Antonio spoke first. "I don't want to read a word of this in tomorrow's papers."

Heads nodded, gathering around him, but Rollin didn't hear anyone else reply.

"We aren't going to lose our focus," Antonio said. "And we are not partnering with anyone."

"What about Sugar Creek?" one of the men asked. Rollin arched his neck, struggling to hear the man's response.

Antonio was quiet for a moment. "Sugar Creek is more of an alignment."

"Without the Puglisis?"

"The Puglisis are irrelevant."

Irrelevant? The families of the men feeding the lake's bottom fish wouldn't settle for irrelevancy.

Antonio slid into his coupe, and the eight hatchet men stalked back to their vehicles beside the mausoleum. Their cars bled into the night as they cruised over the hill.

"Are they gone?" Lance whispered.

"Not yet."

Antonio had climbed into his car, but he didn't start it. Seconds passed, and when everyone else was gone, Antonio stepped out again, cradling something in his arms. He crossed the street, back toward the tombstone with the angel, and he crossed himself as he rattled off a short prayer in Italian. Then he set something on top of the grave.

Back in his car, Antonio putted down the hill, but Rollin continued to wait, five minutes and then ten. He tugged his tie close up to his neck. "Let's go see the damage."

They proceeded cautiously around the stones, across the grass. On the other side of the road, the two of them looked over the cliff at the pristine water below, the calm ripples on the lake's surface reflecting in the starlight.

His partner lit another cigarette. "At least they rid the world of one more Puglisi."

"I wish it had been a Cardano."

"Next time."

Rollin crossed the street again, toward the spiraling column where the men had met, to see what Antonio had left behind.

"Give me one of your matches."

"I thought you didn't want a smoke," Lance said as he held out a match.

Rollin took the match Lance offered and struck it against the stone. The smell of sulfur mixed with the sweet aroma in the bouquet Antonio had rested against the grave. The blaze in his fingertips flickered, and he held the firelight up to the epitaph on the stone.

Dear God.

His fingers shook as he reached, tracing her name in the cold stone, and then his gaze wandered up to the top of the tombstone, to the angel watching over Mayfield. He hoped the angel was taking much better care of the woman buried here than he was of the bribery and fighting down below.

CHAPTER 2

Icy water tingled Katie's toes, and she picked up her pale blue skirt, splashing her son with a swift kick across the surface of the creek. Henry dodged the stream of water, but both of his hands plunged into the creek, and he showered her white *kapp* and face.

"Henry Lehman," she exclaimed as she wiped the water off her cheeks. "Don't you know you're supposed to respect your elders?"

"You're not an elder, *Mamm*." He picked up a stick and twirled it. "But you are old."

"Why you…" She reached out and ruffled the curly hair that, in spite of her rigorous combing, refused to lie flat on his head. "It's a good thing you're so cute, Henry."

He scrunched his lips into a silly face and crossed his eyes. "I'm not cute."

"Cute and *kindish*."

He puffed his chest out. "I'm not a *kind* anymore."

The hem of Katie's skirt grazed the water as she hopped to another rock. Above the pebbles and willow trees, white clouds sprayed the wide sky, and the scents of honeysuckle and sweet hay filled the warm air. August was her favorite month. Work eased a bit as they waited to harvest the corn, and she loved the long sunny days and stolen hours playing with her son.

No matter how fast Henry was growing, he would always be a child in her heart, and she desired the same things for him as any good mother does for her child—to be safe and secure and content with the life God had given him. One day he would be a man, and she prayed he would be a man who loved his family and respected those around him. A man who feared God and God alone.

The putter of an engine interrupted her thoughts, and Henry hopped out of the water, watching the path that led down to the creek. A motorist would be hard pressed to get their vehicle up that bumpy trail, but she'd stopped trying to guess what an Englisher—an outsider—would or wouldn't attempt to do. A tourist might have gotten lost on the main road and tried to take a shortcut back. Or maybe it was a car full of teenagers looking for fun.

The whirring sound grew louder, jarring the stillness, and Katie stepped up onto a rock that jutted from the water. The stone's warmth felt good on her wet feet, but her pulse raced at the growing noise.

Henry looked back at her, his blue eyes wide. "What is it, Mamm?"

"I don't know."

The cattails along the waterside began to dance as a breeze gusted up the creek, and the cascading leaves on the willows joined their dance. Something flashed in the sky, and Katie's eyes narrowed when she saw the airplane over the trees, not forty feet above them. Metal glistened in the sunlight, and the plane's bright green skin looked like papier-mâché pasted around its body. The pilot dipped one of the yellow wings, and she shivered as a dark shadow crossed over her and Henry.

Then the plane disappeared.

His mouth agape, Henry turned toward her. His lips quivered, but no words came out of them.

Both her fists flew to the safety of her hips. "That was an airplane, Henry."

"An airplane." He said the word slowly. Reverently. "How—how does it stay up?"

"It has an engine, like an automobile."

Henry blinked. "Automobiles don't fly, Mamm."

"Some can almost fly."

His eyes searched the sky again for the plane, but the sound had tapered off into a faint buzz like that of a pesky fly. She'd seen that look before on his face when they were in Sugarcreek and a luxury Peerless or Packard drove into the village. He and the other boys stopped their games and practically drooled with admiration. The older men watched the automobiles as well, but most of them kept their admiration in check.

With God's mercy and wisdom, Henry would be different from other men. She would gently guide him until he saw how dangerous the machines—and the outside world—were.

Hopping off the rock, she crossed the creek and placed her hand on her son's shoulder. "People get hurt in airplanes, Henry."

He slowly turned away from the sky to meet her gaze. "Sometimes people get hurt in buggies too."

She sighed, pulling him into a tight hug. Then she released him to look in his clear eyes. "Are you certain you're only eight?"

He stepped back, crossing his arms over the bibs of his overalls. "Mamm…"

"Because you are way too smart for eight."

His chest puffed out a couple inches, and he pounded it. "I'm almost nine."

"I'm sorry, Henry." She shook her head solemnly, glad he wasn't asking any more questions about the flying machine. "I'm afraid I will have to forbid you from turning nine."

"You can't forbid me."

"Oh yes, I'm quite certain that I can."

He laughed. "You are the one being kindish, Mamm."

With a grin, she stuck out her tongue at him. "No, I'm not."

His eyes on her, Henry reached down into the creek and swooped his hands through the water, soaking her arms and her apron. Then he turned and ran down the stream.

"Come back here," she yelled, hopping from stone to stone as she chased after him.

Her heart swelled. More than anything in the world, she was grateful for her son.

"Katie?"

When she heard her name, she turned and slid across the stones. Her arms flailed on both sides of her, searching for a tree limb, a hand, anything to hold onto, but there was nothing there. The world seemed to sink under her as she fell back into the water.

The creek water soaked her skirt and cooled her skin, but her face burned. In the blur around her, she saw Henry turn back to her, yelling to see if she was hurt. As she shook her head, she felt a man's strong hand on her shoulder, the man who had called out her name. Jonas Miller.

Her head felt like it was swimming along with the current as the giant of a man cradled his strong hands under her arms and lifted her out of the water. His hat fell in the water and sun dusted golden waves across his light brown hair and clean-shaven face. A sound came out of her throat, but it sounded more like she was choking on creek water than laughing. And when she tried to smile at him, her teeth chattered instead.

"Are you *shmatza*?" he asked. Hurt.

He sounded distraught, and she knew he was concerned about her condition. But even more than the bruises that would surely form on the backs of her legs, she knew he was concerned about her behavior.

Her toes still in the water, she bunched her skirt together and wrung a gallon of the creek back into its source. "I'm fine."

Jonas plucked his straw hat out of the water and looked toward the pathway that led to the house. She knew exactly what he was thinking. She should be up helping Erma can peaches in the kitchen instead of playing in the creek with Henry.

"Did you see it, Jonas?" her son asked, his eyes as round as silver dollars.

Jonas shook his head slightly. "See what?"

"The airplane! Did you see it fly?"

A shadow crossed over Jonas's handsome face, as if the plane had blocked the sun from his face as well. "*Nay*, I didn't see it."

Henry pleaded with him. "Then surely you heard it."

"The only thing I heard was your mamm falling into the water."

The smile rose quickly on her lips, laughter bubbling in her throat, but Jonas didn't laugh with her.

"He is fascinated with machines," she tried to explain.

She hoped Jonas would say it was no problem, all Amish boys went through a fascination with automobiles and even planes and they all grew out of it. But Jonas didn't offer her any consolation. Instead he studied her like she should be the one consoling him.

"Are you here to see Isaac?"

"No," he started. "We were supposed to…"

She stopped him. "Oh, Jonas, I'm so sorry."

The call of this beautiful day had been so strong that she'd completely forgotten that Jonas was coming. She should have been at the house, ready for him to take her and Henry to his parents' home for dinner.

She wiped the beading sweat off her forehead with the back of her arm. "*Kumma*, Henry."

Her son took her hand, and she turned back to Jonas. "We'll be ready in fifteen minutes."

Jonas nodded his head slowly.

She squeezed Henry's hand. "Maybe even ten if we hurry."

Her bare feet sank into the cool earth and leaves as she turned toward the pathway, tugging Henry along behind her. She wished she could read Jonas Miller's emotions, because he never talked about how he felt. He should be angry with her this afternoon, but it seemed he was just irritated with her that she was playing instead of working and waiting for him.

She never should have forgotten this dinner.

At the top of the hill, hidden by the trees in front of her, was the white farmhouse where she and Henry lived. She would quickly wash up and change into her lavender dress while Henry put dry clothes on as well. Jonas, she assumed, would wait in his buggy since Isaac was in the field.

A green garter snake slithered in front of them, and Henry squealed. As her son knelt down in the dirt, she sighed. If she stopped every few minutes to let Henry explore, they would never be ready in fifteen minutes.

Jonas waited in silence behind her.

During the past three years, Jonas Miller had become quite the expert on waiting for her. He'd asked her to marry him a long time ago, and when she couldn't give him an answer, he told her he would be patient while she made a decision. Many a night she'd lain in bed, trying to figure out why she couldn't just say "yes" to his proposition. Jonas would make a good husband for her. A good father for Henry. She should accept his proposal with grace and gratefulness.

But this decision was about so much more than her and Jonas Miller. It was about marriage, and it was about....

"Katie." Jonas's call to her was low, but it still felt like the icy creek water flooded her veins. She stopped walking and turned, wondering what he wanted from her now. "Could I talk to you alone first?"

Henry picked up the garter snake, and it wove through his fingers. She nudged him and his new friend toward the house. "Go change your trousers," she said. "I'll meet you in a few minutes."

After her son rounded a bend in the curved path, she turned and faced Jonas. His dark blue eyes searched her face, and she felt the smoldering fire in his gaze.

"I really am sorry, Jonas."

"You are always sorry."

"It's this day." She lifted her free hand to the sky as if the soft breeze and sunshine explained everything. "I got distracted."

He ground the heel of his boot into the ground. "And you are always distracted as well."

She stepped back, leaning against the crusty bark of an oak tree. "You shouldn't wait on me, Jonas. There are plenty of less distracted women who'd love to be your wife."

His eyes didn't leave her face. "But I don't want to marry those women."

She looked down at the hem of her skirt, burying her toes in a pile of leaves. "You have been a good friend to Henry and me for so many years, but it's not fair to make you wait any longer."

He took off his straw hat and twisted the wet rim in his hands. "Are you turning down my proposal?"

"No—"

He glanced down at his hat for a moment and then met her gaze again. "Then I will continue to wait."

"I'm not ready to marry."

"You don't have to make a decision until November."

The wedding month.

"I don't know when I will decide," she said. "*If* I will decide."

"One day you will have to make a choice, Katie."

She nodded, but she didn't want to choose. She was content with her life exactly as it was right now.

"You make your peace with God first," he said. "Then we will talk."

God had been just as patient with her as Jonas had been, but the thought of making either of these decisions was daunting. Her word was her honor, and she would never, ever take a vow she couldn't keep, whether it was to the church or to her husband.

"Do you still want us to join you for dinner?" she asked.

He watched her for a moment and then shook his head. "We will talk at the Yoders' on Sunday."

Nodding her head, she watched him walk back up the path. There were plenty of other Amish women across their county who would do just about anything to have Jonas Miller come visiting, but he had chosen her, and she had no idea why. And she had no idea why he continued to wait on her.

She heard the sound again above her, the whir of a plane's propeller. She looked up and watched the machine streak through the blue sky one more time.

She didn't want anything to change and yet things kept changing, even in the timeless hills around the village of Sugarcreek. She wanted Henry to stay eight. She wanted to remain friends with Jonas. And, more than anything, she wanted to run from any decision that would change her and Henry's lives.

CHAPTER 3

Cigarette smoke clouded the dilapidated station on Euclid Avenue, the stench of hard work laced with the acrid smell of smoldering tobacco. Twenty desks crammed into the open room and almost twice as many detectives and cops gathered around these desks in small pods to collaborate on how to stop the organized families in the *Unione Siciliana* from overrunning their city with Prohibition's dual offspring, otherwise known as bootlegging and racketeering.

Profanity spiced the whispered conversations along with the loud banter that volleyed across the room. Metal chairs scraped across the cement floor, and doors clanged from the cells that ringed the building. In the middle of the room, Rollin shoved a mass of paperwork into a pile, hiding it under his desk. In its place he spread a colorful map of Cleveland across the wooden surface.

He'd spent most of his life in Cleveland, and he'd never heard of Sugar Creek before. Was Antonio talking about aligning his family with others at this place? If he could determine the location, he was certain they could find out what Antonio was planning there.

With a sharp tug, he unknotted his tie and strung it over his coat, across the back of the chair, and began to pore over the ridged lines and dots on the map. But the lines on the papers blurred. The dark form of last night's angel seemed to haunt him, following him around the precinct today like she was curious about what he would find.

He rolled his neck and pressed his hands to his shoulders, trying to work out the knots. He had a job to do, and he wouldn't let her distract him again.

He blinked, his eyes on the map as he searched the waterways for a Sugar Creek. No matter how long it took, he would find out what Antonio was planning next, just like he'd found out about the meeting up at Lake View Cemetery last night.

Once their captain confirmed Leone Puglisi's murder, the news would sweep through Cleveland like an oil slick burning across Lake Erie. Half the force was down along Mayfield this afternoon, manning the corners and shops so no more bullets flew today, but the police couldn't stand guard forever. Leone was right—a war had been brewing for well over a year, and this last skirmish could set them up for a battle of unknown proportions. The Puglisis against the Cardanos.

If it weren't for all the innocent bystanders who would be hurt in a battle, he'd try and convince Malloy to let the Sicilians battle it out among themselves. It would make his job a whole lot easier if they could take each other out of the picture for good.

Too many people viewed the government's ban on alcohol as a business opportunity instead of a detractor, and the Volstead Act only swelled the demand for their goods. Everyone from the bottom up in Cleveland's law enforcement knew the Sicilian crime families were competing to be the sole refiner of corn sugar to make liquor, but they covered their tracks well when it came to distributing the corn sugar to their disreputable clientele.

He and Rollin were the only detectives in their precinct dedicated to thwarting families like the Cardanos and Puglisis, and there were only fourteen detectives in all of Cleveland fighting against organized crime.

Fourteen men with limited resources fighting against a stronghold of hundreds who made more money than John Rockefeller himself.

The odds would make a betting man laugh, but Rollin didn't bet nor did he laugh. He didn't care much about the other families, but he would take down the Cardanos, with or without Lance Dawson's help.

Drips of coffee sprinkled across his map, and Rollin looked up to see Lance with a mug in each hand.

The younger detective pushed a mug toward him. "Thought you might be thirsty."

Rollin glanced down at the coffee splattered across the map, but he took the coffee without complaining. "Thanks."

Lance twisted a chair around and sat down beside the desk, hands clutching his mug. "I was a jerk last night."

Rollin took a sip of the coffee, his eyes focused on the map. "Good observation."

"I was tired."

"Me too."

"I didn't think they'd show up." Lance inched the chair closer to the desk.

"And yet they did."

Lance paused. "I've never actually seen someone get a bullet through the head before."

Rollin traced his finger along Mayfield Road, stopping at one of the entrances to the cemetery. "It won't be the last time in this business."

Lance scooted the chair closer, lowering his voice. "How many people have you seen knocked off?"

"Too many to count."

Lance's hand shook, the coffee spilling onto the floor this time.

Rollin looked over at him. "Why did you take this job?"

He knocked on the wooden top in front of him. "I couldn't stand the thought of sitting behind a desk all day."

"Sitting behind a desk probably sounds pretty nice now."

"Nah," Lance said, his grin returning. "I'd rather watch a Puglisi get shot up any day."

"Just as long as it's not you being shot at."

The grin fell a notch. "I'll steer clear of the bullets, boss."

Rollin tugged on his chair, pulling it close to the desk as he contemplated the names on the map. "I can't for the life of me find a creek called Sugar."

Lance took another sip of coffee. "You're limiting your options."

Rollin looked up. "You know something?"

"I'm just wondering if Sugar Creek isn't a place," he said with a shrug. "Maybe it's some sort of code name for something else, like a place they hide their corn sugar. It could be near a creek or something."

Rollin rolled his neck again. Maybe he was limiting his options.

There was one person he could ask, but getting information from his contact was complicated.

There was one person he could ask, but getting information from his contact was complicated.

"We'll have to begin with the obvious first." Rollin took a pen from his top drawer and circled the creeks near Mayfield Road. Sighing, he counted twelve. "We could spend all day sniffing around these, but what exactly are we looking for?"

"A warehouse of some sort, I'm guessing. Someplace they're storing the sugar."

"Antonio said it was an alignment."

"Maybe they're pooling their resources."

Rollin tapped his pen on the map. "Who are they working with and why?"

"Whatever they're doing," Lance said as he tipped his chair forward, "they won't be able to keep it secret for long."

"Wells!" the captain called out from across the room, and Rollin hopped up from his seat.

Lance clapped his shoulder. "Good luck."

Captain Malloy slammed the door behind Rollin, the frosted glass shaking along the wall. Even as Malloy dropped down into the chair, he commanded attention. He was the tallest man at their precinct and probably the smartest looking as well, with his neatly trimmed mustache and tailor-made attire. Even if he didn't always agree with his tactics, Rollin had admired the man since Malloy recruited him eight years ago. Malloy was as devoted to cleaning up their city as he was.

Malloy propped his elbows on the desk, folding his hands together. "I just got back from Dempsey Lake…"

"And?"

"The divers recovered Leone's body along with the body of Sergio Nardelli."

Rollin glanced out between the bars on Malloy's window. His contact said last night would be big, but Rollin had had no clue as to how big. Not only had they knocked off Leone Puglisi, but now Nardelli was gone as well—the criminal who'd been accused but not convicted of taking the life of a Cleveland cop. The case against Nardelli had gone to trial, but the jury hung on the verdict like most juries seemed to do when it came to convicting anyone involved with bootlegging alcohol or racketeering the sale of it.

Malloy scooted to the edge of his seat. "What exactly happened last night?"

"I have a contact—"

"Who?" he interrupted.

"I can't say."

Malloy drummed his fingers together. "Go on."

"My contact told me something important was going to happen last night above Dempsey Lake."

"How did he know?"

Rollin shifted in his chair. "I can't say that either."

"You're just a wellspring of information, aren't you?"

Rollin pressed the soles of his shoes against the hard floor. He wanted to come clean with the captain, but he couldn't compromise his source. Not until they were ready to expose the entire Cardano family. "We wouldn't even know about these murders if it weren't for my information."

"I want you to treat this informer with kid gloves."

"Yes sir."

"We need his information."

Rollin nodded, wondering how much to tell Malloy and how much to keep under wraps until he had more evidence. When they finally unraveled the organization, his boss would hold a press conference and tout their hard work fighting crime in Cleveland. Malloy would have his moment in the spotlight, but Rollin had to make sure they had enough evidence to convict the Cardanos this time. Irrefutable evidence.

"So where exactly did Junior meet up with these men?"

Rollin thought about the tombstone—and the angel. He didn't want to bring her into this.

"They were along the road, near a mausoleum."

Malloy nodded. "We found plenty of blood on the road, but we don't know who shot them."

"Neither do I," he said. "Antonio was there along with about eight other men, but I couldn't see their faces in the dark."

"Antonio never seems to do the bloody work himself."

"He doesn't need to. He pays the other men well enough to do it for him."

"So we have two murdered criminals. No suspects." He eyed Rollin. "And no witnesses."

The captain was fishing, but Rollin didn't waver under Malloy's stare. If Rollin testified against Antonio right now, not only would it destroy any hope of him exposing the Cardano family operations, but his source would never speak to him again. He couldn't risk it, not until the time was right.

"Before they shot Leone…" Even though the door was shut, Malloy's voice dropped to a whisper. "What were they talking about up there?"

Rollin cleared his throat. "Leone was offering Antonio protection."

"I bet he loved that."

"Turns out Leone was the one who needed protection," he said. "Antonio mentioned something about Sugar Creek and an alignment, but I haven't been able to locate a creek by that name."

"What kind of alignment?"

"I have no idea."

"I've never heard of Sugar Creek, but I have a contact down at the library who is a geography whiz." Malloy scribbled down a name. "Visit him and then let me know what you find."

Rollin took the paper.

"Anything else?" Malloy asked.

"Nothing else significant."

Malloy stood up and shook his hand. "Good work, Wells."

"Thank you, sir."

"Why don't you take the rest of the day off?" Malloy opened the door and saw Lance waiting outside for him. "Take that partner of yours with you."

"We have too much work to do this afternoon."

"That's why you're my top detective, Rollin. You never quit."

Malloy shut the door behind him, and Lance stepped forward, a black box tied with a gold ribbon in his hands.

"Did Malloy tell us to go home?" Lance asked.

"I turned him down."

"You never want to have fun."

"Getting the Cardano family behind bars is a good time for me."

Lance shoved the box at him, and Rollin saw his name on the lid.

"What's this?" he asked.

Lance thumbed back toward the front door. "A messenger delivered it a few minutes ago, but he didn't stick around."

Rollin untied the gold ribbon and tipped back the cover to see a dozen pieces of candy, each one neatly wrapped in silver foil.

Lance dug for one of the chocolates. "You got a secret admirer?"

He eyed the note taped to the inside of the cover. "Apparently it's not so secret."

Lance grabbed another piece of chocolate as Rollin opened the note, reading the short sentence twice. He ripped the note into shreds and dropped them into his pocket. Then he grabbed the jacket on the back of his chair. "I'll be back in an hour."

Lance's mouth was stuffed with chocolate when he spoke again. "Can I go with you?"

Rollin shook his head. "Not this time."

CHAPTER 4

Pastries and fancy breads lined the glass shelves in the bakery window. Powdered shells of cannoli stuffed with ricotta cheese and chocolate shavings. Crème puffs. Rum cakes. Sugar cookies iced with pastel pinks and greens.

Rollin eyed the pastries and the CLOSED sign hanging inside the door. The sidewalk was empty for a moment so Rollin ignored the sign and pushed open the door.

She was waiting for him back in the kitchen, her black chiffon dress rustling from the breeze of a fan. The bags under her eyes matched the color of her dress and the feathers that sprang up from the back of her hat. Twenty years ago she may have been a striking woman, but she'd fallen hard from her diva position. The years—and her husband—had erased most of the beauty from her skin.

He took the iced glass of lemonade she offered him but didn't take a sip. "They killed Leone last night," he said.

"I doubt the Puglisis are crying."

"Maybe not crying, but they'll be hopping mad." He set the lemonade on a stainless steel counter. "Did you know they were going to kill him?"

"I suspected it." She took a long sip of her lemonade and seemed to be contemplating her next words. "Who exactly killed him?"

"It was dark, and there were a lot of guns."

"Antonio didn't do it."

He nudged the lemonade glass an inch. "He may not have killed Leone, but he orchestrated it."

Her eyes narrowed. "This isn't about Antonio."

Rollin crossed his arms as he stopped his retort. He knew exactly who this was about, but he had to tread softly with her. She was like an alley cat—one wrong move and she would either pounce with her sharp claws or disappear. He wanted to make sure she pounced, and when she did, he wanted to make sure she was leaping in the right direction.

Rollin brushed his hand across the worktable. "Why did you want to meet me?"

"They planned to take out Leone in secret so the Puglisis didn't retaliate."

"And now they are worried?"

"Antonio is searching for the leak in the ranks," she replied. "We can't meet again until he stops looking."

"He won't stop until he finds the leak."

"Perhaps not." She tapped her fingernails on her glass, the lemonade swirling inside. "But he has bigger things on his mind right now."

He glanced over at the back door and then toward the front entrance. No one was nearby but still he stepped closer to the fan so the sound would drown out his words. "What is Antonio planning next?"

Her gaze drifted over her fingernails, over the trays of cookies on the counter. Seconds passed, and then she looked back at him. "I'm not sure."

He met her eye, and she looked away again. He hated it when people lied to him.

"I've only heard bits and pieces," she said. "Something about a meeting."

Two years ago the Cardanos and Puglisis tried to coordinate a meeting of the *Unione Siciliana* at a hotel in downtown Cleveland, but before they met, the management had grown suspicious and called the police. Rollin and the other cops took in a few men wanted by the law and spooked the others away from the hotel. As far as he knew, the criminal society had never tried to meet again to unite.

Now that the Cardanos and Puglisis were enemies, maybe Salvatore and Antonio were organizing some sort of meeting without their rivals.

"What kind of meeting?" he persisted.

She shrugged, her shoulders swishing the chiffon. "Antonio doesn't talk about things like that when I'm home."

Lie number two.

"I heard him say something about a creek." Rollin stepped closer to her. "Sugar Creek."

Her face paling, she set her lemonade beside his and rubbed her arms like she was cold.

"What is happening at Sugar Creek?" he pressed.

Instead of answering, she stepped toward the door. "I must go home now."

His hand reached out to her shoulder, stopping her. "What are you hiding from me?"

She turned slowly, her weary eyes narrowed into small slits. "I've never heard of Sugar Creek."

"Too bad," he said as he released her shoulder. "Something big is going to happen there."

"There's enough going on around here without worrying about a creek."

"Maybe Antonio will mention something tonight."

"It doesn't matter," she said. "It will be weeks before I can contact you again."

With that, she turned, and her heels clicked against the tile floor as she walked away.

The screen door slammed behind her, but Rollin stayed staring at the place she had stood, like maybe she'd left the truth behind.

* * * * *

The porch swing rocked under her, and Katie leaned back as far as she could to watch the hundreds of stars lighting the night. God's display delighted her soul, and in a strange way, it comforted her as well. God had placed each of these stars in the right place, and with perfect precision, He had placed her and Henry here in Sugarcreek as well. A place they could belong.

A cow bellowed from the pasture, and the crickets chattered like women preparing for a Sunday lunch. Every summer night, after her chores were done, she snuck out to the front porch to enjoy the Lord's creation and thank Him for all He had done. For bringing her here.

The front door opened with a soft creak, and Erma Lehman stepped outside. Her silver hair glistened in the starlight, and the planks groaned under her as she crossed the porch and took her place beside Katie on the swing.

Erma pushed her wire-rimmed glasses up her nose. "Is Henry asleep?"

"He nodded off while he was washing his face." Katie smiled at the memory of her son's chin resting on his chest, water spreading like soft butter across his shirt. "I had to carry him to his bed."

"You won't be able to do that much longer."

"I'll do it as long as I'm able."

Erma patted Katie's knee. "I'd still carry my boys around if I could." Katie pushed the swing again with her heels.

"You should have seen Henry today." She leaned back on the swing again to see the sky. "He watched that airplane with a mix of fear and awe like it was a tornado whipping up over the hills."

"He should be afraid," Erma said. "It was the first time he saw a machine fly."

"I've never seen him so fascinated about anything before." She sighed. "He was still mumbling about it when I carried him to his room."

"It's *neiya*, Katie. It will pass."

"I hope so," she said, trying to sound confident. Erma hadn't seen the wonder in Henry's eyes or heard him shout. "Is Isaac feeling better?"

"He's recovering," Erma said. "I made him a tea with ginger root, oregano, and garlic."

"That sounds dreadful."

"And a teaspoon of honey," Erma added before she laughed. "But it still tastes terrible."

No matter the ailment, Erma always seemed to be able to concoct the right remedy. Tonight Isaac was suffering from body aches and a sore throat that stole his voice, but if his wife's concoction soothed his pain, Isaac would continue drinking the foul-tasting tea.

Silence drifted over them, and there was comfort in the quiet. Even though Erma was an expert at patching up people, her aunt could never fix Katie's problems, but it didn't stop her aunt from loving her.

Nothing seemed to frighten Erma Lehman, not even progress or the question of what would happen in the future. Katie wished her aunt could brew a tea to eliminate her fear as well. She'd drink whatever

Erma recommended if it would calm the anxiety that clenched her chest so tightly some days that it felt like it was about to suffocate her.

Katie pushed her feet on the porch, the swing gently rocking under them. "Jonas stopped by today."

"*Ya*, I saw him."

"I forgot we were supposed to have dinner at his parents' house."

"He cares for you very much." Katie heard Erma breathe in the night air. "And Henry as well."

"I know."

In the distance she could hear the creek trickling over the rocks and the gentle *clip-clop* of horses pulling a buggy up the road that ran in front of the house. Behind them, the windmill rotated in slow, deliberate turns. "Isaac and I would be pleased to see you and Jonas marry."

She took a deep breath. "Do you want me to leave?"

"Of course not, *dochtah*." Erma patted her knee again. "We would be very sad to see you go."

She loved it when Erma referred to her as a daughter.

"I would be sad to go too."

"But we both want what is best for you and Henry." She gently pushed the swing again. "Someday you will have to make a decision about your future, Katie."

Katie rubbed her hands over the edge of her apron. "That's exactly what Jonas said."

"He's right."

Jonas was always right. In fact, in the eight years she'd known him, she had never seen a single flaw muddy his character. Not once. She admired his sense of perfection, envied it even, but she could never live up to the standard of perfection that he placed on himself and everyone around him. Jonas's bar was way too high for her to reach, and she wasn't sure it was right to place those expectations on Henry either.

But then again, Jonas's high standards might be good for her son. It would give him something to strive for. A role model to follow. She could almost see Henry following Jonas's steady footprints across the fields and roads. Jonas's footsteps always knew where they were going—and where they came from.

Henry would thrive with a father who would teach him how to harvest corn and care for the farm animals and raise a barn—Jonas could be exactly what she needed to protect Henry and her both from the future's uncertainty.

Henry would thrive, but what about her?

Jonas Miller thought he knew her, but he didn't. Her past would muddy his impeccable reputation and perhaps even his character. Would he risk marrying her if he knew the truth?

"You have to give Jonas the option," Erma said. Without Katie ever saying the words, her aunt had an uncanny ability to read her mind. "If he knows the truth, he can make a decision—and so can you."

"He'll fly away faster than that airplane."

"Perhaps."

Katie pushed her heels against the wooden porch. "And if he does, what will happen to Henry?"

"Jonas might waver at first, but he'll make the right choice."

"Really?"

"Jonas is an honorable man, and you would bring him honor as his wife."

Katie put her arm around Erma's shoulders and squeezed. "You bring me honor."

Erma shook her head, and Katie imagined the older woman's cheeks were shaded red in the darkness. Isaac and Erma saved her life, but they were too humble to acknowledge their role in her salvation.

"The bishop won't let you marry Jonas until after you're baptized."

She sighed. "I keep hoping he'll make an exception."

"No Amish man can marry a woman before she's taken the vows."

The word vow made Katie shiver. It was so ominous. Permanent. Once she joined the church, she knew in her heart that she would never leave. It should be what she wanted to do. Joining the Amish church would give her a lifetime of peace and unity and contentment. And it would put an end to her fear of change.

But even stronger than her fear of change was her fear of losing Henry. When he grew up, what if he decided not to join the church and left Sugarcreek instead? And what if he did get baptized into the Amish church but then disobeyed the regulations set out in their *Ordnung*? The bishop could shun him for life.

No matter what the church did, she could never ban her son from her home or from her heart.

She wrung her hands together in her lap. "It's just too hard."

"No matter what you decide, Isaac and I will always love you."

"Thank you," Katie whispered.

"We are your family, Katie, but Jonas is not. He shouldn't have to wait for your answer any longer."

She'd told Jonas over and over not to wait for her to decide, but still he waited. Did she need to be firmer with him? Or maybe she needed to tell him a definite no.

But she didn't want to tell him no, and that was the problem. She didn't know what she wanted.

Erma brushed her calloused fingers over her apron. "Last church service, Ruth told me that Greta Hershberger has been following Jonas around like he was the Pied Piper."

"He should marry Greta."

Erma shook her head. "Jonas Miller should marry you."

Katie's gaze wandered across the front lawn of the house to the treed hills beyond. A couple miles up the road was the farm Jonas had purchased two years ago. When he bought the property, he'd implied that he was buying it for her. For them.

Sometimes she envisioned herself in his kitchen, in his yard. She could see herself planting the garden and hosting the church service in the barn. But there was one place she couldn't begin to imagine herself, and that was in Jonas Miller's bedroom.

A brilliant light streaked the black as a star fell from the sky.

Erma was right. She shouldn't keep Jonas waiting any longer. She would tell him the terrible truth about her past, and then together they could decide if she would become his wife.

CHAPTER 5

Cleveland's Main Library towered above the city like a boulder jutting up from the sea. Its columned façade fortified the rows of trees and businesses along Superior Avenue and reminded Rollin of the *Château de Versailles* he'd seen outside Paris. Inside the lobby, electric lights glowed off the marbled floors, and carved balusters accented the staircase that climbed to the top stories of the massive building.

The lobby was quiet on a Saturday morning. The only patron was snoring on a bench beside the front door, his mouth drooped open, his felt bowler hat hiding his eyes.

Rollin tapped Lance's shoulder. "Wake up, soldier."

Lance jumped to his feet and patted down his thigh, searching for his holster. Rollin grabbed both his partner's wrists and secured them until Lance's eyes focused on his surroundings.

His confusion quickly turned to a glare. "You told me to be here at eight."

"The trolley never came."

"You could've paid for a cab," Lance muttered as he stood.

"I needed the walk." Rollin glanced at the clock high up on the wall. It was almost eight thirty.

"Then let's move it," Lance replied. "I've got a date with my golf clubs this afternoon."

Lance followed him through the lofty doors at the side of the lobby. Books were stacked almost to the pressed tin ceiling, and the musty smell of paper and leather permeated the air.

As they walked toward the reference desk, Rollin scanned the rows of books written by novelists such as Louis Bromfield, Zane Grey, and Sinclair Lewis. Before she passed away, his mother read mounds of books, but reading fiction wasn't much of an escape for him—he was too busy fighting against real crime and corruption.

He did enjoy reading about history on the occasional Sunday afternoon when he wasn't working. As King Solomon once said, there is nothing new under the sun. Corruption and betrayal shaded every new century, and people could learn a lot about the present if only they'd take the time to learn about the mistakes and regrets of the past.

Behind the reference desk was a skinny young man with short brown hair and smeared spectacles. When Rollin flashed his badge, the man sat up straighter and looked over Rollin's shoulder like a gangster was about to mug all of them.

He tucked the badge back inside his jacket. "I'm looking for a librarian named Quincy."

The man scanned the vacant room before he focused back on Rollin. "I'm Quincy."

He lowered his voice. "Captain Malloy said you could help us."

Quincy's hands shook as he reached for a pencil and scrap of paper. "It depends on what you need."

"Malloy also said you knew how to keep quiet."

The man tugged on his tie. "As long as you're not asking me to do anything illegal."

"We need your help finding a location."

"Inside our great country or outside?"

"I believe it's near Cleveland," Rollin said. "We're trying to find a place called Sugar Creek."

The guy took off his spectacles and rubbed his eyes. "The village or the actual creek?"

Rollin glanced over at Lance and his partner crept closer to the desk. "Both."

Quincy stood up and motioned to them to follow him. Passing through a maze of shelves and desks, they stepped into a smaller room filled with piles and piles of newspapers. Quincy shut the door and muttered the names of the papers to himself as he crossed the room.

Rollin picked up a copy of the *Cleveland Plain Dealer* and perused the headlines. Yet another story on the famous "Lady Lindy." A recap of yesterday's Olympic Games in Amsterdam. And an entire article about the sweltering heat wave that spiked temperatures in Cleveland to eighty degrees.

There was no headline about Leone Puglisi's murder.

Quincy stopped in front of the papers starting with W and lifted a stack into his arms. Cradling them like a child, he took several steps back and placed the pile on a table in front of the men.

"The *Weekly Budget*," he proclaimed, like he'd struck gold.

Rollin stared at the papers blankly. "What's the *Weekly Budget*?"

"The newspaper in Sugarcreek."

Rollin stepped forward, staring down at the headline that ran below the masthead.

The Sugarcreek Street Fair Starts Thursday.

Rollin looked up at the librarian. "Where is Sugarcreek?"

Quincy held up his finger. "I'll be right back."

Rollin slid into a chair and tossed his fedora onto the table beside the newspapers. Lance took the seat beside him.

The headlines on the front page contrasted greatly with the headlines on the *Plain Dealer*. There was an entire article on the upcoming street fair and an announcement of a band carnival. There were articles about local cheese makers, book recommendations for the upcoming school year, and a long list of people traveling, visits with friends and relatives, and the churches that would hold picnics that week.

Turning the page, he saw letters instead of articles. A dozen or so of them.

Miss Minnie Beachy wore her peacock blue dress to church today.

Bushy Yoder is the proud owner of a new buggy.

Mrs. Moses P. Miller held a quilting on Thursday.

Mrs. Benjamin Bontrager had some bad luck with her canned fruit jars. She had a shelf of two hundred quarts and the shelf broke down.

Rollin slumped back against the chair. What kind of newspaper reported the dress someone wore to church? And the loss of canned fruit?

He turned the page and saw the recipes for prune jam and shoofly pie. And an advertisement for buggy repairs.

Lance looked over. "What is it?"

"This newspaper is filled with letters." He read the ad for the buggy repairs. "Written by what seem to be Amish people."

Lance stared at him. "The group with the bonnets?"

"Bonnets and buggies."

"What would Antonio and his fellas have to do with the Amish?"

"They could be buying corn from them." He tapped the top of the paper. "And storing the corn sugar down there."

Quincy came around the corner with a long blue book in his hand. An atlas. He set it on the table and paged through the maps for a moment. Then he spun it around. Quincy pointed at Cleveland and his fingers traveled down the page, passing tiny towns like Fairlawn, Clinton, and Brewster.

He pushed his spectacles back up his nose before pointing at a tiny dot just west of Dover. "That's Sugarcreek."

Rollin massaged the back of his neck. "Any idea how long it takes to get there?"

The librarian eyed the map. "I'd say about two or three hours."

Rollin reached for his hat and circled his fingers around the curled brim. Then he shoved his hat back on his head. "Can we borrow this?"

Quincy hesitated but finally handed over the atlas.

Outside the library, the sunshine bore down on them. Rollin stepped under a tree and looked at Lance.

"You want to take that new car of yours on a ride?"

A grin swept across Lance's face.

"You betcha…" he started before his eyes narrowed with suspicion. "Where did you want to ride?"

"Down to Sugarcreek."

"Quincy said it was three hours down there."

"Actually, he said two or three."

"That's our entire Saturday."

Rollin shoved his hands in his pockets. "You think golfing is more important?"

"As a matter of fact—"

"Because today might be the day things are going down in Sugarcreek."

"You promised me dinner with a dame."

"So go out to dinner tomorrow night."

"I already asked her out tonight."

"Get a rain check."

"It ain't rainin', Rollin."

He glanced at a small white cloud building toward the lake. "It might be by the time we get back to town."

Lance sighed, eyeing the phone booth across the street. "Let me call Mazie and tell her I'll be late."

After Lance talked to his girl, Rollin tried to call Malloy, but his boss didn't answer the phone.

* * * * *

The stench of manure overpowered the sweet scent of grass in the barn. Midday light washed through the wide doors and tumbled across the mounds of hay, farm equipment, and the four horses penned in their stalls. Katie removed a stiff brush from where it hung on a wall and opened the first stall. Prince nudged his cheek against hers, the white star between his eyes gleaming in the light.

She laughed, pushing his muzzle away. "Keep your nose to yourself, mister."

She held out three cubes of sugar in her palm, and with a slight shake of his head, he devoured the treat.

Lifting the brush to Prince's mane, Katie stroked the rich chestnut hair on his neck and back and brushed the dirt off his barrel and belly. As she worked, she soothed him with a hymn they'd sung in service two weeks past. The words resonated in her soul.

No ear has ever heard, no eye has seen
The joy that God bestows and has prepared for those
Who will behold God, with a bright countenance:
Pleasantly with their eyes, the eternal true light.

She'd sought God as her eternal light, and she believed He had prepared a future for her and Henry, a short future on this earth and a joyous one in the next life. A future that should include Jonas Miller as well.

This morning she'd tried to find a reason why she couldn't visit Jonas today. Erma had moved from canning peaches to tomatoes, and Katie volunteered to help, but Erma refused her assistance. Isaac had woken early this morning, the ginger and garlic combination raging through his veins. He'd snuck to the field after breakfast without asking her or Henry to accompany him.

The Lehmans were conspiring against her. Or for her. She wasn't sure which it was this morning.

She harnessed Prince and led him out of the barn, toward the separate buggy shed where the Lehman family stored their wagons, a road cart, and two buggies. She'd been up most of the night, her mind racing with how to tell Jonas about her past. The truth only Isaac and Erma and the deceased bishop of their district knew.

Once she told Jonas the story, she had no illusions that he would rush his decision about their marriage. He could think about it as long as he wanted, and if he still wanted her hand in marriage, she wouldn't vacillate any longer. She would take her vows and be baptized and become Jonas's wife. Henry would become his son.

Her stomach rolled as she opened the door to the buggy barn. It was the best decision for all of them, so why didn't it fill her heart with joy?

If Jonas decided tonight that he wanted to pursue their marriage, she would talk to the new bishop at their church service tomorrow. She wouldn't wait any longer.

For three years she'd waited for God to answer her pleas as to what she should do about the future, but His voice had been silent. She had no choice but to conclude His silence meant her marriage to Jonas was the right decision. She would rescue Henry from the world like Isaac and Erma had rescued her.

She guided Prince by the spring wagon, surrey, and black-topped buggy. Jonas's house was only three miles away, so they would take the open road cart for their visit today.

The door banged against the wall, and her son bounded into the barn. "Are we going to visit Jonas?"

"Yes." She pulled the shafts of the cart toward Prince, threaded them through the loops on his shoulders, and attached the straps to the breeching on his flanks.

"Do you think he'll let me drive his Belgians?"

"Maybe."

"I can do it all by myself this time."

She sighed, leaning into the horse. She would always be Henry's mother, but she couldn't mother him forever. A boy needed a papa, and it was her responsibility to provide a good papa for him. Jonas would make a fine father. Why couldn't she rid herself of her fears?

As the sound of an engine echoed through the barn, Prince whinnied and reared his head.

"Steady," she whispered, stroking his neck.

Henry popped his head out the door and then turned to her in excitement. "It's the airplane again."

He ran out the door, waving his arms as he followed the flying machine across the yard.

She groaned as she climbed into the cart. The problem was that Henry was too much like the man who'd fathered him.

Her hands clutched the reins almost as tight as the anxiety clutched her heart.

At one time, when she was much younger, she thought she'd been in love with Henry's father. Her heart had trembled and quaked, and she'd spent hours fantasizing about what could be. As she grew older, though, she realized her feelings for him had been a silly infatuation. She'd been too young to know what real love should look like. A love like Isaac and Erma's.

Isaac and Erma respected each other. Admired each other. Even after forty years of marriage, Katie saw the fleeting tender looks pass between them, and every once in a while, she would come upon them in the parlor or on the porch swing and find their fingers intertwined or Erma's head on Isaac's shoulder. Whenever Katie caught their rare physical displays of affection, Erma blushed and scooted away from Isaac like she'd been caught in a scandalous affair.

Perhaps that was what love looked like. Blushing faces of a couple who'd been married for a lifetime and a love that endured even in their wounds.

The sound of the airplane faded away, but Katie didn't drive out into the sunshine.

Would she and Jonas last for forty years? Would she secretly reach for his hand when they were alone and blush if she were caught? Or would she grow bitter with age and hide from his affection?

She tapped her bare feet against the floor of the cart as she waited. Her feelings didn't matter. She wasn't marrying for herself. She was marrying for Henry.

Her son raced back into the room, jumping up into the cart beside her. "The pilot waved at me!"

"Did he now?"

"He tipped the plane and I could see his face. He saluted and waved."

"That was nice of him."

"When I grow up, I'm going to be a pilot."

Her heart racing, she lifted the reins and prompted the horse forward.

It didn't matter what she felt. She would marry Jonas, and he would protect her son from the world.

CHAPTER 6

Sweat balled up on Rollin Wells's forehead, dripping down the sides of his face, but he didn't wipe it off. With the windows rolled up, Lance's new coupe sweltered like a hot boiler—almost as hot as the fire those blasted *Boche* showered over the trenches during his little holiday in Rheims. A decade had passed since he fought alongside French and Americans alike, but he could still feel the heat from the German flamethrowers. And taste the fear.

There were no trenches near Sugarcreek and no German soldiers. Only miles and miles of forest and fields with the occasional farmhouse and barn scattered around for a reminder that people actually lived in these isolated hills.

"You hot?" Lance quipped on the seat beside him.

Rollin groaned. "Shut up."

"You gotta roll the window down." Lance rolled down the glass on the driver's side to demonstrate, like Rollin didn't know how to operate a window knob. Humidity rushed through the open window, and dust settled over the coupe's shiny blue interior.

Lance tapped the steering wheel. "Don't it feel great?"

"Dandy."

"If you've got to be out here on a Saturday, you might as well enjoy it."

Rollin grunted. They'd already wasted their morning and half their afternoon searching for who knew what. If the Cardano boys were down here, they were well hidden.

The car flew over the crest of a hill, and Rollin's head crashed into the ceiling. "Son of a —"

Lance laughed again, and Rollin wanted to reach over and wring the laughter out of his partner's throat. If he didn't do it, some gangster would pummel sense into Lance one day, and the result wouldn't be pretty.

Rollin rubbed the growing bump on his head. "Slow down, would ya?"

"What's the fun of driving a new tin can if you have to go slow?"

"We're not out here to have fun."

"Says you, boss." Lance turned the radio knob, and jazz music poured out of the speakers. "Just listen to her sing."

"Are you nuts?" Rollin flipped off the radio. "Someone might hear us."

"There ain't nothin' out here except cows."

Rollin had been hoping they could scout out some sort of distribution center or meeting place, but his partner was probably right. There was nothing out here except endless fields and trees and cows. No Amish man or woman would sell corn to the corrupt Sicilians, at least they wouldn't if they knew what the gangs planned to do with the corn.

His heart lurched. Maybe Antonio knew they were listening on Thursday night and tossed out Sugarcreek to throw them off the scent. Maybe they were trying to get him and Lance out of town so his men could do something big in Cleveland.

They needed to find a telephone so he could try and call Malloy again.

Rollin braced himself as the car launched over a second hill, but instead of clear road, a curtain of brown and black swung in front of them. A horse and cart turning onto the road. Rollin stomped on the floor like there were brakes on the passenger side.

Lance swore as he slammed on the brake. The back tires fishtailed, and he struggled to regain control.

Rollin clutched the door handle until his partner finally straightened the car. Lance took a deep breath, and Rollin slumped back against the leather seat.

A few seconds later, Lance glanced over at him. "I guess there's some Amish out here with the cows."

A little head popped over the seat of the cart in front of them—a boy with a straw hat. He lifted his hat, waving at the two men until the woman driver tugged on the child's shoulder. The boy turned around, facing the front again.

Rollin wiped the sweat off his brow. "You still having fun?"

His partner's eyes were on the narrow road. "Not so much."

"Good."

Slowly they climbed up another hill behind the cart and horse. In the distance he could see a large red barn. In a field near the barn was a white house surrounded by a cluster of trees. Only one solitary barn and house as far as he could see.

Scanning the fields, his gaze rested on the back of the woman's pleated cap in front of them. "Is it just me or has she slowed down?"

"Methinks she's playing with us."

"I've got to get to a telephone."

Lance pushed the accelerator until they were six feet or so from the cart. "It may take awhile."

The woman driving the cart didn't turn around nor did she prompt her horse to move faster.

"Who do you need to call?" Lance asked.

"Malloy."

"I thought you didn't need to keep him informed."

"I want him to up the security around Mayfield tonight."

"You think there's going to be trouble?"

The car rattled over a bridge before it rolled onto the dirt road again, behind the woman and her cart. "I don't know."

"If you call Malloy, he's only going to grandstand."

"He can't grandstand if nothing happens."

"You do all the work, Rollin, but Malloy gets all the credit."

Rollin glanced down at the atlas.

The newer men didn't respect Malloy like the older ones did. They may have heard the stories about the man who almost brought down Club Cardano seven years ago, but they didn't appreciate it. Even though the jury acquitted Salvatore, the feat of capturing him was legend among Cleveland's veteran police officers.

They came to a crossroad, and the woman stopped her cart. She didn't turn around, but the boy waved at them again. Rollin lifted his hat.

As the horse pulled the cart through the crossroad, Rollin pointed left across the steering wheel. "Go that way."

Lance nodded down at the atlas. "What's over there?"

"I'm hoping a telephone."

"Which means we're lost…"

Rollin slammed the atlas shut. "I'm pretty sure we're still in Ohio."

Lance dropped back against the headrest. "I told Mazie we'd go out tomorrow night."

"We'll be back by tomorrow."

The cart was only eight or nine yards ahead of them, the horse slowed to a crawl.

"I don't care which way you go," Rollin said. "Just stop following her."

Lance opened his window as he turned left and sniffed the humid air. "I can smell it."

"The horse?"

"No." He sniffed again. "The Cardanos."

Rollin rolled his eyes. "You should have gone into theatre."

"You should have gone into law enforcement," Lance grinned. "Oh, wait…"

They came to another crossroad, and Lance closed his eyes, smelling the air again. "We need to go right this time."

The sun dipped toward the horizon behind them. As long as they were going north, toward a phone, and then back to Cleveland, Rollin was happy. He shouldn't have brought Lance down here without more information about where they needed to search.

Lance stretched his neck. "You don't think Mazie will ditch me tomorrow, do you?"

"Mazie'd be crazy to ditch you."

"She is crazy."

"All women are."

Lance shook his head, his voice as serious as Rollin had ever heard. "My mother isn't crazy."

"Then you are a lucky man."

They came to another crossroad, and as they passed through it, Rollin saw telephone poles leading up a long driveway.

"Maybe they'll let me use their telephone," he said.

Lance turned right and the lane narrowed as they sped up the driveway. On one side of the drive was a flat field and on the other was a dark forest.

"Slow down," Rollin said as they bumped over the rocks.

"This ain't no buggy—" The last word hung on Lance's lips.

A black Lincoln crept out of a clearing in the forest and blocked the road.

Rollin stared at the sedan in front of them. "And neither is that."

Lance stopped the car as Rollin edged his pistol out of the holster and held it beside him.

"What do we do?" Lance asked, his fingers clenched around the steering wheel.

Rollin glanced behind them. "You slowly back down the driveway and then take off."

Lance slid the gear into reverse as Rollin squinted at the window in the Lincoln to see the driver, but all he could see was a man with a hat pulled low over his forehead.

These guys didn't know they were detectives. If necessary, he and Lance could take them down, but perhaps the men would let them go without a fight. Then tomorrow he and Lance would return with backup.

Out of the corner of his eye he saw another flash in front of them as a second Lincoln crawled out of the trees.

"Not good." Lance's voice shook, but his foot was steady on the accelerator, inching the coupe away from the bigger cars.

The passenger window of the second Lincoln rolled down. Rollin saw a flash of metal at first, and then the barrel of a Tommy gun edged over the windowsill.

"Get us out of here," Rollin ordered.

Lance punched the accelerator, and the coupe jerked backward.

CHAPTER 7

Dust plumed across the cornfield like the funnel of a tornado, and tires churned on the gravel road. Her fingers entwined around Prince's reins, Katie Lehman rolled her eyes.

Stupid Englishers.

Simple consideration dictated that those who visited these quiet hills would remain quiet as well, but instead of respecting those who were trying to live a secluded life away from radios and automobiles, these Englishers blasted their radios and tore up the country roads with their machines.

All her community asked was to live separately from the modern world, in peace and isolation. Yet the *hoch Leit*—high people—insisted on bringing the world to them. It was almost like they had to muddy these tranquil hills with their own religion of idolatry, including possessions like bright blue cars wrapped in gleaming silver chrome. Frivolous and way too fast.

Beside her, Henry watched the dust cloud with wide eyes. "What are they doing?"

She rolled her eyes. "Some Englishers are playing with their toys."

"Do you think it's the men in the blue automobile?"

"Probably." She glanced at him, and fear washed over her again at her son's fascination with the machine.

A horn blasted across the field, and she groaned. Most men in the outside world never seemed to grow up. They bought their roadsters as soon as they could afford them, revved their engines, skidded on their tires. The years passed, but they never matured. Instead all this frivolity was somehow supposed to make them men, like money and speed equated respect and power. It was a lie, and their mothers should have told them this before they were Henry's age.

One automobile or ten of them did not make a man powerful. A man of true power was a man of character, built piece by piece like the slow, deliberate raising of a pole barn. Every beam, every nail, had to be hammered into the right place for the building to withstand the elements that would surely plague the structure over the years. A few missing planks, a handful of forgotten nails, and the entire barn would be useless in the wind and snow and rain. Eventually the building would collapse on itself, just like most men collapsed under the pressure when the storms of life hit.

"How fast do you think it goes?" Henry asked.

She let go of the rein to rumple his hair. "A fast automobile does not make an honorable man."

"Faster than a whole team of horses?"

Isaac had talked to Henry on occasion about the worldly machines, but her son never seemed to listen. She needed help from another man. A younger man like Jonas. "Maybe you and Jonas could talk about automobiles today."

His eyes shone again. "Do you think he would?"

She secured the reins in both hands. "I'm sure he would talk with you about whatever you'd like."

He rubbed his hands together. "Can I drive Prince?"

"Not today."

"Jonas lets me drive his horses."

She took a deep breath. "You like Jonas, don't you?"

She felt his eyes on her, but she didn't look at him. "Why, Mamm?"

"Jonas and I…" she hesitated. "We have things we must discuss today."

"Lucas says you are going to marry Jonas, but I like living with Isaac and Erma."

"I do too, Henry," she said. "But it is good for boys to have a father as well as a mother."

When he didn't respond, she took a deep breath. "Do you want a father, Henry?"

He shrugged. "Ya, I suppose so."

"Would you like Jonas to be your father?"

It was like he didn't hear her. "I want a father with a red automobile."

How was she supposed to convince her son he could respect a man who drove a buggy as much as he respected those who drove automobiles?

As the road curved, she saw the lane cut between two cornfields that led to the Yoders' home. Ruth Yoder spent hours in her summer kitchen this time of year, perfecting her recipes for pies and cookies. People traveled across the county to purchase them from the shops a mile north in Sugarcreek.

Henry reached over and tugged on her arm. "Can we go see Ruth?"

Even though Henry wasn't her kin, Ruth spoiled him like she did every one of her dozen-plus grandchildren. Love seemed to pour out of her heart like April rain, and Henry never turned down the woman's hugs or her treats.

"Please, Mamm."

"Not today." Their cart rolled past the path. "The Yoders are preparing for the church service tomorrow."

Henry's lower lip slipped out almost as far as his chest had earlier. "Prince is hungry."

She eyed the chestnut gelding that pulled their rig. "He doesn't seem very hungry to me."

"He could eat five pounds of oats." Henry rubbed his own stomach. "And so could I."

Her eyebrows climbed. "Oatmeal cookies, you mean."

"Even better," he said with a grin.

Ahead of them was another crossroads with trees and thick foliage that trimmed the edge of the Yoders' cornfield. The road to the left went toward the Village of Sugarcreek, but Jonas's home was straight.

She wiped the beading sweat off her forehead with the back of her arm.

Jonas didn't own a blue automobile nor was he attracted to the many temptations and distractions offered by the world. Today she would offer her past and her future to Jonas, and if he would have her, she would accept with gratefulness and grace, like she should have done a long time ago.

Katie glanced both ways at the crossroads and clicked her tongue for Prince to cross, but the moment her horse stepped into the intersection, tires squealed on the road to their left. Prince flung back his head, stepped sideways in his traces, and Henry hollered as the horse jostled the cart, gripping the seat beside her as Katie yanked back the reins, trying to steady the horse.

What were the Englishers doing now?

Turning her head, she saw a flash of blue race toward her. The automobile.

She jerked Prince toward the side of the road, clutching the reins as the machine flew past them. Dust flooded over them, and Henry coughed, struggling for air. She lifted the reins to urge Prince across the road, away from the particles of dirt, but before Prince took a step, a streak of black raced by them, followed by another car.

Katie stared at the road in front of them. If Prince had stepped forward, the automobiles would have hit her horse and maybe even killed her son.

Killed her son.

She shook her head, shaking herself free from the memories. She had to protect Henry, had to get them both away, but the reins felt like slivers of ice, frozen to her hands. Who were these people and what did they want?

Her eyes on the road ahead, she lifted her hands to move the horse forward to cross the street toward Jonas's home, but then began wondering if she shouldn't go back instead. Forward. Backward. The decision was simple yet she couldn't seem to make it.

"Mamm," Henry whispered.

"Ya?"

"We should go to Ruth's house."

In the distance, an explosion blasted through the silence and then another boom.

It was a gun.

Henry squeezed close to her side, and she whipped the reins, pushing Prince to turn back toward the path.

Another shot blasted across the field, and she prayed as Prince raced toward Ruth's home. Prayed that the men hadn't seen their buggy. If they had, she had no doubt they'd want to eliminate any witnesses to their crime.

She clicked her tongue and Prince cantered toward the Yoders' driveway.

She didn't know what kind of hell these Englishers had brought to their county, but she wasn't going to let them get close to her son.

* * * * *

The oval window in the rear shattered, but Rollin didn't turn around. He hated playing cat and mouse—especially when he was the mouse—but these guys refused to relent. Whoever was chasing them wanted them dead.

"Keep her steady," Rollin muttered, his head ducked behind the seat.

Lance didn't respond, but his knuckles were seared white against the steering wheel, his eyes locked on the road. All joviality was erased from his face.

In that moment, Rollin was sincerely glad Lance was his partner. If nothing else, the kid was a good driver.

Another blast slammed into the car, but the Lincolns weren't getting any closer. He glanced over at the gas gauge. A half tank left. Hopefully the guys chasing them were closer to empty.

Rollin slid his pistol back into his holster and reached over the seat for his shotgun. Glass shards sliced his fingers as he pulled the gun to the front seat, but he didn't feel any pain. Ducking, he loaded two shells and locked it. Then he lifted his head again to face their attackers.

The man riding in the passenger seat edged his gun out the window again, but before he shot, Rollin pulled his trigger. The gun kicked back against Rollin's shoulder, the blast reverberating in his ear, but he switched barrels and shot again.

The Lincoln swerved behind them, but the shots didn't stop them. Another gun blast, and Lance swerved left and then back to the right like he could dodge the bullets. The sedan was only twenty feet behind them now. The hat had blown off the gunman, and his greasy black hair whipped in the wind. Rollin recognized his face. Nico Sansone, one of the Cardano family henchmen.

"Go faster," Rollin shouted over the roar of the engines.

"My foot's on the floor."

"Faster, Lance." As they started to climb another hill, the automobile behind them edged to the left. "They're going to ram us."

Lance jerked the wheel left. "No, they're not."

Rollin banged his head on the ceiling again as the coupe went airborne, launching over the hill. Time seemed to stop as the auto flew through the air, wind whistling through the window.

"God help us," Lance murmured.

Rollin braced himself for the landing. Was this it? Thirty-one years gone in a flash. He wasn't like Lance—so full of life and hope for the future. Lance had a dame. And a mother.

No one would miss Rollin, but Lance was too young to die.

The car hit the road, and Lance battled the spinning wheel. Rollin held one hand on the door, the other secured against the dashboard. He didn't know where his gun was nor did he know what had happened to the men pursuing them.

The car skidded across the dirt, Lance pressing down on the brake.

"Don't stop," Rollin commanded, but Lance didn't seem to hear him.

With one hand, Rollin searched the seat for his shotgun, but couldn't find it. His hand flew to his holster; his Colt was still there. He secured it with both hands as they plowed over a bank, toward a cornfield.

Metal crunched under them, and the coupe stopped with a terrible jolt. The tires hung on the bank of a ditch. Lance hit the accelerator, and the engine roared back at them, but the car didn't move.

Another gunshot exploded behind them, and when Rollin turned around, both sedans slammed on their brakes, blocking them. Steam poured out of the engine, and when Rollin met Lance's eyes, the horror was palpable. His partner was about to lose it.

Rollin propped open his door. "We can take them."

"No, we can't."

With a quick swipe over the floor, he found the shotgun and shoved it into Lance's hands. "Yes, we can."

A door slammed behind them, and Rollin kicked open his door. Nico Sansone climbed out of the front car, a sawed-off shotgun propped under his arm. Rollin shot twice, but Nico ducked behind the vehicle.

The other men got out of the cars, all of them wearing dark jackets and hats. One bent down and began inching toward Lance's open window. Lance didn't shoot at him.

"C'mon," Rollin growled.

The seconds dragged, the man creeping closer to Lance's door, but his partner didn't fire.

"You've got to fight," Rollin demanded. "We'll take them together."

Lance kicked open his door and Rollin groaned. If his partner ran for the cornfield, it would be almost impossible for Rollin to take down all four gangsters with his pistol.

Rollin slipped out his door and backed toward the engine of their coupe, expecting to see Lance hightailing it toward the tall stalks.

Instead, his partner snuck up beside him, his gun facing the men. "Are we gonna fight, boss?"

"We don't have a choice."

"All right."

Lance lifted his shotgun and fired. The man in the black coat keeled over.

"Nice shot," Rollin muttered.

Nico and another man crept toward them, close to the ground, and Lance reloaded his gun to shoot again. They were two against three now. Two shotguns against one. Their assailants were burly, but Rollin was street smart and as long as Lance stayed focused, they could take their opponents down.

Bullets pinged off their car, whizzed over their heads. Lance kept shooting, ducking to reload, and then shooting again. Rollin looked over the roof, and the men were close enough now to use his pistol, but they were hiding behind the Chevy.

Lance stepped out from behind the car, aiming ahead with his gun. A shot rang out, and Rollin thought he'd unloaded the gun, but when he turned, Lance was on the ground.

His partner met his eye. "Get outta here."

Another gunshot blasted as he crawled to his partner. Blood spread across Lance's chest, and Rollin swore.

"I'm not leaving you," he said.

Rollin glanced up and saw Nico peeking out from the side of the automobile. He picked the shotgun off the ground and shot it. The gangster disappeared behind the car.

Lance reached up, grasping at Rollin's collar. "You can't fight them by yourself."

"Yes, I can," he started, but something hit his shoulder, pain searing his arm.

Lance coughed. "Run, Rollin."

"I can't."

Lance pushed him away, his eyes closing. "You'll find them later, boss."

"Lance..."

Lance opened his eyes again, intent. "Run!"

Clutching his shoulder, Rollin glanced over at the cornfield and then back at his partner. Lance had closed his eyes, his chest bathed in red.

These men would pay for what they'd done.

CHAPTER 8

Cornstalks slapped Rollin's face as he sprinted through the field, guns popping like firecrackers behind him, but he didn't turn around. The men wanted nothing less than his life, and he wouldn't give it to them without a fight. He pressed his hand to his shoulder, the buckshot burning his skin. The flamethrowers never stopped him before and the fire wouldn't stop him now.

An ear of corn pounded his arm, and the pain raged through his arm and chest, but he didn't stop running. Acre after acre.

He should be the one lying at the edge of the cornfield. Not Lance. He should have protected his partner.

Another gun blasted behind him, but the sound was muted now. Farther away. His mind raced almost as fast as his legs.

Why had Cardano's men killed Lance? And why did they want Rollin dead?

He never should have talked Lance into coming to Sugarcreek, not until he was sure about the odds they were playing against. He always pushed too hard. Risked too much. And now his risk had ended Lance's life.

He should have waited until he had more information. Until he could contact Malloy and tell the captain they were coming here today. Now he was out here in the middle of nowhere with no one to back him up. And the only one who knew where they had gone was a librarian.

It would be Monday morning before Malloy even knew two of his detectives were missing.

He had to find a telephone and call Malloy. The captain would send a whole unit of officers down to Sugarcreek tonight, and they would search the area like they'd searched Dempsey Lake. They'd find the men who murdered Lance—the men who probably killed Puglisi and Nardelli as well.

A crow cackled overhead, and Rollin glanced up for the briefest moment. His foot caught on a rock, and his wounded shoulder hit the soil. Stunned, he lay paralyzed in a bed of stalks, blood spreading across his jacket.

Death had never scared him before. Not when he was in the trenches of the Great War nor when he was trailing a gangster in the shadows of Cleveland. He welcomed death, but death never wanted him. It only seemed to want the breath of the good ones. Like Lance and like Liz...

The crow buzzed the top of the corn, its wings clipping the golden tassels.

Maybe he wasn't good enough to die.

A man shouted nearby, his face hidden in the corn, but instead of running, Rollin closed his eyes. His arm burned with pain, and he was so very tired.

The crow called to him again, and he squinted up into the sunlight.

The only reason Lance died was because he was in the wrong place at the wrong time.

His mind spun as he blinked in the light. Both Lance and Liz deserved justice for what was done to them, but justice seemed to elude the courts these days. He had to persist until he made it right, either inside the courts or out of them. He was the only one who could avenge their deaths.

The voice faded away in the cornstalks, death passing him by once again.

No matter how much his body hurt, no matter how tired he was from the loss of blood, he had to force himself to move on. He had to find a telephone and call Malloy. Then he would find a safe place to hide until the captain came to his rescue.

With his good arm, he pushed himself off the ground and trudged on through the field even though his feet felt like they weighed a hundred pounds each and his tongue chafed against his mouth like sandpaper.

Ahead of him was a bright red barn, a beacon in the sea of corn. Sliding open a side door, he stepped inside and his eyes slowly adjusted to the light that shimmered through the cracks in the walls. Patches of hay and grass speckled the floor, and a horse neighed and kicked his stall in the basement below him.

A low wall protected a long granary on the far side of the barn, and he tugged a wool blanket off the top of it. Walking into one of the open doorways along the granary, he threw the blanket on the floor and collapsed on top of it.

He would rest for a moment and then he would find a telephone.

* * * * *

Ruth Yoder slid a plate of hot peanut butter cookies onto the small table in her summer kitchen and brushed the flour off the light green apron that matched her dress. Her peppered gray hair was tied in a bun at the nape of her neck, most of it hidden under her prayer kapp, and her neck and arms were as doughy as the pastries she loved to bake.

Ruth scooted the plate toward Henry, and he swiped a cookie with each hand. Katie didn't have the energy to scold him. He could have ten cookies if he wanted, as long as he was safe from the wicked English men.

A breeze drifted through the open windows, mixing with the oven's heat. The gun blasts had subsided, but the quiet did nothing to stop the racing in Katie's chest. Who dared to pollute the peaceful solitude of their hills with gunfire? And why?

"It's wonderful *goot*," Henry mumbled, his mouth full of cookie.

Ruth patted his shoulder. "Thank you, Henry."

He lifted up his free hand to show both women. "May I have another?"

Ruth giggled and passed him another one. Nothing pleased their friend more than a child or an adult who couldn't resist her baking.

Katie looked out the window, at the larger farmhouse beside Ruth's kitchen. Ruth's son Daniel lived there with his family and three of his eight children who were not yet married. Even though the man would only use his shotgun on a coyote or a deer, knowing he was there along with his gun would ease her mind.

"Is Daniel home?" she asked.

Ruth shook her head. "They drove into Sugarcreek to get supplies for tomorrow."

She sighed. So much for easing her mind.

"Will they be home soon?"

"Oh, I don't believe so. They didn't leave until the last hour."

"Oh…" Maybe she could borrow one of Daniel's guns.

Henry reached for another round of cookies as Ruth chattered about their family's weeks of preparation for tomorrow's church service. There was the cooking and the rigorous cleaning and the racks in the cellar that she'd filled with baked goods.

Katie squirmed in her chair as Ruth continued to talk. Either her poor hearing had muffled the sound of the gunshots or she didn't know what it was. Should she tell her friend about the guns or pretend she never heard them so Ruth wouldn't be afraid?

Ruth picked up the plate and held it out to her. "Have a cookie."

She started to shake her head, but she took one in her hand instead, holding it in her lap. "*Danki.*"

Ruth leaned closer. "Speak your mind, Katie Lehman."

Katie stared down at the crisscross marks on top of the cookie. For the first time in a very long while, she wished she were driving an automobile instead of a road cart. She would put Henry in the back seat, and she would drive him far away from the fast cars and the guns. She would protect him from the evil.

"What is wrong?" Ruth asked.

She started to reply, but her son answered instead.

"We saw some cars," Henry explained as he chewed yet another cookie. "They sounded like they were banging on a drum."

Ruth's eyebrows arched, looking at Katie instead of Henry. "A drum?"

Katie nodded. "A very loud drum."

Henry hopped off the wooden chair and began circling the room. "They were going zoom, zoom, zoom."

In his eyes was delight at their speed. At the noise. But Ruth watched Katie's eyes instead of Henry's.

"Henry?" Ruth turned toward him. "I have a favor to ask of you."

Henry stopped his zooming. "What is it?"

"I've been so busy baking today that I haven't had time to feed my chickens."

Henry's chest puffed out. "I can feed chickens."

"I figured you could do that for me."

Katie stood up. "I'll go with him."

Ruth opened the door. "I was hoping you could help me sweep the barn floor one more time before the men come with the church wagon to set up the benches."

Katie's arm stretched around Henry's shoulders as the three of them walked out the door, to the coop beside the barn. Her son would only be a few yards away from her. He would be okay.

But even as he stepped toward the coop, out from the security of her arm, she reached for him. He nudged her hand away. "I'll be all right, Mamm."

Ruth handed him a metal pail filled with feed. "As soon as you are done, you come into the barn."

Henry nodded, and Katie watched him walk toward the coop.

"I can't leave him," Katie whispered to the older woman.

Ruth lowered her voice but didn't push for Katie to move. "What happened on the road?"

Henry unlatched the door to the coop, and she watched him step inside. "There were two black automobiles chasing a blue one around the south end of your cornfield."

"Chasing it?"

She nodded. "And then there were gunshots."

Ruth's face paled. "Gunshots?"

"Eleven of them." She'd counted every shot, each one reverberating in her head.

"Are you certain?" Ruth pressed.

"Yes."

"The men will be here soon with the chairs," Ruth said. "They will know what to do."

If the English men chose to shoot at each other, there was nothing the elders or the bishop could do, but at least they would know what was happening. And they could pray together for protection.

Several of the Amish men could escort her and Henry back to Isaac and Erma's home. The Lehmans' house was a safe place. Her aunt and uncle held no ill will against anyone, and no one felt ill towards them either.

Henry marched out of the coop, his grin broad as he handed the pail back to Ruth. "The chickens weren't very hungry."

"Come help us sweep," Ruth said, opening the large barn door. "Work will distract us."

Katie picked up her skirt and followed Ruth and Henry into the barn. She wasn't certain that work—or anything else—could distract her today.

CHAPTER 9

The aromas of spicy sausage and tomato sauce permeated the first floor of the Cardano mansion, a good hour before most families in Cleveland ate dinner. The *stracciatella*—little rag soup—was on the stove, and a loaf of bread, fresh from her niece's bakery on Mayfield, was warming in the oven.

Celeste Cardano took a chug of whiskey from a bottle by the porcelain sink and almost spit it out. Her eyes burning, she gulped it down and set the brown bottle back on the counter before stirring the soup again. Salvatore didn't drink, but before the ban, he used to bring a bottle of chianti home almost every night. Even though she despised the taste of whiskey, she knew she was lucky to have it.

She hated whiskey and she hated eating supper before five o'clock every night and then watching the men in her life rush out the door seconds after they finished dessert. And she hated the supposed business that kept them away from home every night, all night long.

She wasn't stupid—she knew where her men spent their night hours—but they thought she was deaf and blind. As long as they thought she was too simple to understand what was really happening in the Cardano family, she'd live up to their illusion.

Antonio walked into the kitchen and kissed her on the cheek. "It smells *fantastico*, Mamma."

"Only the best for my family." She dipped the soup spoon into her pot of sauce and tasted it. Adding another palmful of basil, she kept stirring. Even if Salvatore didn't like the taste of her food, cooking for her family was one thing that gave her a hint of purpose in life. It made her feel like they needed her. "Where are you going tonight?"

Antonio shrugged. "To play cards with Emanuele."

"You need to get married, Antonio." She always called him by the name she'd given him at birth instead of Junior. "Settle down with Rosa Gallo or another good woman."

"You are the only good woman left."

She waved the spoon at him, reprimanding. "Flattery is for fools."

He laughed, his eyes teasing her. No matter how much she scolded, he knew that she thrived on the flattery. Flattery and falsities. Her entire life had been built on deception.

She set the large silver bowl of stracciatella on the dining room table alongside the bowls of olives and roasted peppers. Then she rushed back to the kitchen to take the bread out of the oven.

She never liked being at the table when her husband came downstairs anyway. He enjoyed making snide comments about the food she'd set out on the table, saying he should send her to train with his kitchen staff at Mangiamo's. As if they could cook much better than she.

She pulled the bread out of the oven and slid it onto the cutting board. It wasn't like Salvatore married her for her cooking anyway. He'd never tasted a bite of food she'd cooked until months after they married. When he finally did, he declared it unfit for a Sicilian man to eat.

During those early years, when she thought she was in love with the man, she'd tried to learn how to cook for him. She'd visited the other Cardano wives, the ones who had emigrated from Sicily, and followed them around their kitchens, trying to make sense of all the pasta making, herb-chopping, and meat pounding. But even then, Salvatore wasn't pleased. There were other places he could go for his meals, but he always came home to her at night.

Those days and nights were long gone. Now he suffered through her cooking three evenings a week, mainly to talk business with his son before he went out for the night. Salvatore could pretend he was a family man, and she could pretend her husband wanted to be with her. And she could pretend she still had a family.

Steam rose into the air when she sliced through the hard crust with her knife and the heat washed over her hands and face. She scooped up the hot pieces of bread and stacked them into a basket. After she looped the breadbasket over her arm, she walked toward the door that separated her from the dining room. She would deliver the bread first and come back for the pasta.

On the other side of the door, she could hear her husband and son talking. Arguing. She leaned toward the door to listen.

Salvatore slammed something on the table and the dishes rattled. "I told you to leave the Puglisis alone."

"You wanted Leone dead as much as I did."

"I didn't want you to take him out."

Antonio's voice rose. "It was self-defense."

"Don't mess around with me, Junior. I know you organized it, and now the Puglisis are going to come after you—and after me."

Celeste leaned closer to the door. Perhaps that's what Antonio wanted—the Puglisis to come after his father.

"No one knows we knocked him off," Antonio said. "I told the men I'd kill them if they leaked the information."

"One of your boys isn't as scared as you think."

"He should be."

"You find out who talked, and I'll take care of it. No one will know where they went."

Spoons clanked against their bowls, and the basket on Celeste's arm shook as she pressed her hip against the door. Before she nudged it open, though, Antonio lowered his voice and whispered to his father.

"Everything is arranged for Sugarcreek."

Celeste pressed her ear to the door, straining to hear Salvatore's response.

"For Friday night?"

"The wedding is officially next Saturday," Antonio replied.

Their voices lowered, and as hard as she tried, she couldn't hear their next words.

She stepped back from the door. A wedding? Now she knew why Rollin asked about Sugarcreek. He was right. Her son was planning something down there this week.

Her eyes blurred for a moment, and her head felt light. She had to get more information about what they'd planned, but it wasn't like she could ask either man directly. The only reason she knew so much already was because they didn't think she could hear. Or see.

Her husband had grown lazy over the years with the information he passed along inside their house. And Antonio conducted much of his business in their home, among the deadwood he called friends. As long as she continued to feign stupidity, both men would keep talking.

They saw her as more of a prop around here, like the old furniture that filled their living spaces. They needed her to manage the home for them and cook on occasion and smile like a good Italian wife on Salvatore's arm at the city's political events. But even there, she was only a prop. Salvatore didn't want her to say much to the men he was trying to impress or to their wives even though she could easily impress them with her style and her wit.

Salvatore knew he could use her for whatever he needed and she never would walk out the door—she had no place else to go.

"Celeste?" Salvatore yelled, and she hopped forward. She heard him call her an idiot, the same word he called her whenever she didn't jump fast enough at his bidding.

Taking a deep breath, she tried to clear her mind as she pushed open the door. "Yes?"

"I was looking for some decent bread," he said, eyeing the basket in her hand. "But I guess I won't be finding any here."

Antonio laughed along with Salvatore, his earlier flattery seemingly forgotten in the presence of his father. She should have taken Antonio away from Cleveland a long time ago, but it was too late for that. The boy she used to love with all her being was becoming like the man she hated.

When she set the bread on the table, Antonio reached for the butter and then a slice. Salvatore didn't touch the bread, but he began to retell their son about the kitchen fire she'd started almost a decade ago, while trying to fry bacon over the stove.

It was like neither he nor Antonio remembered what happened during the early hours of that morning, like the fire had been an accident.

She wasn't the idiot in this family. Salvatore was.

* * * * *

Katie plucked a broom off its peg and handed it to Henry. Her son propped the broom over his shoulders and pretended to fly to the far end of the room. She sighed as she reached for a second broom. Clearly, she was losing her battle against the machines of the world.

The bristles on her brush swept across the floor, scattering the chaff and dust. Cleaning a barn was a losing battle as well. No matter how long they worked, they would never be able to remove all the dirt from the floor. Grime stuck to the old wood like a tick on livestock. No matter how hard you swept or scrubbed, there were some things you could never get rid of.

Henry whipped across the barn floor with the broom on his back, stirring up the dust but making no progress in their fight against it. She and Ruth moved toward opposite ends of the barn, and they worked deliberately, moving the remnants of hay and grass into piles so they could throw them out the door when they finished.

For some reason, she felt safe in the confines of the barn, safer at least than in Ruth's kitchen with its open windows and door. No one could see inside the barn, and there were plenty of places to hide.

She glanced at the various hooks, rakes, and equipment hanging on the walls. There were also plenty of sharp tools and shovels to use if she needed to defend them.

Defend them?

She swept the broom hard across the floor. An Amish woman never thought about defending herself or anyone else.

"The men should be here any moment," Ruth said as she swept. "They'll be able to help us."

Katie nodded.

"Several of the elders are coming tonight. And Jonas Miller."

Goosebumps covered her arms. Jonas should have been the first one she thought about when this happened. She should have wanted him to help her. Comfort her. But, from the moment she'd turned at the crossroads, she hadn't thought once about him. Evil had come to Sugarcreek and not even Jonas Miller could protect her or Henry from it.

Backing toward the granary along the wall, she ducked under one of the openings. She'd work hard until the men arrived, trying to distract herself like Ruth suggested.

She turned to face the wall. And then she screamed.

Ruth was at her side seconds later, and Henry joined them. All three stared down at an English man passed out on the barn floor.

Blood had soaked through the man's torn suit jacket and his tan pants were streaked with mud. One of his shoes was missing, and instead of a hat, thick sand-colored hair was tangled across his head. As quiet as Ruth and Henry were beside her, she assumed they all thought the man's breath had slipped away.

But then the man shivered, and she jumped back, clutching the broom in her hands like it was a weapon. They didn't know if this man was good or evil. Or if he was bringing evil with him.

Ruth took a step closer, and with the broom propped over her shoulder, Katie edged toward him too. Her eyes were on his hands and the leather secured around his waist.

Slowly, her gaze traveled up to his face, and even in his sleep, she saw the determination etched around his eyes, the stubble that dusted the firm line of his jaw.

This wasn't just any English man. It was…

The man stirred, and she stepped back toward the doorway, her heart pounding. She and Henry had to run.

Ruth grasped her arm. "We can't leave him here."

"Henry…" she whispered. "Get out of the barn."

"Mamm." She looked down and saw her son's eyes pleading with her. "We have to help him."

She slowly lowered the broom. "I can't."

Ruth's voice was a steady calm. "God brought this man to us, Katie. We must help him."

God brought him to them?

Why was God so angry with her?

Ruth put her hand on her arm. "God is here with us, even when we are afraid."

Katie nodded, but she wasn't convinced God was really with them. Even if He was in their midst, it didn't mean that God would stop the pain. Ruth would be scared as well if she knew what English men were capable of doing.

Henry took her trembling hand and together they knelt. She reached for the man's hand and it was warm inside hers. There were no calluses on his fingertips. No soil under his nails.

She felt for his pulse along his neck, and he stirred again. Then his eyes opened—a steely blue color she'd never forget.

The blue eyes studied her face, held her captive in their gaze.

"Liz?" he whispered.

The name punctured her racing heart.

"No," she insisted. "I…"

Ruth knelt beside her. "What did he say?"

His eyes didn't wander from her face as he repeated the name. This time it wasn't a question. It was a statement. "Liz."

Katie shook her head, jumping to her feet. Ruth looked back and forth between them like she was trying to solve the puzzle of why Katie was so flustered. And why the man kept calling her Liz.

"He's hallucinating," Katie tried to explain.

Ruth reached for the brown holster and slipped out the pistol. She held the gun toward Katie. "We don't need him using this."

Katie clutched the gun with both hands, pointing it toward the ground. Too much was happening at once. She would help Ruth get him to the house, and then she would run back to the Lehmans' home. Her cocoon.

Outside, she heard the steady trot of hooves coming up the drive, and she strained her ears to listen to the horse's gait. She'd heard that sound many times. It was Jonas Miller coming to help set up the benches.

The elders would determine what to do with this man—no one had to find out she knew him. Isaac and Erma had harbored her secret since she arrived in Sugarcreek, and the former bishop took her secret to his grave last year. No one, not even Jonas or the new bishop, could know about her past now. It would endanger them all.

Ruth picked up her skirt and marched toward the stall door. "They will help us take him into the house."

Katie collapsed back against the wall, the gun resting at her side.

She looked over at the man on the ground, her son standing beside him. She tried to meet Henry's eyes, to reassure him that she would care for him no matter what, but her son's eyes weren't on the stranger or even on her.

Henry's eyes were focused on the gun.

CHAPTER 10

Like stone statues, the nine Amish men sat deathly still in the large Yoder living room, their straw hats in their hands. The only sound was the slow hiss of gas from the Coleman lantern hanging above them. With their long scraggly beards, the married ones looked like mountain men in the picture books Katie had read as a child, but there was nothing rough about these men. They were strong, quiet, and determined to do the right thing before God and for their fellow men.

Isaac was in the room, along with Jonas Miller and another neighbor. The other six men were elders from their district—the men who made the decisions when the bishop wasn't there. Some had their eyes closed, thinking and praying and waiting for a decision. Katie was in the corner rocking chair, praying quietly as she watched them.

The men had arrived hours ago and slipped out to the barn in pairs to set up the benches for tomorrow's service. Now the sky was dark, the preparations finished for the morning, and they still didn't know what to do about the stranger in Ruth's guest room upstairs.

Rollin Wells's badge was on the coffee table between them, his name printed on the brass. Plenty of English lived in Sugarcreek, and even more tourists liked to come in the summer to visit the shops and gardens. The tourists often drove their automobiles on their back roads and stopped to picnic along their creeks. Sometimes they caused trouble, wrecking their cars or mocking an Amish man or woman who wouldn't retaliate. One time an English teenager had drowned in the pond at the Yoders' farm.

But never before had an Englisher been shot in their community. And never had a wounded detective stumbled into one of their barns.

The cruel world was at their doorstep, and they didn't know what to do with it.

Henry slept on Ruth's bed upstairs, and the last Katie saw Ruth, the woman was keeping watch over Rollin Wells. He had slipped back into unconsciousness in the barn, and he didn't wake up when the men carried him to the house and up the stairs. Lifting his head, Ruth spooned some chicken broth between his lips and cleaned his wound, but his fever had spiked. He needed a doctor.

From across the room, Jonas met her eye and gave her a slight nod before he looked away. This morning, she'd been so ready to tell him the truth, ready even to be baptized and become his wife. But she never expected to see Rollin Wells again. Especially not here.

Hours ago she'd been so certain of what she should do, but Rollin's appearance stole away her resolve. The truth could hurt Jonas and the others. The reason she came to Sugarcreek was to save a life, not to hurt anyone. And she'd come here so she wouldn't have to run again.

This was her home. Her security. Rollin Wells had to leave.

The light flickered, and the silence unnerved her. These men could think and pray all night, but they didn't know who might be trailing Rollin. They needed to get him out of Ruth's house and back into the world in which he belonged.

She scooted to the edge of the chair and cleared her throat. "This man needs to see the doctor in Sugarcreek."

Several of the men mumbled to themselves, considering her words, until Isaac stood up. The red tones in his bushy white beard seemed to glow in the lantern light. "My Erma is better than any English doctor."

The men were supposed to confer and make this decision, not her. But they didn't know what she knew. "Erma doesn't know how to treat a bullet wound."

Isaac twisted the hat in his hands, his voice raspy from the illness that Erma's tea chased away. "My wife has a cure for everything."

Katie slunk back into her seat. None of them could argue with Erma's ability to heal. Isaac was right—she could cure about anything with her herbs and tonics. But Erma Lehman shouldn't be responsible for patching up Rollin Wells and his bullet wound. Couldn't be responsible for him. An English doctor could mend his shoulder and contact the authorities up in Cleveland. Someone could come pick him up and take him back to his corrupt world.

The men discussed their options in front of her. Take the man to the village. Take him to the Lehmans' home. Leave him here with the Yoders.

She wanted to stand up and protest taking him to the Lehmans, but how could she explain her protest without them questioning her motives? Her past?

The truth would endanger all of them, but so would having Rollin Wells in her home.

The room quieted again, everyone's eyes on the oldest elder in the room. Jacob Hostetler, known in their community as Speaker Jacob.

Jacob cleared his throat.

"God would want us to help this man," he declared.

Katie coughed, thumping her chest to stop, but not even Jonas seemed to notice.

Jacob continued. "I don't know why this man is here or who hurt him, but with Isaac's approval, I believe we should take him to Erma and let her decide if he needs to visit an English doctor."

"He needs an English doctor," Katie repeated, but no one acknowledged her.

The door opened, and another man walked into the room. Daniel Yoder, Ruth's oldest son.

Daniel glanced around the room at the elders and neighbors in his mother's home. "There was a black car driving slowly near the house," he said. "Do we know what they're looking for?"

Jacob nodded and began to tell him what Katie saw and heard on the road. And he told him about the man sleeping in his mother's guest room.

Daniel's face filled with alarm. "We've got to get him out of the house."

With that statement, Jacob called for a vote, and the men voted unanimously to take Rollin to Isaac and Erma's home.

Several of them put their hats back on. One of the men stepped toward the door.

Isaac stopped them. "But how do we get him to my house?"

The men looked at each other, and Katie sighed. It could be hours before they made that decision.

But then Jonas spoke. "I have an idea."

Katie waited in her chair as the men huddled closer together. She hoped his idea came down from the Almighty Himself. It would be almost impossible to get the bloodhounds outside off Rollin Wells's scent.

* * * * *

Dark petals splattered across the wallpaper, and glass shards rained down on Celeste's prized davenport. Her son scanned the room, but there were no more vases to throw so he kicked one of the chairs. And then another.

Tomorrow she would have her housekeeper clean the stains off the carpet and wallpaper and pick up the broken pieces of roses and glass. But tonight Celeste didn't move from her chair. If she pretended she wasn't there, maybe Antonio wouldn't notice her.

The vulgar words pouring out of her son's mouth were some of the worst Celeste had ever heard, but she didn't cower. She sat calmly on the upholstered chair with her needle and thread, weaving the green strands through the cream-colored cloth. In and out, she pushed the needle into the fabric and then pulled it through the cloth, quietly counting as she stitched tiny x's to make the leaves for the pillow top.

Five stitches. Six. Seven.

Antonio slammed his fist on the coffee table, rattling the glass, but she didn't take her eyes off the needle and thread. The monster emerged more often these days, swallowing her son's charm and easy smile. Just like his father.

Stitch number eight. Number nine. Ten.

Salvatore had escaped the house after dinner, but Antonio opted for a nap before he went out for the night. He'd been preparing to leave minutes ago when the telephone rang.

Celeste answered it, her heart racing like it did whenever someone called after dark. She never knew if yet another body had been found or if someone had been sent to the hospital for the night. Or who Salvatore needed to bail out of jail.

She wished she had never picked up the phone. When she answered it, the foul words that poured out of the man's mouth were worse than her son's. The man was terribly rude to her, and she wondered where the mother was who should have taught him his manners. Antonio had a temper and a foul mouth, but at least he still had manners.

The doorbell rang, and she set her cross-stitch on the side table to answer it, but she didn't have time to stand up. Antonio raced for the door.

She picked her stitching back up and waited to see who was on the other side.

When she looked up again, she watched Emanuele Cardano stumble into their house.

Emanuele was Antonio's younger cousin by three years. His black hair was cropped close to his head, and while he always wore the fancy suits like his uncles and cousins, his lanky frame never fit quite right in them. They hung off him like a baggy shirt draped over the straw of a scarecrow.

Tonight, Emanuele's eyes were bloodshot, but he still nodded her way. And slurred. "Evenin', Aunt Celeste."

"Hello, Emanuele," she said. "You look quite dashing this evening."

Antonio glared at her, but she just shrugged her shoulders and kept stitching. Her nephew stumbled forward into their family room, trying to balance himself on the banister. Any drunker, and the boy wouldn't be able to walk at all.

Antonio stepped toward Emanuele again, his hand raised. At first she thought her son was going to offer to help Emanuele down the two steps into the family room. Instead Antonio slapped him across the face. Emanuele fell backward, landing on the floor.

Celeste stitched faster, her eyes focused on the pillow instead of on the man struggling to stand again. And the boy she had raised to be considerate and kind, especially to his family.

Antonio leaned over and jerked Emanuele to his feet. "You are a drunk."

Emanuele rubbed his cheek. "I ain't drunk."

Antonio shoved the younger man toward one of the chairs and demanded that he stay there. Emanuele eyed Celeste for a minute and then his head fell back against the chair, his mouth hanging open and his eyes closed.

One stitch. Two stitches. Three. She mouthed as she started the next row on the leaf.

Emanuele snored beside her.

It was a joke—the way the government thought they were mandating morality in their country by controlling the liquor. No one was in control—except perhaps the organizations that formed to make and distribute the illegal stuff.

Her husband and son wouldn't let alcohol touch their lips, but they made plenty of money off other people's intoxication. They didn't want to lose their heads or their wallets to a drink, so they settled for women and cigars instead. Their various enterprises provided more than enough smokes and girls.

Her needle continued weaving in and out of the material.

Neither her husband nor her son drank liquor, but it would still be the death of them. Probably the death of the entire Cardano family before it was all done.

Antonio stomped back into the living room, a glass of tomato juice in his hands, probably spiked with lemon juice and Tabasco sauce. If he decided to throw the juice too, she would be up all night scrubbing red out of the carpet.

Instead of throwing the drink, he kicked Emanuele's shin and the boy yelped, grasping his leg to his chest. Antonio thrust the juice into Emanuele's hands, and his cousin sputtered and choked as he sipped Antonio's concoction. His eyes were still bloodshot when he set the glass on the table, but he didn't fall back into the seat. Instead he leaned forward, coughing one more time before he spoke.

"I thought we were meeting down at the club."

Antonio towered over him. "Something came up."

"I was playing poker," Emanuele said. "And winning."

Antonio reached out, grabbing Emanuele's crooked tie as he pulled his face close. "I don't care a lick about your poker hand. We've got a situation to discuss."

"A situation?"

He released Emanuele's tie. "A couple cops were sniffing around down in Sugarcreek this afternoon."

Emanuele's eyes shifted to her. "Junior—"

"She won't talk." Her son glanced her way, waving his arm. In his eyes, she saw pity—and disdain. "Will you, Mamma?"

Antonio didn't wait for her response, inching closer to Emanuele's face instead. "I need you to round up three other guys and get down to Sugarcreek. Tonight."

Emanuele stood up. "Are you coming?"

"Not yet, but Nico will be waiting for you."

"Did the cops find anything?"

Antonio's face turned red. "Stop asking stupid questions."

Celeste didn't take her eyes off her stitching, but she couldn't help but wonder the same question as Emanuele.

What were the police looking for in Sugarcreek?

And did they find it?

CHAPTER 11

Sunlight stole around the evergreen-colored drapes and rippled across the golden floor. The light crept up the edge of the quilt and lingered for a moment on each square until it reached Rollin's face. He lifted his hand to the light, like it was a firefly he could capture and squash in his palm, but the light continued to pester him.

An antique trunk rested at the base of the window, a treadle sewing machine beside it. By the door was a narrow bench, and above the bench were four bare knobs.

His right hand flew to his side, searching for his holster, but the strap was gone, along with his Colt. Pushing himself up on his elbows, he wanted to fling his legs over the side of the bed, but a searing pain shot up through the blood-soaked cloth someone had wrapped around his other arm.

He collapsed back onto the pillow, trying to remember how he got here and what had happened to his arm. And his gun.

The memories came back to him in flashes. Lance's new coupe. Their country drive. The men in the Lincolns, chasing them.

He and Lance tried to escape, but they hadn't gone fast enough. Nico Sansone and the others forced them into a ditch. And then they started shooting.

Bile filled his throat. His partner was dead.

Lance Dawson had a girl. He had a family.

Long before Lance became a threat, the Cardano family stole his life so they could get more money. Or power. Life held no value for people like the Cardanos. They killed just because they didn't like someone. Or because they got in the way.

Maybe, in some sick way, it was good that Lance was gone before this fight got any messier. The kid would have turned cynical in a few short years. Just like Rollin.

He shifted against the pillows until the pain in his arm subsided, and then he closed his eyes.

After she died, Liz wandered often through his dreams, teasing him with her smile. He'd stretch out his arms, trying to touch her, but he couldn't seem to reach her.

It had been years since he'd dreamt about Liz, but last night he saw her again. Her hair had been a glossy black, like the rich fur of a mink. Her eyes bluer than the water on the Great Lakes. He rubbed his fingers together. And her skin—her skin had been softer than anything he'd ever touched in his life.

For an instant, he thought perhaps Liz had been sent to take him to the next life, but even in his dream, he knew that couldn't be right. God only sent angels to pick up the good guys. A guy like him wouldn't be welcomed at heaven's gates.

He opened his eyes again and stared at the light. He had to stop thinking about the woman he'd loved a long time ago. The woman who was never coming back.

Clutching his left arm, Rollin slipped out of the bed and stepped to the window. He'd expected to see the barn and the trees and the fields of wheat and corn beyond the barn, but he hadn't expected to see more than a dozen buggies lined up outside the red barn. And a long black-topped wagon at the end of the row.

With one arm, he cracked open the window, and he heard the gait of a horse trotting up the drive. Men with long beards and black coats milled around the yard, and women with white aprons and black bonnets walked with trays of food between the house and barn.

Had the Amish rescued him from Cardanos' hatchet men?

Someone knocked on the door, and Rollin turned to answer the knock, but before he could take a step, the door opened. A man with a tangled white beard and bulbous nose walked into the room and tossed some clothes, a pair of black boots, and a straw hat on the bed. He didn't smile when he looked at Rollin, but the light in his eye matched the warm sunshine that flooded through the window.

The man pointed at the clothes. "It's time for you to go to church, Rollin Wells."

"Church?" Rollin sat down on the bed, shaking his head. "I can't go to church."

The man shuffled to the side of the room and shut the window, pulling the drapes across it.

"I don't have time for church," Rollin tried to explain. "I have to find a telephone."

"I'm afraid we don't have a telephone booth near here, and you can't go to town."

"Yes, I can," he replied, releasing his grip on his bloody arm. "I need to call my boss so he can send someone to help me."

The man's gaze traveled toward the window. "Others are looking for you right now, and I don't think they are the kind of company you want."

"Black Lincolns?"

"The only Lincoln I know had the first name of Abraham." The man stepped away from the window. "But there are four cars that keep driving up and down our roads, searching for something or someone. We're assuming they are looking for you."

Rollin pressed his fingers against his arm again. "Your assumption is correct."

"Which leads us to wonder why you are a wanted man."

"I'm not exactly sure."

The man nodded toward the window. "It probably won't be long before they come on the Yoders' property."

Rollin rubbed his fingers over the stubble on his chin. "I've brought trouble to you."

"It seems to be so." He paused. "Are you the good guy or the bad one?"

"I'd never presume to be good," Rollin said. "But my job is to fight those who defy the laws of our land."

"These men—they seem to know you are close." The man peeked back out the curtain. "We have to get you out of here before someone is hurt."

"How do you plan to do that?"

"We're still working on our plan," he said. "But I need to know you will cooperate."

Rollin's head felt heavy. His stomach woozy. He closed his eyes for a moment then opened them. "I'll do whatever you ask."

The man eyed him for a moment before he stretched out his hand. "My name is Isaac Lehman, and my wife is better with medicine than any doctor around. Before we move you, we'd like her to look at your arm and have her give you something to dull the pain."

"Is your wife here?"

Isaac walked toward the door. "She's waiting outside."

Rollin's arm throbbed, and the pain rushed through his entire body. He would take whatever medicine this woman offered, especially if it would help him walk out of this room.

He propped up his arm. "I'd like her to look at it."

Isaac nodded and then he opened the door and introduced Rollin to his wife.

Dressed in a light green dress and white apron, Erma Lehman was a petite woman who looked much younger than her husband. It was hard to tell her exact age without the fancy face paint and attire of the women he knew in Cleveland, but her hair was white and small wrinkles trailed the corner of each eye. He guessed she was in her mid-fifties. Maybe sixty.

Her husband stepped back, sitting down on the bench along the wall. The woman didn't speak. Instead, she set her satchel on the night-stand and leaned down to listen to his heartbeat. She lifted his arm above his head. When she pressed her fingers around his wound, he groaned.

Then she looked him in the eye. "With God's help, Rollin Wells, we will have you back on your feet in no time."

With God's help?

Erma sounded like Matthew Kennedy, the soldier he'd spent hours with in the trenches. Matthew used to pray for God's help almost as much as he talked about God's love. Matthew relied on God for help, and it got him blasted by a *Boche* into the next life.

Erma began rifling through her satchel until she found a glass vial. Pouring a light brown liquid onto a spoon, she held it toward his lips. He didn't ask what it was. Instead he swallowed, and the bitter concoction burned as it went down his throat.

As she unwound the cloth around his arm, his skin pulled and stung. She said something to Isaac in what sounded like German, and her husband walked to the dresser and poured water into a basin. With a rag, she wiped off the blood on his arm, and when she pressed the wound, he couldn't help but groan again.

"Isaac said you were going to give me something to dull the pain."

She pressed around the wound again. "I already did."

"It feels like you shot me again."

"You didn't really get shot," she said. "The bullet just grazed you."

Pain tore down to his fingertips. "You could have fooled me."

She made a clicking noise with her tongue as she took a clean strip of cloth out of her bag. "But the bullet took a nice chunk of skin with it."

"It feels like it took my entire arm."

She laughed as she smeared an ointment over his injury and then wound the cloth around his arm. At least one of them was enjoying the process.

"You've lost a lot of blood," she said. "But my greatest concern is infection."

"My greatest concern is those Lincolns."

"What does Lincoln have to do with it?"

He sighed. "The cars that were chasing me are called Lincolns."

"Don't you worry," she said as she cut the cloth. "We'll take care of the Englishers."

After what the Englishers had done, they should all worry. "Why are you helping a stranger?"

She pinned the cloth. "We don't consider you a stranger. More like a guest from God."

God must have them fooled.

"Have you seen my gun?"

"Not recently, but I found this." She handed his holster to him, and he clutched it in his hand.

"Whoever took my gun might want to give it back as well if they'd like us to have any chance of defending ourselves."

"We don't concern ourselves with defense—only with healing."

"You're going to be quite busy with healing and burying if those men start shooting."

For a moment he thought she would crumble and find his gun, but she gathered up her things. "The Lord giveth, and the Lord taketh away. Blessed be the name of the Lord."

He stared at her like she was speaking another language. "But what if He takes away someone you love?"

Isaac glanced at her, and in the man's look, he saw an intense love for his wife.

Erma stuffed the remaining cloth back into the satchel. "It is not for me to condemn our Lord for what He does or does not do. Even when He takes someone I love, I bless His name."

He leaned back against the pillows. There was no arguing with someone who wasn't afraid of death. Still, he would not be responsible for the loss of a single Amish man or woman.

"I have to get out of here."

"In time," Erma said, patting his arm again. "God's perfect time."

She nodded down at the clothes lying on the bed. "Isaac will help you get dressed, and then you come worship with us in the barn."

CHAPTER 12

Katie slipped onto the threshing floor of the barn and sat down on the hard bench beside her aunt. Her white organdy apron was starched and pressed, and her toes were aching, crammed into the black oxfords Amish women wore only on Sundays.

She set her bonnet in her lap and straightened her prayer kapp as she and the thirty other adults and children waited for the elders to finish praying together outside the barn door.

"How is he?" she whispered in her aunt's ear.

"He lost a lot of blood, but he is recovering."

"So he will survive," she said, more a statement than a question.

"Ya. If the Lord wills it."

Katie's gaze wandered toward the open door. "Where did you hide him?"

"Isaac helped him back to where you found him." Erma nodded toward the granary wall, now lined with black straw hats. "The elders are hoping the men in the Abraham Lincolns won't bother him during the church service."

Abraham Lincolns?

Katie bit her lip as she tucked her skirt under her legs. She'd laugh later, after Rollin Wells was gone.

She eyed the open doors on the granary and hoped Isaac thought to cover him with a canvas or something. A church service wouldn't stop the bad men if they were desperate. Sometimes she doubted God Himself could stop them, even with His army of angels.

Isaac stepped out of the granary, pulling the door closed behind him. Katie watched him wink at Erma, but instead of smiling at the sweet gesture toward his wife, the knot in her stomach swelled. As long as Rollin was under their roof, the people she loved were in danger.

Henry sat on the second row across from her, swinging his bare feet under the bench as he waited for Isaac to join him. He looked quite handsome in his dark Sunday suit and slicked back hair. When Isaac took his seat beside him, Henry straightened his shoulders. He would be nine in October, and she was afraid the next decade would pass in a flash. Nine for a moment and then Henry would be nineteen. In no time, he would be as tall as Isaac, and he would be catching his wife's gaze across the room, winking at her.

The elders shuffled into the barn and stood to the right of the benches. Erma opened the *Ausbund* beside her and Daniel Yoder began singing in Pennsylvania *Deitsh*. Even as Katie mouthed the words to the hymn, she didn't focus on the meaning. Instead, her gaze wandered back to the wall of the granary.

It was so strange to have Rollin Wells under the same roof with her again after all these years.

Much had been given to her over the past decade and much had been taken away. Most of it she'd given away willingly, but she couldn't give up Henry. No matter what Rollin did or said, she wouldn't let him near her son.

God would never require that of her, would he? He couldn't require it.

She dropped her gaze back to the rows of boys and men in front of her. Jonas Miller sat toward the back, his head bowed, singing with the rest of them.

In righteousness at all times. Be prepared for Him,
Him alone and no other. On this earth neither fire nor sword,
Nor any other affliction, shall frighten you
From God, so will He indeed let all your sufferings be turned to joy.

Katie brushed her hands over her apron, singing the words a little louder.

Nothing should frighten her. Not fire or sword or black Lincolns or bad men with guns. So many of their ancestors had suffered under the sword when they were in Europe, killed for their faith. They'd truly suffered for their belief, and yet they'd remained steady. Even in their sufferings, God had turned their grief to joy.

She didn't need to be afraid either. God had protected her before, and she prayed He would protect her again. But if He didn't this time, He could turn her fears and her pain into joy.

Even as she sang the words, her hands trembled. She couldn't stop herself from being afraid.

An hour passed as the men and women sang together and prayed. When Speaker Jacob stood up to dismiss the young children and their mothers for a break of cookies and milk, Daniel Yoder's teenage son ran into the room.

"There's a black car coming up the drive," the boy said.

Jacob lifted his hands and the congregation stood. There would be no eating cookies today.

Closing his eyes, Jacob blessed them through his prayer. "May God go with each one of you," he said before he opened his eyes again and spoke. "You know what to do."

* * * * *

Rollin drifted in and out of consciousness for what seemed like hours of mournful singing and long prayers in a language he didn't understand. People shuffled in the barn's heat, and he'd tried to stand up to look over the wall. Losing so much blood had filched his energy.

Erma's bandage wound tight around his upper arm, and the broadcloth shirt Isaac lent him chafed his skin. Pain continued to pulse through him but the bleeding seemed to have stopped.

The threshing floor exploded with activity when a boy shouted that a car was coming. Shoes pounded the oak planks. Benches scraped the wood.

At first, he thought they'd forgotten about him, but then the door next to him swung open. He looked up, expecting to see Isaac, but a woman stepped inside instead. Her head was bowed, her black bonnet pulled close to the sides of her face. Stepping close to him, she held out her hand and helped him stand.

"You will hold up your head, Rollin Wells," she whispered her command. "And you will pretend you have the strength of an Amish man."

"But my arm…"

She stopped him. "Pretend like it doesn't hurt one bit."

"Easy for you to say," he mumbled.

She stepped close to his ear. "I don't care what happens to you, Mr. Wells, but I care very much what happens to the people outside, and I don't want a single one of them hurt because of you."

He brushed the hay off his pants with his good arm and checked the holster he'd hidden under this plain jacket. It was still empty. "Understood."

"The elders have appointed me to be your wife for the afternoon, and as much as I don't want to even pretend we are married, I will comply as long as you don't give me trouble."

He tried to catch her eye, but her head was still bowed. He pitied the man who was really married to her.

"Where are you taking me...Mrs. Wells?"

"It's Katie," she replied. "Katie Lehman."

He moved past her, his shoulders back and eyes straight ahead. When he turned to look back at Katie Lehman, her gaze was still focused on the ground. "How does everyone know my name?"

She held up the badge in her hand and tossed it to him. "Stick this inside your shirt or something. We don't want your friends to find it."

"They're not my friends," he said. "What about my gun?"

"You'll have to learn to live without it."

His legs felt anchored to the barn floor as he plodded out of the granary in front of the woman posing as his wife. A crowd of Amish people milled around outside, all eyes on him. He nodded, wanting to say something to express his gratitude, but another man spoke to the entire group. Rollin didn't understand the words, but when he finished speaking, all the men and women flooded out the two open doors.

"Hurry now," Katie said, tugging on his elbow. "We have to be in the middle."

"Middle of what?"

She didn't answer.

When they stepped into the sunlight, Rollin followed her lead as she walked toward the long wagon. Men were loading benches into the wagon, and he thought they were going to hide him with the benches, but she stopped at a buggy in the center of the pack. His arm throbbed, crying out for him to brace it with his hand, but he didn't press his hand to it.

On both sides of him, men hitched horses to their buggies, and Isaac hitched a horse to the buggy in front of him. Out of the corner of his eye, he could see one of the cars at the corner of the yard, waiting in the driveway. Watching. He kept his eyes focused on the horse.

Were they planning to hide him in the back of the buggy? Nico would find his hiding spot in a second and pick him off faster than a cat taking out a field mouse. And it wasn't like they could outrun the car in a buggy.

He stepped close to Katie. "I need my gun."

"No, you don't," she said.

"Yes, I do."

She climbed up into the buggy, and he could feel the eyes of Nico and the others watching him. Even in this attire, he looked like the clean-shaven city man that he was. Eyeing the barn door again, he thought about hiding back inside, but if all these Amish men and women left, the gangsters would come for him. And they would kill him.

It was better to leave the farm.

"Kumma," Katie whispered from the bench above him.

"Where am I going?"

She patted the left side of the seat. "Right here."

Placing his foot on the tiny step, he pulled himself into the buggy with his good hand. Behind the bench were two narrow seats, too small for an adult, and a wide crevice that cut through the back of the leather to expose them. He couldn't hide there.

He collapsed back against the upholstered seat and closed his eyes.

Katie jabbed him with her elbow, and he jolted upright. "No sleeping, Rollin."

"I'm just resting my eyes."

"These men and women are sacrificing their lives to protect you," Katie said, her gaze focused on the rump of the horse. "You will not put them at risk because you are tired."

"I'm far beyond tired."

Katie nodded at the horse. "Prince, this is Rollin Wells, and Rollin, I'd like you to meet your new best friend, Prince."

He stared at the horse, wondering if Katie was trying to lighten the mood with a joke or something, but when he looked back at the side of her head, she didn't crack a smile. Did she want him to shake Prince's horseshoe or something? Tell the horse he was glad to meet him?

He had to find a telephone and get back to Cleveland before he completely lost his mind.

Katie set the leather reins in his lap. "Have you ever driven a buggy before?"

"Have I ever driven—" He shook his head. "Of course not."

"Well, you better learn fast."

With a click of her tongue, the horse stepped forward, and Rollin grasped the straps. This woman was insane.

She pointed to the left strap. "Tug on it."

He did as she instructed and the horse faced the drive and started walking toward the road.

"C'mon, Prince," she whispered as the horse slowed behind another buggy. The car was about forty feet in front of them, and behind them was the long covered wagon.

"C'mon, Prince," Rollin repeated, eyeing the cornfield again beside them. Either the horse needed to make him look good or he needed to run.

"Hello, Rollin Wells."

Rollin jumped and glanced behind the bench to see the wide grin of a boy. The boy who'd waved at him from the cart. No wonder Katie Lehman was so irritated at him. Lance had been on her tail, annoying her on the road.

What would she think if he told her Lance was dead?

Katie turned around, scolding the boy. "You were supposed to go with Isaac and Erma."

"I wanted to ride with you."

"Henry…"

"I'm pleased to meet you, Henry." Rollin held up the reins. "Do you know how to drive one of these?"

"Mamm won't let me."

"Maybe you can start now."

"No, he can't," she said, pushing on the boy's head. "Get down, Henry."

The boy slipped back behind the seat.

Nico Sansone was leaning against the Lincoln, his arms crossed. Rollin only allowed himself a glimpse at the man, and then his eyes went forward, his fingers weaved around the reins. At least Prince seemed to know what he was doing.

The buggy in front of them passed beside the car, and Nico examined the driver. Rollin cringed. The Amish attire wouldn't fool Nico. In seconds he would recognize Rollin, and he had no gun to defend himself against the man's attack.

He mumbled a prayer to himself, just in case the God of Erma Lehman and even Matthew Kennedy happened to be listening. He prayed that the man wouldn't hurt the innocent woman beside him or the boy in the back or anyone else in the driveway risking their life to help him.

Prince marched past the hood of the car, and Rollin bowed his head like Katie, his hat low on his forehead. His hand instinctively patted his empty holster.

A moment before he rode past Nico, he heard a voice. Glancing behind him, he watched an Amish man hop off the long wagon.

The man marched right up to Nico. "Is something wrong with your vehicle?"

Rollin didn't dare look again. If the Amish man could distract Nico for just a moment, he would be safe.

"We're looking for someone," Nico said. "A dangerous man."

"A dangerous man?"

"A man wanted for murder."

Rollin's hair stood up on the back of his neck. If the Amish thought he had murdered someone, they might turn him over to Nico.

"Are you a police officer?" the man asked as Rollin's buggy rolled past the car.

"We're helping out a friend," Nico told him. "Have you seen any strangers today?"

The man's voice was muted behind him now, but Rollin heard his words. "We don't have any strangers here."

"Thank you, Jonas," Katie whispered.

He glanced in the mirror, and he watched Nico step in front of the long wagon and tell his men to search it.

Rollin didn't know who Jonas was, but he assumed it was the man who'd spoken with Nico. He'd like to shake that man's hand.

"Turn left," Katie said.

He tugged the left rein, and Prince actually responded to his lead.

"Good job," Henry's voice piped up from the back.

A brief smile crossed his lips. "Thank you."

The buggy in front of them turned right onto the country road, and as they turned left, he saw another black Lincoln at the end of the drive. Waiting. A quick glance over his shoulder, and he shivered when he saw two more automobiles on the other side.

The Amish couldn't outsmart the city boys. The Cardano family had found him, and they'd smoked him out. The gangsters wouldn't want the publicity that would come if they took out a group of Amish men or women, so they would wait until he was alone. Or almost alone. Now it was just him along with a woman who didn't like him and a boy who didn't seem to understand the danger they were in.

In the side mirror, he watched as one of the parked cars turned into the road and began following them. Another buggy continued behind them before a second car joined the slow-moving parade.

No matter how fast Prince went, there was no outrunning an automobile, and he couldn't take off running through the fields and leave this defenseless woman and her son behind.

They hit a pothole, and it jostled his arm. He groaned, trying to keep his hands on the reins and his eyes on the road.

"Keep driving," Katie said, and he could hear the fear echoing in her voice.

The automobile was driving on his tail, and he wondered if they would pull beside the buggy and gun him down while he was driving or wait until they stopped.

He kept his eyes focused ahead. "What do we do now?"

"I don't know," Katie mumbled.

A road crossed in front of them, and the first buggy went right. The buggy directly in front of him turned left. Prince followed the buggy to the right.

"He knows where he's going from here," Katie said.

Rollin hesitated before he looked in the side mirror, hoping the automobile went left, but when he looked behind them, the black car was still there.

"Did you make a plan for this?" Rollin asked.

"We will not go to our home until they stop following us."

"And if they don't stop?"

"Prince will last longer than any automobile."

He nodded, but he could feel the adrenaline seeping out of him. The exhaustion returning. The horse would last, but would his body make it longer than the automobile?

Another road crossed in front of him, and he watched as the lead buggy turned to the right again.

Katie pointed ahead. "We're going straight."

The horse started to roll through the intersection when Henry leaned into the opening beside him and waved at the car behind them.

Katie turned around, swatting him. "Sit down," she commanded.

The automobile seemed to hesitate for a moment, and then it turned right to follow the other buggy.

Rollin sighed. "Well done, Henry."

Katie didn't say anything as they drove under a canopy of buckeye trees, but he could feel the anger emanating from her skin. They had all been in danger, but her son's wave seemed to disarm the men. Maybe they guessed there wasn't room for Rollin to be hiding in the back with him.

He didn't know why the men turned, but even if Katie wasn't happy, he was glad to be free of them. "Is everyone angry at me or is it just you?"

"It's just her," Henry piped from the back, and Rollin smiled again.

Katie cleared her throat. "The Yoders won't go back to the house for a few hours."

He nodded. "I'm grateful they let me spend the night."

"And everyone was disappointed to miss the big lunch today."

"Okay," he said slowly, trying to empathize with the trauma of missing lunch. "Hopefully, they'll enjoy it next Sunday."

"Two Sundays from now. Next week is no-church."

There were men with guns chasing them around the countryside. Why were he and Katie talking about lunch?

A honeybee flew into the buggy. He expected Katie to scream like many of the women he knew in Cleveland, but she just swatted it away.

"Turn here," she directed as the bee dodged her hand and flew back out of the buggy, but he didn't need to prompt the horse. Prince went left at the bend.

They traveled over another steep hill, and in the distance, he could see a cart in front of them. Dairy cows ate grass inside a fence on the left of the road, and in the field on the right side, the white petals of Queen Anne's lace embellished the acres of red clover. In the valley beyond was a scrap of trees and a house in the distance surrounded by barns.

It was strange and a bit exhilarating to travel across the countryside like this without a car. He noticed details he'd never seen before and the smells of the steaming fields and livestock.

His eyes edged shut, and Katie elbowed him again. "Stay awake, Rollin."

"I'm trying," he muttered.

"Try harder."

Prince's hooves clapped as they bumped over a wooden bridge and the trickling water of a creek loping over and around a stone path. Minutes later, the horse paused at a driveway, and Rollin looked up the hill at a white farmhouse. A barn was to the right of the house, and beside the barn was a forest. There were acres and acres of fields to the left and on the hill above the house.

As they rode up the steep hill, they passed several outbuildings painted red to match the barn, and a large garden dotted with neat rows of green plants and staked vines bulging with tomatoes. Beds filled with colorful petunias, impatiens, and other flowers decorated the yard.

A dog barked, and two English shepherds and a brown collie ran toward them. Katie directed him toward a shed that housed a larger buggy and two wagons, and he watched Isaac unhitch his horse from the cart. Rollin handed the reins to Katie and scooted down on the seat, his knees crunched up in front of him. "I'm going to sleep now."

Katie leaned over, looking into his eyes, and he saw the blue in them again. Liz's eyes.

"You did good, Rollin," she said as she took the reins. "Wonderful goot."

His eyes fluttered closed. "And you made a goot wife."

"I'm not your wife," she insisted, but he barely heard her words.

For the briefest of moments, though, Rollin wondered where Katie Lehman's real husband was.

CHAPTER 13

Celeste ducked under the metal stairwell as the trolley rumbled down Mayfield, and she clipped her gloves onto her beaded purse. She snapped the purse open, and as she reached inside, her fingers brushed the cool metal of the pistol Salvatore gave her for her fortieth birthday. She didn't take out the gun. Instead her fingers slid past the metal, into a side pocket, and she pulled out a small smooth stone. Stepping out of her shelter, she flung the rock toward a third-floor window.

Salvatore's society friends would be aghast if they saw her tossing rocks at an apartment window, but when she was a girl, she had been quite adept at throwing stones. And she always hit her mark.

The rock bounced off the glass, the sound reverberating down the alleyway, but no face appeared in the window. She sighed, taking a second rock out of her pocketbook and pitching it up to the glass.

Still, no one came to the window.

The gray apartment building looked like it had been bombed in the Great War. The siding didn't look any sturdier than kindling, and she assumed the interior was just as dismal. It was a bit sad. Rollin's father gambled away their family's inheritance, but Rollin still could have lived in a nice home on the hill if he wanted.

Officers and detectives in every rank and unit across Cleveland supplied information to the local gangs and turned blind when necessary to the crime in their city. Their pockets were bulging with cash, and none of them came home at night to a dilapidated tenement.

Rollin's mother, God rest her soul, had such high aspirations that both of her sons would become men of notoriety in their city. Then her oldest son was killed in the Great War and her second son chose to live his life fighting the Cardanos instead of joining them. Rollin probably would never climb much higher in rank than a detective at the precinct, but he didn't seem to care about titles.

Celeste stepped away from the building again, hoping a light would appear in Rollin's room. And his face in the window.

Salvatore would kill her if he found her there, but she had to warn Rollin that the Cardanos were planning something in Sugarcreek. He had to force the Cardanos out of there before they dug too deep.

The streetlight blinked above her as she continued to wait.

How different life would have been for her—for all of them—if Rollin had married Elizabeth and become her son-in-law. But Elizabeth and Nicola were gone and neither of her girls was coming back.

Footsteps echoed down the street at the end of the alley, and she stepped back under the stairwell as a shadow crossed by on the sidewalk. Even though the night was hot, goose bumps rippled across her skin.

Rollin Wells wasn't living in a hillside mansion, and maybe because of it, he was the only man she trusted. He needed her information, and even though he didn't know it, she needed him even more to help her with her plans.

She waited until the footsteps faded away, and then she took the last rock out of her pocketbook and threw it.

Rollin didn't come.

Ducking her head, Celeste backed down the alley and walked out into the street. Tonight, more than any other, she felt very alone.

* * * * *

The orange glow from a kerosene lamp spilled under the door, into the hallway on the second floor of the Lehmans' home. Her hand on the doorknob, Katie hesitated before she walked inside Henry's room. The room where Rollin had collapsed eight hours ago and, as far as she knew, hadn't awakened again. Erma stayed beside him the entire afternoon and evening while Katie played with Henry and then sliced ham, baked potatoes, and cooked green beans for the family.

Now the dishes were done and Isaac was settled in his room downstairs. Henry fell asleep on a mat in her bedroom before the sun dipped over the hill, and she no longer had an excuse to avoid Rollin Wells. Erma needed her help, and even if she didn't want to see Rollin, she'd do just about anything for her aunt.

She cracked the door and saw Rollin in Henry's bed, sweat beading on his forehead. The light blue drapes fluttered in the breeze, and Erma rocked in the chair Isaac carved for her when their first son was born. On the dresser beside Erma was a basin filled with water and a stack of dry cotton cloths.

Rollin moaned as his head tossed on the pillow, and for a moment, she wanted to reach out and comfort him, but her fingers remained clutched around the knob. Rollin didn't deserve her comfort or her compassion.

"Does he still have a fever?"

Erma nodded, sponging cool water on his forehead. "He should have been resting instead of driving the horse all the way here."

Katie reached for the rag in Erma's hand and dipped it back into the basin of water. "We didn't have a choice."

"His head must stay cool for the night, until the fever breaks."

"Ya," Katie sighed. "I will help you."

Erma turned toward her. "What is wrong, Katie?"

She wrung out the rag and handed it back to her aunt. "A lot has happened today."

"Are you tired?"

Her heart was more weary than her body, but she couldn't tell Erma about it. "No more than usual."

Erma wiped off the sweat from Rollin's head, her gaze on Katie's face. "Is it because he's an English man?"

Wind breezed through the window again, flapping the strings on Erma's kapp over her shoulders. She removed the pins that held it in place and set her kapp in her lap.

Erma knew almost everything about her and her past, but there were some pieces she hadn't told her. Couldn't ever tell her.

She replied slowly. "I'm more concerned that we don't know who is trying to hurt him or why."

Erma unfolded the rag and spread it across Rollin's forehead. "I don't understand why one man would ever want to hurt another."

Unfortunately, Katie understood, but her aunt would never comprehend the struggles for money and power outside their community. Or the reason a man would kill an innocent woman.

Katie let go of the doorknob. "I will take over for you."

"I'm all right."

"You need to rest."

Erma glanced toward the dark window. "Maybe for a few hours."

"For as long as you want to sleep."

Erma nodded toward the door. "Did you check on Henry?"

"Not yet."

"Go," Erma said, waving her toward the door.

Katie stepped back into the hallway, her heart pounding. She didn't want Rollin to be in her house, near her son, nor did she want to be alone with him in the darkness, but she would do it to help Erma. This was her cross to bear—a cross she could never escape, no matter how far she ran.

Opening the door to her room, she looked down at her son asleep on the floor. His blond hair rested in soft ringlets around his face. Even in his sleep, she could see his inquisitiveness. His mischievousness.

Henry was God's gift to her, and the love for him swelled within her. She'd tried to give him a life away from the world, a place where he could be protected, but the outside world kept finding her. Was there no place she could take him to keep him safe?

She knelt down, kissing his cheek. No matter what happened, Rollin could never know the truth.

* * * * *

A gun blasted into the night, and Rollin ducked under a tree. Someone was chasing him, trying to kill him. He sprinted through the forest again, running for his life, but the roar of the guns was growing louder, like thunder echoing through a canyon.

In the distance, a light glowed in the blackness and he raced toward it. As he drew closer, the light ballooned into a sphere that was bigger and brighter than a harvest moon. Then a face, a woman's face, formed in the light. He stopped running.

The woman teased him with her eyes, her smile. He reached for her, but he couldn't feel her skin.

Another gun blasted behind him, and he threw his body in front of the light, trying to stop the bullet from wounding her. But he couldn't stop the bullet.

The light faded away.

Rollin swiveled around, begging the invisible assassins to shoot him too, but they didn't shoot. The guns had faded away with the light.

Rollin groped in the darkness for Liz, but instead of his fingers slipping through the air, he felt her skin this time. Her hand. He grasped her fingers, squeezing as hard as he could. This time he wouldn't let her go.

"It's going to be all right, Rollin."

Her tender words soothed him for a moment, but it wasn't going to be all right. When he woke up, she would slip into the darkness again.

Cool water dripped over his forehead, and he tried to shake it away. But he wouldn't let go of the hand.

Minutes passed. Or hours, perhaps. He didn't know. When he finally opened his eyes, the room seemed to whirl around him, and he squeezed the gentle hand again, afraid to face the woman who let him grasp it. Afraid she would disappear.

Slowly he turned his head and saw those beautiful blue eyes looking back at him. Her black hair had turned into a honey brown, resting in soft waves across her shoulders. He released her hand and reached for her face.

"Your eyes…" he said, brushing his hand over her cheek. "Liz?"

She pulled her hand away. "You're hallucinating again."

"No, I'm not."

She removed the cold cloth from his head, looking away from him. "My name is Katie Lehman."

His head hurt when he shook it. She shouldn't lie to him. "Why are you here?"

"I live here," she said.

"They killed you."

"Who killed me?"

He tried to scoot up on the pillow, but his entire body ached. "I don't know."

He watched her move toward the basin, soaking the cloth and wringing it out. He wanted to hold her hand again. Touch her cheek. But the moment had passed. She'd only let him touch her when he was asleep.

She dabbed the cloth over his head again. "Who is this Liz?"

"A girl I knew in Cleveland."

"Is she still in Cleveland?"

"She's…" he started. "She died a long time ago."

Katie paused, rocking back on the chair. "Did you try and rescue her?"

"I couldn't save her," he said. "I wasn't there."

She looked out the open window. "You should have saved her."

He nodded. He hadn't protected her, and the guilt had haunted him for almost a decade.

The door opened, and Erma slipped inside. As Katie stood up, her gaze lingered on him for another moment before she looked over at Erma. "His fever has diminished."

Erma scooted around her and placed her hand on his cheek and then his neck.

"He is better." Erma sat in the chair. "I'll watch over him for the rest of the night."

"Liz?" he called again.

She didn't turn around, but she stopped by the door. "I'm not your Liz."

CHAPTER 14

"I need to talk to you, Mamma," Antonio said as he pounded on her bedroom door and jostled the locked knob.

She rolled over and checked her clock. It was barely five. "Come back in two hours."

His voice escalated. "I need to talk to you now."

She eased her feet over the side of the bed and rubbed her eyes. Her son's late-night footsteps were as familiar to her as the hourly toll of the bells at Holy Rosary. She'd heard Salvatore come home around an hour ago, but she hadn't heard Antonio until now.

She tugged her floral wrapper around her and tied it before she put on her pink house slippers. Then she opened the door.

She barely recognized the angry, bloodshot eyes of the child she'd birthed twenty-nine years ago. The boy she'd tried to rear to be a God-fearing man. Instead, her only son didn't fear anyone or anything expect perhaps his father. And even then, she wasn't convinced that Antonio was actually afraid of Salvatore.

Her son craved Salvatore's pride like she craved the comfort of alcohol, but Antonio's obsession to earn his father's approval would never be realized. Salvatore reserved all pride for himself.

"Is something wrong?" she asked.

Antonio shoved his hands in the pockets of his jacket, like he was afraid he might use them if they weren't secured. "Giuseppe told me he saw you out on Mayfield last night."

Celeste took a deep breath, calming her nerves. Her own son didn't even trust her anymore.

"Why is Giuseppe reporting my whereabouts to you?" she asked.

He crossed his arms. "What were you doing out last night?"

"I went on a walk."

"A walk?" Antonio snickered. "You never go for walks."

"You don't know everything about me, Antonio." She fussed with the belt on her wrapper. "I can take a walk whenever I want."

"Giuseppe said you were close to Wells's apartment."

"Whose apartment?"

His eyes narrowed. "Rollin Wells."

"Rollin Wells?" She forced herself to sound appalled. "I despise that man."

"Then why were you at his place?"

Celeste slipped around her son and padded down the long hallway. She heard Salvatore's snores as she passed his door, and Antonio didn't dare say anything. There would be hell to pay if either of them woke him up.

Antonio followed her down the back stairs and through the kitchen. She didn't need coffee to wake up this morning. She needed something to calm her nerves.

In the corner of the living room, she poured herself a glass of whiskey at the bar and took a sip of the wretched drink. Her son stood across the room, watching her closely, as if the truth would pour out of her if he waited long enough.

She drained the whiskey glass and set it on top of the baby grand piano that Antonio used to play almost every night until Salvatore convinced him that gangsters didn't play piano. She missed the music and

MELANIE DOBSON

she missed the laughter that used to ring from his lips when his fingers danced across the keys.

"Why were you at Wells's apartment?" he repeated.

"I don't know what is wrong with you, Antonio." She reached for the glass again and tried to take a sip, but it was empty. "But I don't appreciate the accusation in your voice."

He stole the glass from her hand, and for an instant, she thought he was going to hurl it against the wall, but he slammed it onto the coffee table instead. "I want to know what you told Wells."

She met his stare, her eyes hardening to match the anger in his. "I didn't tell him anything."

"Then why were you with him?"

"With him?" she huffed. "It's like you're not even listening to me. I don't know where Rollin Wells lives, but I couldn't sleep last night, so I took a stroll to enjoy some fresh air, something you'd know I do regularly if you ever stayed home at night.

"Maybe Giuseppe can join me next time instead of following me around, so he won't be confused about who I did and didn't visit."

"He said you were throwing rocks at a window."

Her head flung back, and she laughed from her belly. "Throwing rocks?"

Antonio shifted in his socks. She knew he couldn't imagine it either.

She eyed the empty glass on the table. "What was Giuseppe drinking?"

He shook his head, conceding to her. "I don't know."

She reached for her glass and filled it with whiskey again before turning back to her son. "How much did you pay Giuseppe for this information?"

Antonio shook his head as she downed the second glass, but he

141

knew the same as she did. As long as Giuseppe was paid well, the man would say anything.

Her son teetered a moment. "If you ever contact Rollin Wells, Papa will be the first to know."

With his crisp words, her nerves curled under her skin. Would Antonio really tell his father if he caught her visiting Rollin?

The malice in his voice drained. "I'm just trying to protect you, Mamma."

"Protect me from who?"

He reached down and picked up the glass again, clutching it in his hand. "From yourself."

He leaned over, kissing her cheek, and it stung.

"You know I love you," he said.

She nodded. "I love you too."

And she did love her son. With all her heart.

* * * * *

The aroma of coffee and salty bacon filled the large kitchen. Katie yawned as she flipped the hotcakes on the stovetop. The four hours of sleep made her feet drag, but even though her body was exhausted, her mind felt like it was on fire. She rubbed her hand on her skirt, the hand that Rollin had clutched in his sleep last night, like she could rid herself of his touch. Her muscles still ached from his grip, and the warmth from his skin lingered.

Why had she let him hold it? Even worse, in the darkness, she hadn't wanted him to let go.

Katie refused to look at Erma working at the counter beside her, afraid the woman would guess the emotions warring in her head. When she left Cleveland, she left everything behind, including her friends and her family and Rollin Wells. But now Rollin was here, and she couldn't figure out why God brought him back to her.

Erma set plates on the table behind her, and Katie picked up the coffeepot, filling a cup for herself. Today she would do her best to help Erma get him well again, and then Isaac would take him to Sugarcreek to call whomever he needed to take him back to Cleveland. He would leave, and she would never see him again.

A plate clattered as Erma set it on the wooden top. "How does Rollin know?"

Katie took a long sip of the black coffee and then placed a stack of fried bacon in the center of the table. She could pretend she didn't know what Erma was talking about. Pretend she hadn't even heard Rollin call her Liz as she slipped out the door.

But Erma had heard, and playing stupid would only deepen the guilt she already felt. Besides, Erma would know she was lying.

She placed a fork on the platter of bacon. "Rollin is only guessing."

Erma stopped working for a moment, watching her. "He's a mighty good guesser."

"That's why we have to get him out of here."

Her aunt lifted a handful of utensils out of a drawer and set them on the table, letting the silence rest like a sleeping dog between them before she spoke again. "What are you hiding from me, Katie?"

Leaning back against the counter, Katie weighed her next words. When she arrived in Sugarcreek almost nine years ago, she told Erma as much as she needed to know. She'd been too terrified to tell her aunt everything.

The same night she knocked on Isaac and Erma's door, her aunt recommended that she wash her mind and her heart clean of the past through Christ's love and forgiveness. She asked God to give her peace, and He had done a miracle in her heart since that awful night. Even when her mind wandered back, her heart was at peace. He'd given her grace, and He'd given her a passion to fight for the future.

But now Rollin was under the Lehmans' roof, and he thought she was Liz. Erma deserved some sort of explanation.

She took another sip of coffee and set it back on the counter. It needed some milk.

"Rollin was a..." Katie started, stepping toward the cellar door. "He was a friend of Liz's in Cleveland."

"A friend?"

"A good friend."

"Katie—" Erma started, searching for her words. "How good of a friend?"

She opened the door. "I'm going to get the milk."

Erma stepped toward her, gently taking her arm. "Don't run, Katie."

Tears started to fill Katie's eyes. "What else am I supposed to do?"

"You can't hide forever."

She wanted to say she wasn't hiding, but they both knew that wasn't true.

Erma brushed her hand over Katie's arm. "Tell Rollin the truth."

She blinked back the tears. Her aunt didn't know what she was asking.

"I can't tell him."

"Why not?"

Katie slipped down into the darkness of the cellar, away from her aunt's questions. She couldn't tell Rollin nor would she ever tell him. The truth would change everything.

CHAPTER 15

The front screen squeaked open below, and Rollin inched himself up in his bed. In the moonlight, he read the clock beside his bed—almost midnight. He stole to the dark window and pushed his nose against the cool glass. He didn't see any vehicles, but lantern light spilled across the driveway, and he watched Katie's silhouette slip into the barn.

Was she meeting someone tonight?

He sat on the edge of the windowsill and watched the barn door. He didn't know what happened to Henry's father, but if Katie was a widow, he assumed the single men in their community must be vying for the attention of such a beautiful woman. If he were Amish, he would be vying for her attention too.

Not that he would ever become Amish.

He eyed his bed before looking out the window again. He should go back to sleep, but he would wait until Katie came out of the barn, safe for the night.

He lifted the window, and the breeze rocked the chair in the corner, its wooden back beating a steady percussion against the wall.

Two days had passed since the Lehman family stole him away from the Cardanos and hid him away in their home. He didn't remember much about his first night in the Lehmans' home except he'd felt like a train had rolled over him. In the following hours, Erma froze his fever out of him with cold water and rags, and she filled him with terrible-tasting concoctions, but his strength slowly returned. The woman warded off the infection along with the pain.

He rubbed his hands together. Even though two days had gone by, he could still feel Katie's fingers woven through his. He'd touched Katie's skin, but his mind had wandered back to the woman he once loved. Even as the years passed, he would never be completely free of her or the guilt that accompanied her face whenever he dreamt about her.

Still it had been a long time since he'd dreamt about Liz, and he'd thought perhaps he was almost free. Then he watched Antonio put the flowers on her grave. And he saw Katie.

It was almost like Liz was haunting him, even as he was trying to let her go.

It was wrong for him to cling to Katie's hand. And it was wrong of him to watch over her from this window, jealous over the beau coming to court her.

Still, it was uncanny how much Katie looked like Liz. It had been almost a decade since he'd seen Liz, but he would never forget the passion in her blue eyes or the sheen in her black hair. Katie's hair was much lighter, but her eyes were almost identical to Liz's, except he didn't remember gold flecks in Liz's blue eyes. Maybe he'd forgotten the gold.

He blinked, waiting for the barn door to open again. He remembered Liz's eyes, and he remembered her peculiar toes, the two smallest ones gracefully curved away from the others. Like they were dancing their own dance, isolated from the rest of the troupe instead of dancing alongside them.

It sounded ridiculous, but if he could see Katie's toes, he would know for sure she wasn't Liz.

He shook his head. He would never see Katie's toes, and he might never actually speak with her again, at least not alone. She'd avoided him for the past two days. He could hear her voice in the house, but Henry delivered his food and Erma took care of his medications during the day. His arm still ached, but his energy had been restored.

He had to get out of here and find out why Cardano's men were staking out the area near the Yoders' house. And he had to get away from the memory of Liz.

His gaze remained focused on the barn door below, but it didn't open again. Through the trees, he watched headlamps from a car careen down the road on the east side of the Lehmans' property. There were plenty of non-Amish men and women living in the countryside who drove cars, but it was late and in his experience, the Cardano men and the other gangsters did most of their work at night.

Standing up, he dressed quickly and rushed down the stairs. One of the English shepherds—Bennett—slept by the door, and he peered up at Rollin with dark, lazy eyes before dropping his head back onto his paws.

Fireflies lit the darkened yard, and a barn owl hooted from the trees. Headlights no longer shone through the trees, but that didn't mean the driver had left. He'd been a witness to Lance's murder—the Cardanos wouldn't stop searching until they found him. Before they did, he would find out what they were trying to hide. For Lance's sake and for Liz.

His hand on the barn door, he paused and listened to Katie whispering inside. Even with his ear pressed against the peeled paint, he couldn't hear her words nor could he make out someone responding to her.

The door scraped over the dirt when he cracked it open, and she stopped talking. Then he heard a hiccup.

Not wanting to startle her or whoever she was with, he pushed the door wide open and called her name. "Katie?"

She held the kerosene lamp above her waist, the lavender of her dress glowing in the soft light. Her cap was gone, and her long hair rested over her slender shoulders. And she hiccupped again.

"Whenever I get frightened—," she said, pointing to her throat. "I can't make them stop."

He cleared his throat. "I heard you talking to someone."

"I couldn't sleep." She reached up, petting Prince's nose beside her. "He's good company."

His hands fidgeted behind his back. He felt awkward and a bit silly. He'd allowed himself to worry that a gangster might find her. And allowed himself to assume she might be meeting a man out here when she was spending her night hours talking to a horse.

Katie nuzzled her face against Prince, and the hardened shell around his heart began to crack. Katie Lehman didn't need to hear his questions or his frustration. She didn't need to hear about Liz or his doubts about her honesty with him.

What Katie Lehman needed was a friend.

"I couldn't sleep either," he said.

Her gaze drifted to the open door behind him. Her hiccups were gone. "It seems almost a shame to miss out on a beautiful night like this."

He looked back over his shoulder at the stars flickering in the sky.

"Should we take a walk?" The words tumbled out of his mouth, surprising him.

Her bare feet brushed through the hay and dirt on the barn floor, and he braced himself for the rejection. After all, she'd spent the past two days avoiding his room.

When she looked at him, her eyes were wary, but she stepped forward.

Her voice was barely a whisper. "Would you like to walk to the creek?"

He nodded. "I would."

Light trickled across their pathway as Rollin followed Katie Lehman and her lamp through the trees. Branches dipped and swelled in the breeze, and the creek bubbled below them as it bumped across the rocks. In the dim light, he tried to catch a glimpse of Katie's toes, daring to hope that somehow she really was Liz, come back to him. But Katie's skirt covered her feet, leaves crackling under it as she walked.

He wished he could reach for her hand, diffuse the tension between them, but she'd only think he was holding it because he missed a woman he once loved.

Why couldn't he just let her spend her night in the barn alone, talking to the horse? He didn't have to come out here to be with her. But he wanted to be with her tonight.

Even as he stole another glance at her covered feet, he knew she couldn't be Liz. Katie was much calmer and more thoughtful than Liz. And Elizabeth Cardano would never sneak out to a barn to talk to a horse. She would simply wake someone up to keep her company.

Liz had never been a considerate person, but he'd loved her fiery spirit. Her zest for life. She wasn't afraid to ask questions nor was she afraid to love with all her heart. He'd been the one who'd been afraid.

Liz embraced life where he had tolerated it. When he was with her, though, part of her zeal embraced him as well. If they had married, he often wondered if the years would have mended their differences or pushed them apart. If, after almost ten years, he would still appreciate her zeal or if she would grate on his nerves like Lance had done in a few short weeks.

Katie broke the silence. "How's your shoulder?"

"Much better," he said. "Your mother is a saint."

She nodded at the trees. "Those men are still out there."

"How do you know?"

"People have seen them driving around."

"Have they been back to the Yoders'?"

"No, but the Yoders have seen their cars."

He and Lance had stumbled onto something big. These men wouldn't stop searching for him until either he was dead or they were in prison. His goal was the latter, but he needed help to do it.

"It's not safe for me to stay here any longer," he said. "But no one will tell me how to get to town."

"What do you need in town?"

"A telephone."

In front of them was the stream, and Katie hung her lantern over a tree branch. She sat on a wide rock and tucked her feet under her skirt, watching the light dance across the ripples in the water. Rollin sat on a rock beside her.

"Why are those men chasing you?" she asked

He leaned back against a trunk behind him, the coarse bark rubbing rough against Isaac's shirt. "They are trying to sell the materials needed to make alcohol, and my job is to stop them."

"And they shot you for this?"

"I think they were guarding something near the Yoders' house, and we stumbled onto it."

The lantern swung in the breeze beside him, trailing light across the path. "Or maybe they were waiting for you."

Her words silenced him. He'd wondered why the men had chased them so relentlessly before knowing who they were. The Cardanos wouldn't want the attention drawn to them of killing a civilian unless there was a very good reason.

But there was no way they could have known he and Lance were looking for them. No one except Quincy knew about their plans, and he couldn't imagine that the librarian knew the Cardanos.

Could Celeste have told Antonio he was asking about Sugarcreek? Maybe his little bird was playing them both.

"Do you know what they could be guarding?" he asked.

"The only thing over there is a barn," she said with a shrug. "A barn and a farmhouse. An English family owns them."

"Which English family?"

"Bowman is their name, but they moved to Maine a few years ago. They left their furniture here and they rent the place out to different people. The last family who lived there was Amish."

"Who is renting it now?"

She shrugged. "I don't know, but I heard there was supposed to be a wedding over there soon."

He mentally filed through the Sicilian families near Murray Hill, but he couldn't think of any who were planning weddings. "Any idea who is getting married?"

"*Non lo so.*"

He stared at her. "What did you say?"

She cleared her throat. "I said I don't know anything about the wedding."

"In Italian?"

She shrugged again, her eyes fixed on the creek. "Henry said there was someone else with you in the car."

His questions were overpowered by the guilt. He didn't want to talk about Lance.

"Who was with you?"

"My partner was driving the car," he said. "His name was Lance Dawson."

She looked over at him, her eyes sad. "What happened to Lance?"

He broke her gaze, looking back at the dark waves in the water. He didn't want to answer.

"What happened to him?" she persisted.

He took a deep breath. "They killed him."

"I'm—I'm sorry."

"He told me to run, but I should have stayed with him."

"You were injured."

"I still could have fought for him."

"Sometimes it is better to run."

The breeze rested on his arms, and he shivered. "You never have to run."

Quietness enveloped them, but it wasn't a comfortable silence. He didn't know what to say.

"Rollin?" she whispered again, her voice softer than the breeze.

"Hmm..."

"When you were sick, you called me by another name," she said. "Liz."

He flinched at the sound of the name. "I'm sorry."

"Did you love this woman?"

"One time I—I loved her very much."

With the gust of another breeze, he was back more than a decade ago. Back when Liz used to sneak out in the night hours to meet him at the park or at his house when his mother was summering on the lake. They'd been reckless back then. In love.

But then he'd been sent to France for the war. He was only gone a year, but after she welcomed him home, everything changed. He thought she'd fallen for someone else during his tour, but she refused to say if there was another man. She just didn't pine for him like he'd pined for her while he was in France.

"Why didn't you marry her?" Katie asked.

"She…" He scooted farther back against the tree. "She didn't want to marry me."

Katie turned her head. "Didn't want to marry you?"

"She wouldn't accept my proposal, and then—" He paused. "Then she was dead. The same men who killed Lance killed her too."

Katie inched closer to him. "Why doesn't someone stop them from hurting people?"

"I'm trying to stop them, but there are too many people in law enforcement who are on their team."

"So you expose them."

He glanced over at her. "It's not as easy as it might seem."

"It's never as easy as it seems." She rested her head against the trunk behind her. "How did they kill her?"

"They said she and her sister died in a fire."

"But you don't think they did?"

He shook his head. The evidence had been muddled, but in his gut he thought someone murdered them. Someone in the Cardano family.

He just didn't know who in the family had killed Liz and her sister or why.

"I think they were already dead and their family was covering it up."

"Why would her family kill her?"

"A friend of mine answered the call that night to help put out the fire. He said both girls should have escaped."

"So maybe they slept through the fire."

"That's what the medical examiner said, before a car bomb took his life."

Another gust washed over them, and he felt his eyelids grow heavy. It must be past one by now. The Lehmans would be awake in four hours, ready to start their day.

"How about you?" He forced his eyes back open. "Are you courting one of these Amish men?"

"There's one man," she said. "His name is Jonas Miller."

"Do you love him?"

She hesitated. "He would make a good father for Henry."

"A good father…" His voice trailed off. "You would marry him to care for your son?"

"I would be a good wife to him."

"I'm sure you would, but does this Jonas Miller know the real reason you are marrying him?"

Her silence answered his question.

"That doesn't seem very fair to him."

Something splashed into the water, and he heard the throaty croak of a frog.

"Where is Henry's father?" he asked, but Katie didn't answer. Her eyes had closed, her breathing slowed. Her head slowly sank over, resting on his shoulder, and his body froze with a mix of terror and pleasure. Her hair brushed his cheek, and she smelled like wildflowers and dust.

He should wake her up, tell her they needed to go back to the house, but he didn't want to disturb her quite yet.

In her sleep, she stretched out on the rock, her bare feet traveling over the edge. He couldn't take his eyes off her toes. He'd known in his heart that this woman wasn't Liz, but now he knew for certain.

There was no curve to her smaller toes, all of them dancing in harmony together.

He sighed, surprising himself with the relief he felt.

What would he do if Liz were still alive? Much would have changed between them in the past decade. He had no doubt that she wouldn't appreciate the bitter man he had become and his heart would break again. Or not. He didn't know what kind of woman she'd become.

Even though she stayed memorialized in his dreams, she was gone from this life. And she would never come back.

Liz was gone, but Katie was here with him tonight. An outspoken Amish girl who loved her son and tolerated Rollin.

In the darkness, he wanted to reach his arms out and circle them around her, but he didn't. She was an Amish woman, and he was a city man. Even if he allowed himself to entertain thoughts of them together, nothing could ever happen between them.

CHAPTER 16

Celeste's hand brushed over the carved walnut banister, its purple tones mixing with the browns to warm the second floor, and as she stepped down the grand staircase, her sharp heels sank into the cream-colored carpet that concealed the steps.

Salvatore hired a team of Sicilians to build the house back in 1914, and he insisted that every detail be the model for the entire Cardano family. He'd spent months poring over the plans and the décor, trusting no one else's opinion or even expertise.

So he built his castle along with his kingdom, and when it crumbled, he rebuilt it four years later. The second time around, he didn't pay as much attention to the details. Instead of replacing the charred hardwood floors, he had them sanded and covered with carpet. The smell of smoke faded with time, but the heat of the summer sun reawakened the memories engrained in the fibers of their walls and floors.

Two Cardano brothers were dead by the time they rebuilt the mansion so Salvatore could no longer impress them. As they restored their home, his younger brother Raymond was still alive, but Raymond didn't care about furniture or the color of carpet. He was too busy jockeying to get rid of his brother and lead the pack of Cardano enterprises and suppliers along with the scores of Cardano nephews and cousins.

Then Raymond disappeared.

In this world, no one was secure near the top.

Halfway down the stairs, she stopped. Antonio was speaking into the telephone hidden in the small room below the staircase, and the words that spewed from her son's mouth were spiked with venom.

"Find him," Antonio commanded, calling the man a name she couldn't repeat. "Find him today and get rid of him."

She took another step down, wanting to hurry into the kitchen to see if Olivia had returned, but she didn't want to startle Antonio or interrupt his discussion about the man he wanted to kill.

At one time, she'd felt sympathy for the men who lost their lives when her husband—and her son—gave the word, but she'd learned these men usually deserved a bullet in the head, like Leone Puglisi and the other gangsters along Mayfield Road. If one of the Cardanos didn't kill them, it was likely someone from another family would.

The families usually protected their own, and at one time, she believed Salvatore would have protected her—her and their three children. But reality crushed her naïveté, and she realized that Salvatore never protected anyone except himself. If he suspected that she shared information with Rollin Wells, he would send one of his cronies to remove her as well.

She stepped down again as Antonio's yelling quieted to a murmur. As far as she knew, her son hadn't said a word to Salvatore about her visiting the detective, and with the bumbling Giuseppe watching her, she hadn't gone back to Mayfield to attempt another encounter. Yesterday morning, she'd sauntered by the precinct, when Antonio and friends were all asleep, but she hadn't caught a glimpse of Rollin either.

She never should have told Rollin they couldn't have contact until Antonio stopped looking for the person who'd ratted out his plans to murder Leone. Now she'd scared the detective away—and he was one of the few people she trusted anymore.

She trusted Rollin, and she trusted her housekeeper, Olivia Green-feld. She'd met Olivia at Ernie's Dance Hall, back when she was eigh-teen. Then Celeste married, and when Olivia was too old to dance any longer, she came to work at the Cardanos'. Her friend had kept her mouth shut for the two decades that she'd taken care of their house, and she'd kept Celeste's secrets for more than thirty years now.

The door to the telephone room slammed against the wall below her, and she stopped moving, her fingers wrapped around the banister as she fixed her eyes on her toes instead of on Antonio. He crossed the base of the staircase and stomped down the hallway toward Sal-vatore's study. Sometimes she felt like one of the marble busts resting in the alcoves along the staircase, except the marble was prized more by her husband.

With Antonio gone, she hurried down the steps and into the kitchen to find her housekeeper, but Olivia hadn't returned, so she pulled out a kitchen chair and sat down. Rollin had to meet with her again. She couldn't sort all this out on her own. She needed his help.

Voices rose again, this time from the east wing of the house, and a shiver ran through her body. When Salvatore was angry, his voice usu-ally sank to a steely low, almost a whisper. She knew to brace herself when he whispered.

But screaming? The last time she'd heard him screaming…

She held out her arms, reaching to cradle a daughter who wasn't there. Trying to wake her up. Salvatore had screamed that night, yelling at Celeste to fill a pan with grease. Turn the burner on high.

Her head in her hands, Celeste's body began to shake. Her tears had burned up with the fire, but the memory clung to her like the smoky smell on their floors. Memories that would never go away.

The yelling grew closer, out in the dining room, and she could hear Salvatore railing at Antonio for his incompetence. He was telling Antonio he was an idiot for not leaving the house already, telling her son that he was a failure.

Her heart cringed at Salvatore's cruel words. Antonio wanted nothing more than Salvatore's approval, and his father thought even a hint of approval would make his son weak. Antonio Cardano needed to be strong if he were going to take over their clan one day. Strong enough not to run when he was scared. Strong enough to kill his fellow man.

Nothing Antonio had ever done as a child made Salvatore happy, and apparently he couldn't make him happy as an adult either. Like a forlorn puppy, Antonio always slunk away from his father's verbal beating and then he would return again for more. She wanted to shake her son, tell him there were so many other things he could do with his life and talents, but it was too late for that. The only aspiration he had was to please his father, and he planned to do this by eventually taking over his father's role and force friends and opponents alike to respect him.

The only trouble was, Salvatore wasn't stepping aside anytime soon. He didn't think anyone could ever take his place.

The yelling outside the kitchen escalated, Salvatore tearing Antonio apart piece by piece with his words, and Celeste's heart felt like it was about to rip in two. She didn't care where the artillery was flying, didn't even care if it hit her. She wasn't going to sit here and listen to her husband destroy the only child she had left.

Swinging open the kitchen door, she marched into the dining room. "Stop yelling, Salvatore."

Both men turned, staring at her in disbelief. No one ever told Salvatore to stop doing anything. If she were one of his men, he'd probably knock her off right now.

"No matter what happened, we are still family," she said, her voice shaking. She needed a drink. "Antonio is your son."

Salvatore's dark gaze penetrated her, and he pointed the gold handle of his walking stick at her. "This is none of your business, Celeste."

At least he remembered my name.

She stepped back. "I want peace in our home."

Salvatore's laugh was soaked with malice. "Then you shouldn't have birthed such a stupid boy."

Antonio's broad shoulders fell, and she wanted to reach out and pull him into a hug like she had when he was a child and his father told him he was stupid. But they were far beyond simple hugs, twenty years beyond it. Any attempt to comfort him would insult him instead.

Still, she couldn't help but defend him with her words. "He's a man, Salvatore, and he's not stupid."

Antonio shook his head, his eyes panicked. "Shut up, Mamma."

"You aren't stupid," she repeated, but the words bounced off him, ricocheting back to her.

For the first time she noticed the satchel in Antonio's hand. The jacket in his arms. "Where are you going?"

Salvatore's tone dipped to a low roar and he poked her with his walking stick. Hard. "He told you to shut up."

"Idiot." She heard him mutter. "Just as stupid as her son."

She stepped away, letting both of the men pass by her to the kitchen door.

They may think she was stupid, but neither of them knew where she'd sent Olivia this afternoon, nor did they know what Olivia was doing. They didn't realize the power she held in her hands.

Salvatore opened the door to the kitchen, and Antonio stepped through it so he could go out the back door. Celeste followed them.

"Get him," Salvatore told Antonio as he opened the back door.

"I will."

"Because if you don't..."

Antonio stopped him. "I said I will."

Her son walked out the door, leaving her behind with the monster. Salvatore watched their son round the back of the house, and then, with a shake of his head, he left her alone in the kitchen.

She checked the clock over the door and looked back out the window. Any minute now, Olivia would return.

CHAPTER 17

Katie dipped the ceramic bowl into the soapy water and scrubbed off the sticky remnants of oatmeal and maple syrup. All through breakfast, she avoided Rollin's gaze. She never should have gone on a walk with him last night. Never should have allowed him to see her at her weakest.

When she couldn't sleep, she'd only wanted to go outside and spend time with Prince, who was much more than a driving horse to her. He was the only one whom she entrusted with her secrets.

Instead of spending the night hours with Prince, she'd ended up by the creek with the one man she'd never wanted to see again. And she'd fallen asleep on his shoulder.

She scrubbed the bowl even harder. At first she'd only pretended to be asleep, when he asked about Henry's father, but it felt so good to be close to him. Warm. He'd awakened her long before daylight and they'd snuck in through the back door. Even so, what had she been thinking?

Apparently she hadn't been thinking at all. She didn't want to know Rollin Wells, and she didn't want him to know anything about her. She wanted him to leave this house and go back to Cleveland where he belonged. Far away from her and Henry.

Footsteps rumbled down the staircase in the next room, and she dipped the bowl into a tub of water to rinse it off.

Isaac said he would take Rollin to Sugarcreek today. If she worked it right, she wouldn't have to speak with him again.

She heard Henry laughing in the dining room, and she turned

as he and Rollin walked into the room. Rollin looked handsome in his Amish attire. A combination of humility and strength. A tremor rushed through her skin, and she slid the bowl back into the water so they wouldn't see her hands shake.

She crossed her arms, looking back and forth between Rollin and her son. Her eyes rested on Henry. "Where are you going?"

"Down to the creek."

"Isaac thought you might be able to help him repair that fence today."

"He's going to town instead."

She didn't want to speak with Rollin but she had no choice. "Are you going with him?"

"Isaac or Henry?"

"Both of them."

"I was going to fish with Henry until Isaac is ready to leave for Sugarcreek."

She reached out, clutching the side of the kitchen table. "I don't know."

"Non lo so," he said.

She blinked. She'd worked so hard to harbor her secrets, but he'd shaken her up and caused her to regress. What must he think of her? An Amish girl speaking Italian.

She would not be unnerved by this man.

"I had an Italian friend when I was a child."

"Mamm knows lots of Italian," Henry said.

She squeezed the table even harder. "Did you get your fishing pole?" she asked but immediately regretted her words when Henry rushed toward the doorway and disappeared into the next room.

She met Rollin's gaze for a moment and then turned around, focusing on the dishes left in the sink. She washed one glass. Two.

"Katie…" Rollin started.

She spun around again. "Please don't corrupt him, Rollin."

His eyebrows climbed. "Corrupt him?"

"Don't talk to him about automobiles or guns or fancy machines."

"I don't know anything about automobiles."

She brushed her wet hands on her apron. "I'm serious, Rollin. I don't want you to tell him how wonderful the world is outside of Sugarcreek."

He shrugged. "We're only going fishing."

Henry rushed back into the kitchen, a willow branch pole in each hand. "Let's go."

Rollin tipped his hat to her before he left.

She stole out of the kitchen with the ceramic bowl and a dishtowel in her hands, wiping the bowl as she watched the two of them walk down the path to the creek.

Liz never told her that Rollin asked for her hand in marriage, and Rollin had no reason to lie to her now about it. He didn't know who she was. For years she had been furious with Rollin for abandoning Liz, but if he had proposed to her…

It meant he hadn't run away.

"Are you trying to polish that bowl?"

She spun around, and Isaac was watching her with a wry smile on his lips. She dropped the bowl to her side.

"I was…" she started, but she couldn't think of a good excuse for drying the dishes in the living room.

Isaac plucked his hat off the rack and placed it on his head. "Erma heard you sneak into the house in the middle of the night."

"I couldn't sleep," she said, her gaze dropping to the floor. "So I went for a walk."

"She said there were two people."

She nodded, not able to lie. "Rollin couldn't sleep either."

Isaac glanced out the front window as Rollin and Henry disappeared into the forest. "You can't ask for a finer man than Jonas Miller."

"I know."

"Jonas will make a good father for the boy."

Her gaze followed Isaacs's to the window even though Rollin and Henry were gone, and she thought about Rollin's words to her last night. Jonas deserved a woman devoted to him and his faith, not a wandering—and scared—heart like hers.

Isaac turned to her. "Are you certain you want Henry to spend time with Rollin?"

"No," Katie replied. "But Henry seems to like him."

"Erma says his arm is healing fast," Isaac said as he opened the door. "There is nothing more she can do to help him."

"What about the men who are looking for him?"

"It would be safer for Rollin to go back to Cleveland."

Safer for them, but not for Rollin. These men would find him wherever he went. They never forgot.

She swiped the towel over the dry dish again, afraid for him. "You will take him to Sugarcreek?"

"Ya. This afternoon."

Turning back to the kitchen, she smacked the bowl against the counter and the bottom cracked.

She wasn't angry at Rollin. She was angry at herself.

Angry that she didn't want Rollin Wells to go back to Cleveland.

* * * * *

Water splashed on both sides of Henry as he sprinted up the creek, like the wake of the wooden boats on Lake Erie.

"You're scaring the fish away," Rollin shouted to Henry.

"Nah," the boy said as he raced back toward him. "I'm just rounding them up."

Rollin pushed a worm from Henry's pail through a curved pin that doubled as a fishing hook and threw the string into the creek. "What kind of fish do you have in here?"

"Perch, catfish, minnows."

"Maybe we'll bring a few minnows back for lunch," he joked.

Henry sat down on a rock and tossed his line beside Rollin's. "I don't like to eat fish."

"Me neither."

Rollin leaned back against the tree trunk. The sun warmed his face, and he breathed in the aroma of cloves and honey that sweetened the air.

When he was a kid, he'd wanted to go fishing, but the nearest stream was a good mile from their city home. He spent most of his childhood playing in his bedroom and at the manicured park nearby. Even if he'd lived closer to the water, it wasn't like his mother would let him play in it. She believed cleanliness trumped even godliness, and he spent his boyhood as scrubbed and polished as the Wells's family silver.

Cleveland.

For a moment, he'd almost forgotten he was supposed to be going back today. He couldn't remember when he'd enjoyed himself so much.

Henry stood up and splashed back in the water. "I'm going to round up some more fish."

The boy picked up a stick and began to prod the rocks near the bank. Rollin watched him closely to see if his ploy would work.

From over the hills, Rollin heard the whirr of an airplane engine. He strained his eyes, searching the sky until he found it. The bird was a brilliant green color with dual yellow wings. And she flew low, right above the trees.

Henry squealed as he raced back to Rollin. Both of their necks were arched, watching the airplane as it passed over them. The only times Rollin had flown in a plane were when he was being shot at. He often wondered what it would be like to fly in one for the sheer pleasure of it.

"It's an Eaglerock," Rollin said, his eyes on the green tail as it disappeared over the trees.

The boy was beside him, his eyes shaded like Rollin as they watched the plane travel away from them. "A what?"

"An Eaglerock," he repeated. "An Eaglerock biplane."

"What's a biplane?" His voice trailed off in marvel of the word.

"It means they have two pairs of wings instead of one."

Henry turned to look at Rollin. "Have you flown in a biplane?"

He nodded. "When I was in the Great War."

The boy's eyes were wide, watching him with open admiration. "You were in a war?"

He heard the crack of a stick behind him, and he turned on the rock to see Katie. Her arms were folded, and she was glaring at him.

"Come along, Henry," she growled, with as much warmth as an arctic bear.

He'd promised her not to talk about machines and here he was telling the boy about airplanes and the Great War.

"He asked me…" he started, but quickly realized it was pointless to defend himself.

She reached for Henry and pulled him close to her. "Are you okay?"

"Did you hear what he said?" the boy asked, his eyes still on Rollin. "Rollin was in a war!"

Katie's eyes were on him as well. "Isaac said he's ready to take you into town."

CHAPTER 18

Olivia stole quietly into the kitchen of the Cardano house and shut the back door. Often Celeste thought her friend and housekeeper looked like a fairy, with her long black hair and lithe frame that she'd managed to maintain even after she stopped performing on the stage. Today, though, her breathing was laborious as she collapsed in a kitchen chair. Celeste pushed a glass of cold mint tea across the table to her.

Olivia guzzled the drink in the time it took Celeste to take another sip of her own glass. Her lips craved something harder than mint tea, but right now she didn't need comfort as much as she needed clarity.

"Did you find someone to deliver it?" Celeste asked.

Olivia wiped her lips with her hand. "My nephew took it into the precinct for me."

"And Rollin received it?"

Ice rattled in Olivia's glass when she shook her head. "He wasn't there."

"What about his partner?"

"Detective Dawson wasn't there either."

Celeste's head began to pound as her voice dropped to a whisper. "Where were they?"

"My nephew is only fourteen," Olivia said. "Sometimes he gets things wrong."

She pushed her glass away. "What exactly did your nephew say?"

Olivia cleared her throat. "He said that Rollin and Detective Dawson had been sent away for an assignment."

"Sent away?" She paused, thinking. Their job was to stop bootlegging on the streets of Cleveland. Federal agents were responsible for the rest of their country. "That doesn't make any sense."

"I didn't think so either."

"Did your nephew happen to mention where Rollin and Dawson were sent?"

Olivia looked away like she didn't want to tell her.

"Where were they sent?" Celeste pushed her.

"Miami," Olivia mumbled. "Miami, Florida."

Celeste wiped her sweaty palms on her skirt. "Who are they trying to capture—Al Capone?"

"I don't know," she replied. "My nephew probably got the information wrong."

"Did the boys down at the precinct happen to say when they were coming back?"

"They didn't know."

"Rollin better get himself home soon."

She needed him in Sugarcreek.

* * * * *

Rollin laced his shoes beside the front door as he waited for Isaac to drive the buggy to the house. Katie watched him closely, examining his face when he wasn't looking at her. After a decade, he was still a handsome man, with his sharp nose and blue eyes that had mesmerized her and a number of other girls along Mayfield. His strength was still there as well, but the old charm had worn off. She wondered if he'd lost it around the same time her youth had been stolen away.

He looked over, catching her gaze. He leaned against the doorpost. "I'm sorry for telling Henry about the airplane…and the war."

"There is a reason I've chosen the plain lifestyle."

He searched her eyes again, as if he could find Liz in them if he searched long enough. "Why is that, Katie?"

She paused, wondering if she could make him understand without sharing her story. "You see things like airplanes as progress, but I see them as a threat."

"Progress isn't always bad," he said.

"Perhaps not, but fighting is bad. And so are the guns."

"At least we can agree on one thing," he said. "But sometimes you have to fight."

She bit her lower lip as she tried to think of a response. Forgiveness was at the heart of the Amish culture, not defense. The stance on defense was one of the core beliefs she struggled with, though, and perhaps was one of the reasons she'd yet to be baptized. She wasn't as concerned about defending herself, but if someone tried to hurt Henry, she didn't think she could keep herself from fighting back.

"Jesus said that if someone smites you on one cheek, you should turn the other to him," she said, repeating what she'd heard at the services many a time.

Rollin didn't hesitate. "Jesus also blessed those who keep justice."

"Where did you hear that?"

"From a buddy of mine in the army. We called him Preach."

"You can keep justice without shooting anyone."

"Not in France."

Her head felt like it was spinning. The questions berating her again. "It's complicated," she said.

"Yes, it is."

"Jesus taught us to love."

"And sometimes the best way to love someone is to fight for them."

Isaac maneuvered Prince around the front of the house and stopped the buggy. She was relieved not to continue the conversation. She already had enough questions without adding to them.

Katie pointed toward the doorway. "Your ride is here."

He backed toward the door. "I'll stay in Sugarcreek until someone comes from Cleveland to get me. Then we'll go check out that wedding."

She nodded, telling herself this is exactly what she wanted him to do. "I'm sure there will be plenty of people relieved that you are okay."

His laugh was gruff. "My captain will be relieved, but no one else cares."

"Someone else must care, Rollin. Your family?"

"Most of my family is gone." He hesitated. "I'll have to visit Lance's mother and tell her what happened to her son. She cares about him."

The tears came unbidden again, and she blinked them back. "I don't envy you."

"He was a terrible detective," Rollin said. "But he was a good kid."

"His mother will be devastated."

Rollin took another step away from her. "Yes, she will."

In the yard, Erma handed Isaac a basket of eggs to sell in town and then stepped away. Isaac waved his hat at them.

"He's ready for you," she said.

Rollin nodded, watching her. "I have to go."

He lingered for another moment by the door before he went outside. There was nothing else for either of them to say. She and Henry would go back to life as normal when he was gone, and she would marry Jonas Miller.

Marry Jonas Miller.

The thought made her heart tumble.

Moving toward the window, she watched Rollin climb into the buggy. Henry hollered from the barn and came tearing across the yard like a swarm of bees was chasing him. Rollin hopped back down and held out his hand, but Henry didn't shake it. Instead he wrapped his arms around Rollin's legs and hugged him.

Katie tapped her fingers against the glass, her tears brimming now. If only she could tell Rollin the truth. Maybe she wouldn't have to marry Jonas Miller. Maybe she could…

Rollin turned, catching her face in the window, and he lifted his hat to wave to her again. She turned away from the window and escaped back into the safety of the house.

The outside was Rollin's world. She belonged inside these walls.

* * * * *

Buggies rolled slowly by the crowded IGA market in Sugarcreek. Outside the store, wooden crates and bins were filled with raspberries, blueberries, and bananas, and inside the window, Rollin could see the aisles packed with customers and their carts.

Across from the store, people were setting up booths for the Sugarcreek Street Fair that he'd read about in the newspaper. Part of him wished he could stay one more day in Sugarcreek so he could take

Henry to the fair. Katie would never allow her son to go up in an airplane, but surely she couldn't argue with a merry-go-round.

He rounded the corner of the grocery store and eyed the automobiles and buggies in the parking lot before he opened the telephone booth door. No one seemed to be watching him in his Amish shirt and straw hat, but he still nudged the hat a little lower on his forehead before he dialed the precinct number.

As the telephone rang, he could only imagine the uproar at the precinct today. Malloy yelling at his subordinates to find him and Lance, worried out of his mind with two of his detectives still missing from the weekend. They'd be down here in a few hours, and they'd sniff around until they discovered what the Cardanos were doing.

When the dispatcher accepted his call, he wanted to cheer.

"Peter!" he said. "I'm so glad to speak with you."

"Wells?"

"I'm all right."

"How's the sunshine?" Peter asked.

"Sunshine?" He glanced up at the blue sky. "Is Malloy there?"

"He left for a meeting down at city hall an hour ago, but he was anxious to know if you called," Peter said. "A few of us don't think you or Dawson are ever coming back."

"What are you talking about?"

"You know, with all that Florida water and sunshine and beautiful dames. We're all jealous that Malloy sent you down there."

"Sent us?" He switched the receiver to the other ear. "We're not in Florida."

"Right." Peter laughed. "Malloy said you might play it dumb, but he let me in on the secret."

Rollin twisted the mouthpiece in his hands, trying to understand why Peter wasn't worried about him. And why he kept talking about Florida. "What secret?"

Peter lowered his voice. "That you're working undercover in Miami."

Miami? "Malloy doesn't know where I am."

"The captain said what you and Dawson were doing was very important, but he wouldn't tell us specifics. A few of us are betting that you followed Raymond Cardano down there."

"Followed Raymond… On second thought, don't tell Malloy that I called."

"But he'll want to know."

"I'll call him back tonight when I have more information for him."

"He hates surprises."

"He hates the wrong information even more."

Peter agreed. "I told the boys that Dawson probably went to the beach the moment you got down there."

The memory of his friend clenched his gut again. "I haven't seen him for a while."

Peter pounded something. "I knew it."

Rollin slumped back against the wall as he hung up the phone. The precinct was supposed to be frantic right now, searching for him and Lance. But Malloy wasn't there, and even worse, he'd told the others that he and Lance were in Miami.

Why would Malloy lie to the men?

Either he didn't want them to panic that two of his detectives were missing, or… He was working another angle.

He shivered. So many of the police and judges had been bought out by corrupt families like the Cardanos and Puglisis over the past ten years. They served the gangsters instead of the people in Cleveland.

Was it possible that his boss had turned on them too?

Malloy had hired Rollin back in 1920. He'd told him that he recognized a thirst for justice in Rollin that few men had—a drive to find out who had murdered Liz. Malloy was legendary in their precinct. He'd brought down more criminals than any other detective in Cleveland.

A bee buzzed over his shoulder and landed on his hand. Rollin held up his hand, examining the fuzzy yellow and black stripes on its back. The bee was an unassuming creature, if you didn't know about its powerful sting. But if it were startled, it would fight back with a vengeance, even though using its stinger would end its life.

Malloy had directed Rollin and Lance to his friend at the library, and Quincy pointed them here. Did Quincy tell Malloy where they were going? And if so, what had his captain done with the information?

He reached out and fingered the black cord on the phone. He didn't want to alert anyone on the force who may be working for the other side.

Gilbert Simmons, his old partner, had retired to the shore along Lake Erie last fall. He could ask Gilbert to do a little sniffing around, but he didn't want to put him or his family in danger. He needed to speak with someone who was already in danger.

Picking up the mouthpiece, he dialed the telephone again. Celeste might pretend she'd never heard of Sugarcreek, but she knew something about what was happening here. And she had to tell him what was going on.

He gave the operator the name of Raymond Cardano and waited as she tried to connect his call to the Cardano residence. If Salvatore answered his call, he would hang up.

In the corner of his eye, a black automobile turned at the corner and into the IGA parking lot. One of the Lincolns. He slammed the mouthpiece back onto the phone.

The Lincoln cruised through the parking lot, and Rollin turned his face away from them. He shouldn't stay outside while the Cardano men were sniffing around. There was nothing he could do to defend himself or any innocent bystanders who might get in their way.

His hands behind his back, he forced himself not to rush as he walked into the IGA and found Isaac standing dumbfounded in an aisle, trying to pick out Jell-O for Erma.

"Which flavor does she want?" Rollin asked.

Isaac shook his head. "She told me to surprise her."

"Surprises are dangerous," he muttered.

"Peach. Cherry. Chocolate," Isaac said, reading the labels.

Rollin stole a glance back toward the front of the store, but he couldn't see the window. "What would your grandson like?"

Isaac turned to him. "Grandson?"

Rollin rolled his neck. Why did everything seem so confusing today? "Henry," he said, like Isaac didn't know the name of his own grandson.

Isaac picked up the cherry Jell-O. "Henry's my nephew."

Rollin watched Isaac examine the Jell-O box. He'd been referring to Erma as Katie's mother, and she hadn't corrected him. Not that it was any of his business, but why was she trying to hide her relationship with the Lehmans from him? These days, it felt like everyone was trying to hide something from him.

Isaac put the cherry Jell-O back on the shelf and reached for the chocolate one, studying it in his hand.

Rollin felt like he was a modern-day Robinson Crusoe, stranded on an island with a friendly native named Isaac who didn't know what to do with him or how to get him home to Cleveland. He didn't know who he could trust outside the island to help him either. He was helpless, and he hated being helpless.

Isaac put back the chocolate one and stared at all the flavors again.

If they didn't leave soon, the gangsters might trap them in here. "Maybe you should surprise Erma and buy all three."

Isaac contemplated the idea for a moment and then pulled three boxes off the shelf. "Did you make your call?"

Rollin nodded his head.

"When are your friends coming for you?"

He hesitated. "They're not coming."

Isaac turned, searching his face. "Why not?"

"I'm not sure," he said. "Something strange is going on."

Rollin followed Isaac and his three boxes of gelatin to the register. Outside the store's front window, he could see the black Lincoln parked in the midst of the other automobiles and buggies. The market door opened and two men in suits and dark fedoras walked inside.

Isaac stepped beside Rollin to block him from the men's view as the cashier handed Isaac the change for his dollar. Rollin didn't turn, but he felt someone behind him. Isaac nudged his arm, and they hurried out of the store.

As he and Isaac walked through the door, Rollin glanced back at the men paying for something at the register. He recognized both men from the Cleveland streets, but he didn't know their names. He hoped they wouldn't recognize him.

Rollin climbed into the left side of the buggy, waiting for Isaac to speak.

"What are you going to do now?" the older man asked.

Rollin leaned back against the seat. He would have to find out what the Cardanos were planning by himself. "Go visit the Bowman farm."

CHAPTER 19

Jonas pushed the porch swing back and forth with his boots as Katie and he watched the colors of the sunset seep across the sky. Her bare feet were tucked under her skirt, and in the quietness, she struggled to keep her eyes open. Her chin dropped to her neck, and she jolted back up, blinking her eyes. Trying to stay awake.

Jonas glanced over at her. "Are you cold?"

"No."

He pushed the swing again. "Thirsty?"

"I'm fine," she said with a sigh. "Just tired."

"You should go to bed."

She shook her head. "I want to wait until Isaac comes home."

Days ago, she had been driving to see Jonas to tell him the truth about her past and to tell him that she had decided to join the Amish church, but now she didn't know what she wanted. Marriage was forever, and she wasn't certain that an Amish life was what forever should look like for her and Henry.

Her gaze wandered to the road below the house. Isaac would be back any minute now, without Rollin Wells. It was good that Rollin was gone from their lives, but he still left behind a vacancy that she couldn't explain. She didn't want to feel this vacancy nor the thrill that Rollin brought to her heart. She wanted to stay contented with the life she'd built for her and Henry in Sugarcreek.

She closed her eyes again, leaning back against the swing.

When she left Cleveland, she didn't have many options. The Amish lifestyle was the only choice she'd had at the time, the best escape from the people who wanted her dead. Isaac and Erma welcomed her and Henry into their home with open arms.

Now she was no longer Nikki Cardano. She was Katie Lehman. Even though she was plain in her dress, she felt like she had come alive as Henry's mother and Isaac and Erma's niece. People needed her, and they loved her. And she loved the people in her community.

Still, she wasn't convinced that she should join the Amish faith. Some days, when she visited the village, she dreamed about what it would be like to live on the outside again. As long as she didn't go back to Cleveland, she could be free from the strict rules of her family and the Amish community.

But if she married Jonas Miller, she would trade any hope of freedom for security.

She rubbed her hands over her bare arms. Freedom was overrated. She needed security for her and for Henry.

Jonas scooted closer, and she opened her eyes again. The bright colors of the sunset rained down on her.

"What are you thinking about?" he asked.

"All my blessings."

"They are many. For both of us."

"How are the Yoders?" she asked.

"They are well." He pushed the swing again. "Whoever was chasing Rollin Wells has left them alone."

"They are afraid," she whispered.

He turned to look at her. "The Yoders aren't afraid."

Biting the side of her lip, she didn't respond to him. She hadn't meant the Yoders. She meant the men chasing Rollin were afraid—of losing their prey and of being exposed.

"Have you seen the automobiles again?"

"Ya, I have seen them on the road," he said. "But they haven't come on the Yoders' property again."

"Goot."

As long as the men didn't approach the Amish members, she and the others would be fine.

"I was thinking about going to the street fair this weekend." He paused. "Would you like to get ice cream with me on Sunday?"

She smiled. "Henry loves ice cream."

"I wasn't asking Henry." He cleared his throat. "I mean, I was hoping to spend time with just you."

"I see."

He hesitated. "You don't want to go with me alone, do you?"

Her answer would wound him, so she stayed silent. She didn't want to hurt him.

"The last time we spoke..." he said. "You were going to make a decision."

The chains on the porch swing creaked as they rocked again. There was too much happening in her mind right now to make a decision about the church or about him.

"I'm still thinking, Jonas."

"What...what is stopping you?" The questioning in his voice panged with hurt. In her attempt not to wound him, she was being more than unfair. She was being cruel.

"It's a big decision for me to decide if I want to spend the rest of my life as an Amish woman."

"I thought you decided that when you came to Sugarcreek."

She shook her head. "I was only planning to visit for a time."

"And yet you stayed."

"I love it here, Jonas, but when I decide to join the church, *if* I decide, I will never turn away from that decision."

"Do you have a problem with our church?" He hesitated, pushing the swing again with his heels. "Or is your problem with me?"

"Jonas…"

He stopped her. "Because you can join the church without marrying me."

She looked at him, but his eyes were focused on the hills beyond the house and on the setting sun.

It didn't matter that Rollin was gone from her life forever. It didn't matter that she may never marry at all. She had waited too long to give this good man her word.

If she married Jonas, she would marry him for security—not love. And because he would be a good father. Jonas didn't want to marry her to have a son—he could always have children. He was marrying her because he wanted a wife

"You're right," she finally said.

"About what?"

"I almost joined the church so I could marry you."

"You aren't planning to join it?"

"Not now."

His heels stomped on the porch, stopping the swing, and when his eyes bored into hers, she struggled to catch her breath. Jonas Miller was the best catch in their whole community, but he wasn't for her. And she couldn't marry him when her mind kept thinking about another man, hadn't ever stopped thinking about him since she left Cleveland so long ago.

"Do you think you will ever want to marry me?" Jonas's words hung between them, and in that moment, the decision couldn't be more clear. The time had come for him to begin visiting Greta Hershberger or another Amish woman who would thrive on being Jonas Miller's wife.

She hoped she wouldn't regret it.

"I can't marry you, Jonas."

His gaze dropped, and he scooted against the far side of the swing, the gulf between them widening until it seemed like they were on opposite sides of a canyon. If either of them crept too close to the edge, they might plunge over and injure themselves.

"You are certain?" he asked.

"I am."

He paused. "What about your baptism?"

"I don't know."

He stood up in front of the swing and placed his straw hat on his head. "You need to do what God requires of you."

"I wish I knew what He required."

The whisper of Prince's gait traveled up the driveway, and she was grateful for the interruption. And grateful that Isaac was home again. She stepped off the porch to greet Isaac, and in the fading light, she realized that Isaac wasn't alone in the buggy.

The passenger's face became clearer, and her heart seemed to stop. Isaac had brought Rollin back to them. To her.

When the buggy stopped, Rollin hopped off and grabbed the hat on the seat beside him. Walking slowly toward her, he eyed Jonas and then reached out his hand to the man.

"You are the one who spoke with the driver at the Yoders' home."

Jonas nodded, shaking Rollin's hand.

"I'm grateful," Rollin said.

Katie's voice trembled when she spoke. "I thought you were going back to Cleveland."

"Something happened," he said simply, and she didn't press him for information. Not with Jonas beside her.

"I best be leaving," Jonas said, stepping toward his buggy.

"I'm sorry," she whispered as Jonas stepped away, but he didn't turn around. She didn't know if he heard her.

"What are you sorry for?" Rollin asked.

Shaking her head, she rushed back up the stairs. Why couldn't she leave Rollin Wells behind?

CHAPTER 20

Celeste waited up for Antonio most of the night, until she succumbed to sleep in one of the upholstered chairs in the front room around four. After the sun rose, she checked on Antonio's room, but his bed was still made. Neither her husband nor her son ever told her when they were leaving the house or when they planned to return, but she'd hoped Antonio would return from Sugarcreek last night.

In the kitchen, she brewed a pot of coffee and drank a cup with one of the raspberry pastries she purchased yesterday from her friend's bakery.

What was her son doing in Sugarcreek?

She'd spent most of her life being told what to do and where to go. Even in her late teens, when she was a dancer, the stage manager told her what she needed to do and when. Never once had she rebelled against the management at the dance hall. The hours were grueling, but she was glad for the work and the freedom it offered her when she wasn't on stage.

She brushed the golden crumbs into a small pile and dumped them into the trashcan before taking another pastry back to the kitchen table with her. A cream puff sprinkled with sugar.

Salvatore first saw her when she was onstage at Ernie's Dance Hall. He watched her dance for hours, and he called for her after the show. She'd been enamored by his attention and the cash that flowed from his billfold. When he asked her to marry him, she didn't spend time considering whether Salvatore would be a good husband. He was her ticket to leave the stage behind and lead the life that she'd desired since she was a little girl—a life of money and prestige and all the fine foods she could eat.

The justice of the peace performed their wedding before Salvatore's family got wind that he was marrying a girl born in the Americas instead of in Sicily. And before he found out about her past. His family snubbed her for years because she wasn't Sicilian. They never welcomed her into the family, but eventually they accepted her as Salvatore's wife.

Fortunately, none of them ever probed her for details about her childhood, and her husband never bothered to ask.

Salvatore wasn't as wealthy as he'd led her to believe at the time, but he had enough. Because she wasn't dancing, she didn't concern herself with the extra pounds that came with her obsession for pastries and the birthing of three children. Salvatore didn't seem to notice the extra weight in the first years of their marriage.

Celeste brushed her hands over the bulge around her stomach, a bulge she covered well with yards of expensive fabrics and drop waist dresses, but Salvatore knew it was there. At some point, the extra weight began to irritate him. She tried to lose it, but the temptation for sweets—and for alcohol—was too strong.

He complained for a year or two after Nicola was born, and then he stopped noticing his wife at all.

She took another bite of the cream puff and savored the buttery crust and sweet filling.

Her husband stopped noticing, and there was nothing she could do about it except continue to play her role as the compliant wife. She was a coward when it came to confronting Salvatore, too scared to protest his lack of affection. Afraid that she would have to leave the security of her Cleveland mansion and the comforts of her life as Salvatore Cardano's wife.

She'd hoped that Salvatore's love for her would reawaken, but it stayed dormant over the years. She poured her life into her children instead of her husband until two of her daughters were taken from her. The only child left in her home was just like his father. Antonio no longer wanted to be around her either.

When she said good-bye to Nicola, she never thought she would see her youngest daughter again. She promised never to contact her, and she'd kept that promise. Even the slightest contact could risk her daughter's life.

But Antonio was down in Sugarcreek right now, and she didn't know why. What would happen if he stumbled onto Nicola's secret? Or if one of her cousins found her instead?

She trembled.

She couldn't let Antonio or those other men near her daughter.

The back door opened, and Olivia stepped into the house with a bag full of bread and groceries. "It's a beautiful day," her housekeeper sang.

"Is it?" Her gaze wandered toward the window, and she realized the sun was up.

Olivia placed a loaf of bread and a bag of apples on the counter followed by brown paper wrapped around meat. "You want me to start with the vacuuming this morning?"

"No," she replied. "Salvatore is still asleep."

"The bathrooms then."

Celeste stepped to the sink and dumped the crumbs of cream puff into the trash before looking out the window at the slope of the hill behind their house. There was a garage that held Salvatore's car and a small guesthouse where Eligio Ricci, their driver and one of a handful of Salvatore's bodyguards, lived.

Celeste spun around. "Did you take the trolley today?"

"No." Olivia put a jar into the refrigerator. "I drove Benjamin's car."

Celeste looked out the window again and saw the shiny bumper of the Ford that belonged to her friend's husband. She tried to smile. "Can I use your car today?"

Olivia tilted her head. "Eligio should be up soon."

"I don't want him to drive me."

Olivia put the meat into the icebox. "Where do you want to go?"

Celeste sighed. "I want to go home."

Olivia watched her for a moment, like she was trying to determine if Celeste was in her right mind. "Why would you want to go there?"

"Antonio is in Sugarcreek right now, and I don't know why."

"I can't go with you. Not that far."

Celeste folded her gloved hands together. "Could I borrow your car for the night?"

Olivia's eyes narrowed. "Do you still know how to drive?"

"Enough to get me there," Celeste said, but she could read the doubt lingering in Olivia's eyes.

Her friend folded the bag and tucked it under the sink before turning back to her. "I'll ride with you as far as my house, and then I'll decide if you can take it."

Celeste had learned to drive a car about fifteen years before, when she and Salvatore first purchased an automobile. The machine scared her, but she refused to let Salvatore see her fear. She'd driven it when she had to, for about three years, until Salvatore hired a chauffeur for them both. She was glad to give Eligio her keys.

Even though she preferred to walk, she let Eligio cart her around when she had to go downtown. Salvatore used to forbid her to go walking alone because he thought it was too dangerous, but it had been a long time since he told her she couldn't walk by herself. Maybe he was secretly hoping someone would bump her off so he could invite one of his girlfriends to move into her bedroom. Her death would take care of two problems for him. His wife would be gone, and he would have a good excuse for an all-out war against the Puglisi family, blaming them for whoever killed her.

Slipping upstairs, she snuck past the closed door to Salvatore's room and packed an overnight satchel with another skirt, two blouses, and a bagful of toiletries. If she left before he woke up, she wouldn't have to answer any questions until she returned. Maybe he wouldn't even notice she was gone.

"Are you ready?" Olivia asked when she stepped back into the kitchen.

She paused, eyeing the drawer near the back door before she took out a notepad and pencil and scribbled the words. *Visiting my sister.*

She stared down at the words for a moment, and then she ripped off the paper and crumpled it. Salvatore didn't even know she had a sister.

She picked up the pencil again and wrote, *Gone to visit a friend.*

Maybe it would be good for her husband to wonder which friend.

* * * * *

All Katie wanted was a cup of coffee, but as she poured it, the dark liquid spilled out the sides of the cup, pooling on the counter in front of her before it began to drip onto the floor. Reaching for a rag, she quickly wiped the spill off the floor and counter before she willed her long sip of coffee to wake her up.

Even though she'd been exhausted, sleep eluded her for much of the night. She'd tossed off her covers, counted the stars outside her window. The knowledge that Rollin was back under the roof with her, across the hallway, stole her sleep.

She'd made her peace with saying good-bye to Rollin yesterday, yet he was back in the house. And it made her wonder.

What would he do if he found out she was Liz's younger sister? There was no doubt he would be angry at her for hiding the truth from him, but once he calmed down, she wondered what he would say.

Her back against the counter, she surveyed the dirty dishes and pans left behind after a whirlwind breakfast. Henry left with Erma a half hour ago to pick blueberries from the other side of the hill, and Isaac was cutting the alfalfa field by himself.

And Rollin? As far as she knew, Rollin was still asleep in his room. After breakfast, Isaac said he was going to pound on Rollin's door and put him to good use helping muck out the horse stalls, but Erma stopped him, saying Rollin was still recovering. Isaac mumbled something about lazy Englishers, and then he told Katie to send Rollin out to the field if he ever decided to roll out of bed.

Everyone had a job to do this morning, and it was her job to clean up after breakfast. She pumped water into the sink and scrubbed bar soap over the greasy dishes. With each dish, she thought about the man asleep upstairs. At least one of them had no problem getting rest.

She picked another greasy pan off the pile and began to scrub it.

What would Rollin think when she told him that she wasn't going to marry Jonas Miller? That she didn't know what she was going to do with her life. He probably wouldn't care, but she needed to make a decision for Henry's sake.

She'd always known the day would come when she would have to decide where she would go after living with Isaac and Erma, but the day was approaching much faster than she wanted. She wasn't ready to decide, but she couldn't keep their lives in limbo forever. Either she was going to become Amish and hope Henry would one day join her, or she was going to make the decision to live outside this community.

Her gaze wandered outside to the bright blue summer day.

Ever since she was a little girl, she'd dreamed about living by the ocean. Her parents took her and Antonio and Liz to the coast in Florida once when she was young, and she loved running in the waves and digging her toes into the warm sand. When she returned from her trip, she found a picture book with photos of the rugged California coast at a bookstore and her father purchased it for her. She spent hours enchanted by the boulders, cliffs, and miles of sea.

Even though Henry had never been to a beach, sometimes he dreamed about the ocean with her. And sometimes she dreamed alone of running away with Henry to a coastal village on the West Coast. No one from Cleveland would find her there.

It was only a dream. She didn't know anyone in the West nor did she have the resources to get to California.

The last pan scrubbed, Katie dried all the dishes and put them away. With the counters wiped and the floor swept, she glanced up at the clock and realized it was almost nine. At some point today, Rollin would have to get up and help Isaac in the field, or Isaac would take him back to Sugarcreek tonight and leave him there with or without a ride back to Cleveland.

She climbed the stairs to Rollin's room, but instead of knocking, she whispered his name through the cracked door. When he didn't respond, she said it again, a little louder, but he still didn't say anything. Her ear against the door, she listened for sounds of him breathing, but the room was silent.

Had he grown ill again during the night?

"Rollin," she said again as she nudged the door open.

The bed was made, but Rollin wasn't in it. He and his Amish attire were gone.

She pounded her fist in her hand. She knew exactly where Rollin went, and after what happened to him and his partner, he never should have gone alone. Only an idiot would face the Cardanos alone, unless the person didn't care about dying.

Maybe Rollin didn't care.

She walked to Rollin's bedside, picked up his pillow, and sat down on the bed, clutching the pillow to her chest. Memories flooded back from her childhood. The hours she'd spent dreaming about her sister's suitor.

Rollin never knew how much she admired him when she was a much younger girl. At thirteen, her young heart raced every time he came to their home, and she would pester him and Liz like an annoying fly until Liz shooed her from the room.

Liz had to know she adored Rollin, but she didn't think Rollin ever really noticed her. He only had eyes for her sister. With the exception of an occasional hello to Liz's kid sister, he didn't know she existed. She was just plain Nikki Cardano, the dull one of the pack.

Still she'd dreamt about him for years, after he went off to France for the Great War. Perhaps that was the reason she never married. Perhaps those feelings were still there, sheltered not-so-deep within her.

She shouldn't have trusted her heart back then, and she shouldn't trust it now. But, even so, what was she going to do about Rollin Wells?

In the distance she heard the crunching of gravel at the end of the driveway, and the dogs barked below her. She tossed the pillow back onto the bed and rushed to the window. A black Lincoln climbed up the lane to the Lehmans' house, and she caught her breath. They had come looking for Rollin.

Rushing down the stairs, she hurried out to the porch. She wasn't afraid to die, but she didn't have a death wish like Rollin. For Henry's sake—and for the sake of Erma and Isaac—she had to get these men off her property. Before Rollin came back, and before Erma and Henry hiked down from the blueberry bushes.

Bennett and the other dogs joined her side, looking much more threatening than they were. She smoothed the light green apron that covered her dress as the car stopped in front of her.

The driver opened his door, and she recognized his face. Nico Sansone. One of her distant cousins and her father's minion for as long as she could remember.

As she walked confidently toward the car, she prayed that Nico didn't recognize her.

"*Kann ich dich helfa?*" she asked in Pennsylvania Deutsch, and then she fanned her face, pretending to be embarrassed before she repeated the words in English. "Can I help you?"

Nico watched the dogs for a moment, and then his gaze slowly traveled from the hem of her long skirt up to her face. She wanted to clobber the man, but she kept her head bowed and silently thanked God for the long dress and kapp that kept most people from really looking at *her.*

"We're searching for a man who goes by the name of Rollin." Nico spit toward her feet, and she took a step back. "Rollin Wells."

"An Englisher?"

When Nico cocked his head, questioning the word, her sigh hinted at exasperation. She wouldn't let him know that she was afraid. Only irritated. "Is he Amish or one of you?"

Nico looked back at the other man in the car before he answered. "One of us, I suppose."

"Oh." She glanced toward the top of the hill, hoping Erma and Henry had a lot of berries to pick. "I haven't seen any of your kind around here."

Nico opened his mouth and closed it, like he wasn't sure how to respond. She was glad her ambiguity set him off-kilter. If only she could prompt him to leave as easily.

He took off his hat and his gaze roamed the property around them. "Rollin is a dangerous man, Miss…"

"Lehman," she said.

He took a step closer to her, his jacket bulging from the bulk of his gun. "Have you ever known a dangerous man before?"

She met his eye, pulling from a reservoir of strength she didn't know she had. "I'm not afraid of danger."

He ground his toe into the dirt. "You should be, Miss Lehman."

"Do you work with the police?"

"Sometimes."

Bennett growled with a low rumble beside her hip, and she petted the back of his neck. "Then thank you for protecting us from so many dangerous men."

She stepped back, hoping the man would leave. Over his shoulder, she eyed the other man in the car. He wasn't looking at her, but she caught her breath when she looked above him.

Henry's head appeared over the hillside. He was swinging his bucket, waving at her, and probably calling her name. She was thankful she couldn't hear him.

Erma appeared next on the hillside, her kapp gleaming in the sunshine.

If only she could grab Henry and run again, far away from the men in black automobiles and the detective who kept coming back into her life. But no matter how much she wanted to go, she couldn't leave Erma and Isaac to face the anger and madness of her father's men alone. Nor would she leave Rollin with them.

Nico blinked when she met his eye, searching her face like he was trying to place where he had seen her before.

"What does this Rollin Wells look like?" she asked.

Nico shrugged, but his eyes were intent on her. "He's rather tall, I guess. Blond hair."

"Brown hair," the man inside the car shouted out at them.

"Brown hair and an angry sort of face."

"Angry?"

Nico scrunched up his lips and forehead. "He always looks like this."

She glanced back up the hill again, and her son and Erma had disappeared. She brushed the strings from her kapp over her shoulder.

Erma would know to hide Henry until the black vehicles were gone.

"I'll watch for Rollin Wells." She turned, dismissing the man.

And today she'd search until she found him.

CHAPTER 21

Rollin ducked under a branch and crept closer to the Bowmans' barn. Through the trees, he could see the bright red siding and farm equipment piled up under a bay that stretched half the length of the barn, to the wide doors in the back. His colleagues in Cleveland may not be able to assist him this morning, but he didn't need them to discover what the Cardano family was planning out here. Only to stop it.

He wiped the sweat off his forehead, and through the leaves, he watched two burly men in white short-sleeve shirts and black ties stand guard by the back door. Instead of talking, their eyes scanned the forest behind the barn like they were expecting company.

Taking off his jacket, he padded the bark of a tree, and then sat down on the pine-needled ground. He needed to get inside the barn to find out what the Cardanos had planned. Either the barn was being used as a storage center or speakeasy, or they were getting ready to form some sort of alliance here. An alliance he had to block.

He glanced around at the dense trees and branches that fortified the barn. Whatever was happening on the other side of those red walls, the Cardano family had picked the perfect location for it. Without a foolproof tip, no one from the Cleveland force would venture down here to investigate, and unless someone complained, the local police would never notice what was happening out here in the hills. And who would complain about the preparations for a wedding, no matter how many black Lincolns attended the union?

If Antonio's men hadn't mentioned Sugarcreek at the cemetery, he wouldn't be here either.

He fidgeted against the tree, his stomach rumbling.

When he left the Lehmans' house this morning, he should have taken more than a slice of bread to eat. But he'd wanted to get out of the house before anyone woke up with questions, especially Katie. He'd seen the questioning in her eyes last night when he came back with Isaac. He didn't have answers for her, nor did he want to endanger her or any of the Lehmans by telling them too much.

This battle was between him and the Cardano family, and it was a battle he planned to win. But right now wasn't the time to fight. It was time to wait. And it felt like that was all he was doing lately. Waiting for Antonio and the others in the cemetery. Waiting for his arm to heal. Waiting to find out what was happening in the Bowmans' barn.

And waiting to find out why Malloy didn't have the entire force out looking for him.

He closed his eyes for a moment and saw the kindness and beauty in Katie's face again. Something had happened between her and Jonas Miller last night, but he didn't dare ask. It didn't matter to him if Jonas and Katie were breaking off their courtship or if they'd decided to marry. That was their decision to make.

After Liz died, he decided he would never marry. If the Cardanos could kill a member of their own family, they would have no problem murdering a detective's wife or children. It didn't matter anyway. His entire life was focused on bringing down the stronghold of the Cardano family. He could never risk having his own family.

In the distance, he heard the airplane again, flying toward him. Yanking his jacket out from behind him, he ducked and held it over his head. The airplane swept low over the trees, and when it had passed, he peeked out from under his jacket and saw the green tail streak over the barn. The engine whirred for a few moments on the other side of the barn, and then it stopped.

Had the plane landed in the field on the other side? If so, who was flying to the Bowmans' place?

The two guards remained stalwart at their posts, so he leaned back against his jacket again.

Henry Lehman had watched that airplane like it was a shark, and Rollin understood. Even though he'd seen countless planes during the war, he found himself gawking at the flying machines as well. Someday, perhaps, he would actually learn to fly one.

If he wanted to, Henry certainly would be able to fly one when he grew up. He was smart and determined and didn't seem to be afraid of anything.

Rollin, on the other hand, grew up afraid of almost everything. It wasn't until after his father committed suicide that he decided to face his fears and go fight in the war. His mother was angry at him, but he discovered that opposition didn't frighten him like it once had. He had confronted his own fear, but he was still afraid for the few people he cared for in his life, afraid of a criminal's revenge.

Sometimes he wondered what it would be like if he hadn't signed up to join the police force. If he had married and fathered several children. What if he left the police force and strove for a simpler life? Instead of chasing criminals, he could take his son down to fish in a creek every weekend and dote on a daughter who was as pretty as her mother. As pretty as someone like Katie.

He heard voices by the barn and inched up to see two new men join the others by the back door. He recognized one of them—Antonio Cardano. Junior. He couldn't see the other man's face.

As Antonio scanned the forest, Rollin eased down again so Antonio wouldn't spot him.

"Have you seen anything?" Antonio asked the men.

"Nothing but squirrels and birds."

"Rollin Wells is still around here."

He slunk even closer to the tree. They didn't know how close he was.

One of the men spoke. "Should we tell the others about him?"

"No," Antonio insisted, his voice chilling Rollin's skin. "We can't tell a soul."

"But so many of the men already know."

"Then tell them to keep their mouths shut. We're close to finding him."

"How close?"

Antonio paused. "We should get rid of him today."

Rollin scanned the trees behind him, like there was a battalion with guns pointed his way.

"This meeting is going to happen," Antonio said. "No matter what."

He clapped one of the men on the back. "Go search the forest and eliminate any unwanted guests."

"Yes, sir," the man said, stepping forward.

"But don't go any farther than the trees," Antonio said. "Rollin Wells will come to us."

Rollin didn't hear if Antonio said anything else. Crouching down, he rushed back through the trees, away from the barn. Antonio's men wouldn't be eliminating him today.

* * * * *

Celeste edged her friend's Ford to the side of the country road and leaned back against the headrest. Earlier today, she found Isaac and Erma's former house—the address she used to write to when she mailed letters to her sister.

A Mennonite couple lived in the house now, and as the woman bounced a baby on each hip, she said that she thought the Lehmans still lived near Sugarcreek, but she didn't know where they'd gone. The woman recommended she check with the post office in Sugarcreek. Celeste didn't want to go into town. Not that someone would recognize her after so many years, but she didn't want Antonio or any of his men spotting her.

A horse clopped up the road behind her, and she saw the animal's dappled gray neck in the mirror, the blinders over his eyes. A buggy passed slowly by her car, and she watched the Amish couple laughing together, sharing some joke like her parents used to do when she was young.

As the buggy passed, Celeste watched the young girl riding in the back, her feet kicking through the dust stirred up from the tires and horse's hooves.

Celeste never dangled her feet over the edge of a buggy—her parents were much too strict for that—but she and Erma spent much of their childhood perched up on the narrow seat in the rear of a buggy, visiting friends, since her parents' families lived east in Lancaster County. She and her sister made funny hand motions across from each other as they bounced along the country roads. While most of her friends had seven or even nine siblings, it was just she and Erma in their family, plodding through life in the back of a buggy.

Her sister embraced the Amish culture and heritage. She loved the morning hours as she cooked and cleaned and even sewed before most of the world awakened for the day.

Celeste, however, hated the morning hours, and she hated to sew and cook. Her mother insisted she learn how to care for a home. She had no choice but to comply or bow to her father's belt, but during the nights, when her family was asleep, she'd slip down to the cellar and dance to the music playing in her head.

Celeste caught a train to Cleveland on her eighteenth birthday and never came back. After she married Salvatore, she never breathed a word of her past to her new husband. He thought he'd married a savvy, worldly girl, and she intended to keep her identity a secret for the rest of her life.

In the earlier years of her marriage, she'd written to her sister in secret, even after Erma met a man named Isaac Lehman and moved into her own home. Even after Celeste had birthed her three children, and Erma birthed Laben and Josiah—the nephews she'd longed to meet but couldn't without exposing her secret.

Erma and her family lived just hours away from her, and yet they hadn't seen each other in more than thirty years. She guarded the secret of her past like it was a poison that could infect everything around her. Not even when Erma got married or their parents died did she breathe a word of this secret so she could attend the wedding or the funerals. Her old life passed away when she married Salvatore.

Now, after all these years, here she was in Sugarcreek, searching for her sister—and her daughter.

Last night she'd slept in a cramped room, at a forlorn Dover inn. She no longer recognized any of the countryside where she'd grown up, but after discovering Erma and Isaac had moved, she spent most of the afternoon cruising the back roads and reading the mailbox signs. She'd

MELANIE DOBSON

gotten excited when she saw the name Lehman on one mailbox until she saw the much smaller name of Timothy before it.

Perhaps Timothy was a relative, but she'd been afraid to stop and ask an Amish person for directions to her sister's. Afraid of calling any more attention to herself than she already did.

She repositioned the black satin cloche over her hair and crept back onto the road.

It was strange to see automobiles around Sugarcreek, vying for the roadway with the buggies and horses. Besides the automobiles, not much had changed since she'd grown up. Not like the outside world, where the music was sassier and women's hemlines seemed to lose an inch or two each year.

Women in the cities held respectable positions now at offices and department stores. If she had been born a few decades later, she would have joined the working ranks instead of dancing at Ernie's. And instead of marrying Salvatore.

When Celeste was young, the restrictions of the Amish lifestyle felt like they would strangle her. She craved freedom from regulations and rules, so marriage to Salvatore seemed like salvation to her—never again would she have to return to the Old Order restrictions on her life. Even when she was too old and too ugly to dance.

But salvation by marriage was only masked as freedom. There was no bishop to define the world's rules, so she had to learn by herself which ones to follow. And there were plenty of rules in the Cardano family and in society. She learned quickly who could deliver the greatest penalty if she stepped outside the boundaries. In the normal world, these enforcers were usually the police and judicial system, but in her world, it was the men with guns who didn't answer to any judge.

Celeste drove to the next mailbox and inched the car forward as she read the name. Yoder. She pulled back onto the road again.

She didn't think Erma would ever move away from Sugarcreek, but maybe she had. Maybe she and Isaac took their boys back to Isaac's family in Lancaster when Nicola and Henry showed up at their door. It would make sense to protect them all.

The thought should have brought relief, but it saddened her instead. After she sent Nicola and Henry here, she received one last letter from Erma saying they'd arrived, but she never heard another word from Sugarcreek nor had she written Erma again. Anyone could intercept her correspondence—Salvatore, Heyward, even Rollin Wells. She didn't dare let anyone know where her daughter had gone or that Celeste had any part in her departure.

Since the fire, she hadn't allowed herself to hope that one day she would see her daughter or grandson again. Salvatore didn't know where Nicola had fled, and in his mind, both his daughters were dead. Celeste assured him they would never see or hear from Nicola again but refused to tell him where she'd sent their daughter and little Henry.

After the fire, Salvatore paid off the firemen, and the medical examiner identified two bodies in the ashes. No one outside their immediate family knew about Henry, and Salvatore never acknowledged the baby's existence. Even though the medical examiner was on Salvatore's dole, he met with a tragic death a few months later.

On her drive south, Celeste began to hope again. She wanted to see her daughter—tell Nicola how sorry she was for everything that happened. And she wanted to hold her grandson close. She wouldn't stay long, just enough time to warn them to leave the area until Antonio and all his cousins and cronies were gone.

She turned right at the intersection and followed the road through the trees and up yet another hill.

She envisioned holding that child close to her breast, kissing the wisps of blond hair, but Henry wouldn't be a baby anymore. She'd have to give him a quick hug instead, if she could catch him.

A gaggle of geese swarmed over her, blocking the sun for a moment as she crested the hill. They honked like they were cheering each other on their journey. Like they enjoyed being together.

Henry would be almost nine now. Would he be like Antonio when he was nine, playing with the frogs and snakes in the trees behind their house?

Antonio spent a decade playing outside before they moved into their mansion on Murray Hill, back when Salvatore and his brothers were trying out several different business ventures to determine which one would bring them the wealth they'd craved ever since coming to America. The Cardano fruit stands and laundries had been moderately successful, but the nightclubs brought in the most income until Prohibition.

With Prohibition, their family's income exploded, but she often wondered if Salvatore's life was really what he dreamed about growing up in Sicily. She had all the luxuries she'd dreamed about as a child, but it certainly wasn't the kind of family life she'd wanted.

Family was everything to her as a girl, and when she married Salvatore, she'd thought it was important to him as well, with all his brothers and their wives and a dozen Cardano children. Then she'd discovered family was a tool for him instead of a tie.

Celeste was searching for the Lehman house, but it was possible Nicola didn't even live with Isaac and Erma any longer. Perhaps Nicola had met a nice Amish man and married him. She was old enough to run a household by now and have a home full of children who loved her.

Maybe Nicola had a baby Celeste could hold or even two.

Around the curve, a cloud of dust bloomed from a field. She stopped at the next mailbox, checked the name, and continued driving.

She wanted to see Nicola and Henry, and she wanted to see them today. If they were no longer in Sugarcreek, she would find out where they went. Now that she was on the road, she'd drive to Pennsylvania or Indiana or anywhere else if she had to in order to see them.

Her car bumped over a bridge, and she glanced at the creek trickling underneath. On the other side of the water, she saw a young boy splashing in the water with his pants' legs rolled up. She stopped by the bridge and watched him pick up a rock and throw it into the water.

The boy turned, catching her eye, and he waved to her.

She slowly opened the car door and stepped out. She wouldn't ask an adult about the Lehmans, but it wouldn't hurt to ask a child. Maybe he could tell her if Isaac and Erma still lived near Sugarcreek.

As she walked toward the bank, the boy's sandy brown hair became clearer. And his wide smile.

Could it be?

She swallowed hard.

Henry looked just like his father.

CHAPTER 22

With a basket of eggs balanced on the floor of the buggy, Katie directed Prince carefully around the curved roads, toward the Yoders' home. If Nico stopped her, she would show him the eggs. Tell him she was going to town to sell them. If Nico didn't believe her, maybe she would throw one at him.

A smile slid across her lips. They wouldn't let her laugh long, but she'd enjoy watching the egg yolk slide down Nico's slicked-back hair and haughty eyes and his expensive suit.

The sun beat down on her kapp, and the nape of her neck burned. When she lifted her skirt a few inches, her bare toes and ankles welcomed some relief from the heat. She would find Rollin and convince him to come back to the Lehmans' until they could figure out a way to either get him to Cleveland or get someone down here to help him, preferably in the cool of the evening or the dark cover of night.

At the Yoders' house, she unharnessed Prince and opened the pasture gate to let him roam beside the barn. Ruth was inside the house, baking oatmeal cookies, and she visited with the older woman for a few minutes. Before she left, Ruth insisted she take fresh cookies back to Henry, so she tucked the package in the basket beside the eggs.

She didn't tell Ruth where she was going, but Ruth still stopped her before she stepped out the front door.

"God be with you, Katie," the older woman said.

She hoped God was with her today. With her and with Rollin.

The pathway through the cornfield, to the Bowmans' house and barn, was familiar. The last people to rent the house had been an Amish family, and Katie attended services multiple times in their barn and in the house.

Hidden in the cornstalks, she felt protected for the moment. Her cousins wouldn't know their way around a cornfield or a barn, for that matter. Their world consisted of dark alleys, smoky clubs, and the warehouses off Mayfield Road. Most of them had never even been outside of Cleveland.

Katie smiled. They must be going crazy out here in the country. No alcohol and certainly no girls swooning over them. Just endless trees and corn and fields of cows and other livestock. The men were probably more afraid of a bull than they were of meeting a Puglisi gunman.

At the edge of the cornfield, she paused at the forest that led to the back of the Bowmans' barn. If Rollin were still here, she was certain she would find him close to the barn, and she would convince him to come back to the Lehmans' before the men started shooting at him again.

When she stepped into the forest, someone wrapped their arms around her and yanked her back into the corn. She opened her mouth to scream, but the man covered her mouth with his hand. Eggs rolled out of the basket, cracking around her feet, and she struggled against him. When he wouldn't let go, she clamped her teeth into his skin.

He swore as he pulled his hand away from her, and she whirled around on her heels, the basket above her head, ready to swing. She expected to see Nico or one of the other men, but instead, she saw Rollin Wells.

She dropped the basket.

"What are you doing here?" she demanded as she pulled away from Rollin's hold. He didn't fight her.

He rubbed his thumb across his palm. "Be quiet, Katie."

"What are you doing?" she repeated, this time in a whisper.

He met her eyes, the blue blazing in them. "Right now, I'm trying to keep both of us from getting killed."

She huffed, stomping her foot. An eggshell cracked under her heel, the yolk sliming across her toes into the dirt. She slid her foot back, wiping it off in the dirt.

He eyed the egg yolk mixing with the dirt. "I could have eaten those."

"You're that hungry?"

"I will be in about an hour. There's not a lot to eat out here."

"Yes, there is, but you have to know where to look."

"Neither tree bark nor leaves sounded appetizing to me."

Sighing, she leaned down to the basket and picked through the broken shells and muck until she found the package of Ruth's cookies and lifted it out. She held it out to Rollin. "You might enjoy these a little more than tree bark."

He slipped farther back into the corn, and she followed him through the stalks. When he stopped again, he quickly unwrapped the twine around the paper. He inhaled the cookies almost as fast as Henry did whenever they visited Ruth.

She inched closer to him. "What are you looking for out here?"

He looked deep in her eyes, like he was trying to understand her question.

"Are you trying to find the Cardano men, or are you searching for something else?"

"Of course I'm trying to find the Cardano men." He paused, examining her face again. "How do you know about the Cardanos?"

"Oh, Rollin," she said with a sigh. "There is much you don't understand."

He hesitated and then reached for her hand, the strength in his fingers reviving her. She led him away from the Bowmans' barn and the forest, to the north side of the cornfield. There was a small watering pond at the end of the Yoders' property, and they sat on a log someone had propped beside it to use for a bench.

Rollin waited for a moment before he spoke again. "Who are you, Katie Lehman?"

She shoved her toes through the muddy ground, and the black oozed between them. "It's a long story."

"Why don't you start with how you know about the Cardano family?"

"The Cardanos," she began, her tongue burning even as she said the word. She didn't want to tell Rollin anything about her or her past, but he was too close to the story. He deserved to know part of the truth.

"I know about the Cardanos"—she took a deep breath—"because they are my family."

His jaw dropped so far, and for so long, that she nudged it back up with her fingertips. His eyes were frozen on her face, like he was searching for even more answers without asking the questions.

"Which Cardano?" he finally asked.

She held out her hand to him.

"My name is Nicola Cardano," she said as she gently shook his hand. "It's nice to see you again."

"Nikki?" His eyes grew larger. "Liz's baby sister?"

She cringed. "I'm not a baby anymore."

"No, you're not," he said without even a hint of a smile. He rubbed his hands together, looking back over the small pond. "You're supposed to be dead."

"That's what they wanted everyone to believe."

He turned to her again, wiping his forehead with the back of his hand. "And Liz?"

She dropped her gaze. "They murdered her."

He looked at the water, and she knew her words were like dropping a bomb on Rollin's head. He'd been told Liz was dead, but since he'd never seen her body, a thread of hope probably remained that she might still be alive. That someone had hidden Liz away as well.

"How did she die?" Rollin whispered.

She pulled her legs close to her, the mud chilling her toes. "Several of them had guns that night."

"They shot her…" His voice trailed off.

Dark memories from her last night in Cleveland flooded back to Katie. The guns pointed at her and Liz. The terrible sound of the gun firing. She'd kicked off her shoes and run all the way home to her mother, thinking her mother could make the men stop.

Salvatore didn't know Nikki was hiding in the house when he stomped through the front door with Liz in his arms. He didn't know Celeste already knew about her oldest daughter's death.

Her mother sobbed over Liz's body even while Nikki waited for her signal to run. After Celeste turned the kitchen stove on high, Nikki and Henry ran out into the dark night. She'd been running up the hill behind their house, Henry in her arms, when she saw the first flames light the back windows. Salvatore thought Celeste agreed to set the fire to hide the cause of Liz's death, but her mother wasn't trying to protect her husband. She was trying to protect Nikki and Henry.

She'd known her father's men would search for her all over the snow-covered Murray Hill, so she didn't stop running until she got to the bus station. And she watched every man on the bus intently, wondering if one of them would follow her to her aunt and uncle's home in Sugarcreek. But no one had followed her. She and Henry escaped from Cleveland, and she only returned in her dreams.

"Did they try to kill you too?" he asked.

She nodded, fresh tears wetting her eyelashes and her cheeks. "Liz shouted for me to run. She took the bullet for me."

"I don't understand why…"

"They were meeting about a new partnership so they could get a monopoly on the corn sugar business. Someone was with them. Someone we shouldn't have seen."

"Who did you see?"

She shook her head, twisting her hands in her lap.

When Rollin looked at her again, the steely blue in his eyes had softened. "You don't have to be afraid of them anymore."

"Yes, I do."

"As soon as I find out what's going on, I'll stop them from hurting you or anyone else."

"By yourself?" She didn't mean to sound so sarcastic, but it would be impossible for Rollin to fight them alone.

"No," he said, but the strength drained from his retort. "My police captain will help us bust this ring."

"What's your captain's name?"

"Heyward Malloy."

A bitter laugh burned her throat. The surprise on Heyward Malloy's face when he saw her and Liz was seared in her mind. And the smirk on his face as he pulled out his pistol. She didn't know if he'd been the first to pull the trigger—it could have been one of her uncles. She just didn't believe Antonio or her father shot Liz. Couldn't allow herself to believe it.

"Is that funny?" Rollin asked.

Once again, she was backed into a corner. "My uncles were at Mangiamo's that night. And Antonio. And so was Heyward Malloy."

* * * * *

Heyward was there.

The words pierced Rollin's mind, and he shook his head like he could relieve their sting.

Heyward Malloy was there the night Liz was murdered, meeting with the Cardanos.

For years, he'd trusted Malloy. Admired him for his courage against the strongholds in their city and for his tenacity to bring down the crime families in Cleveland. But the whole time, Malloy was scheming with the Cardanos instead of fighting them.

Every time Rollin thought he was getting close to exposing the Cardano family, every time he thought for certain he had the evidence to stop them, something would happen to botch his plans. If Katie was right, no wonder his plans failed over and over. He'd probably been channeling information to the enemy ever since he became a detective.

He stood up, and mud and water slogged against his shoes and pant legs as he paced. Katie had deceived him for the past four days. She could be lying to him again, but why would she deceive him about Malloy? It didn't make sense.

He glanced back over his shoulder at Katie. If she dressed in a fancy chiffon dress and trimmed her hair, she would look exactly like her older sister. It was strange, but he didn't remember Nikki Cardano looking like Liz. All he remembered was a lanky girl, tromping through the pristine Cardano mansion in her braids and bare feet.

He remembered her bare feet and the fact that she'd been a constant nuisance to him and to Liz. It seemed whenever they were finally alone in the sitting room, Nikki would bound through the door to offer them tea and scones as if she were serving the President and First Lady. He hadn't wanted scones and neither had Liz.

Nikki's demeanor had calmed since she left Cleveland. And her beauty had blossomed.

Was it life in the Amish community that sobered her, or the reality of watching her sister die?

He looked back at her again, and Katie's bare toes raked through the mud again. Maybe she hadn't grown up as much as he thought. Perhaps under the weight of her bonnet and apron was a woman who still savored the joys of childhood. She'd never be completely carefree again—the cares of the world had followed her into one of the most peaceful places in the world. But, in his mind, he could still see the lively girl who wanted to be at her sister's side.

No wonder Katie hadn't welcomed him into their community. She'd known who he was from the moment they found him collapsed in the Yoders' barn. She'd known who he was, but she didn't know to whom he answered.

He moved back toward her.

"Heyward Malloy…" he started. "Malloy was one of the city's top detectives in 1919."

She nodded, the sunlight shimmering the gold specks in her eyes. "How do you think he knew so much?"

"Because he was a good investigator."

"Because my father paid him well to help take down the Puglisis."

"Salvatore fed him information?"

"By the truckload," she said. "Back when he used to work with the Puglisis."

He sat beside her, searching her eyes for her motivation. For the truth. "But how do you know?"

"Before I ran away, my mother told me what was happening."

"But after you left," he refuted, "Malloy gathered enough evidence to take down Salvatore."

"Did he succeed?"

He shook his head. "The jury found your father not guilty in spite of the evidence."

"A nice ruse, don't you think? Taking the Cardanos to court." She fidgeted with her apron. "No one would ever guess Heyward was on the Cardano payroll."

"Maybe he got off the payroll after you left Cleveland."

"He knew too much to get off the payroll."

The consequence for jilting the Cardanos would be fatal.

"Did Heyward help pick the jury that heard my father's case?"

"I suppose so."

"Then he did his job well."

Rollin leaned over and cupped his chin in his hands. He'd sat in the courtroom during Salvatore Cardano's trial, three rows behind Malloy. He'd been so proud of his boss during the proceedings. The evidence about Cardano's illegal business dealings seemed to be irrefutable with Malloy's delivery of detailed records and reputable witnesses. During the trial, his admiration for Malloy grew stronger along with his hatred for the Cardano family.

The suspicious fire at the Cardanos' home, along with his daughters' deaths, were mentioned during the session, but it was only mentioned, along with the subsequent murders of Salvatore's two brothers. Most people assumed the Puglisis killed the brothers. No one had the evidence to convict anyone for murder, and Rollin guessed the man who examined Liz's body was on the Cardano payroll.

The trial judge was an upstanding man, though, and Rollin had hoped the jury members were as well. He, along with most of the gallery, was shocked with the not guilty verdict.

Had the Cardanos really handed the evidence to Malloy with the assurance of an amiable jury? His arresting Salvatore would certainly up his credibility with the Puglisi family, and it would have erased any question of him working for or with the Cardanos.

Rollin had seen the smirk on Salvatore Cardano's face right after the judge said *not guilty*. Like he already knew what the judge would say. With pressure from the mayor, Malloy and the prosecutor opted not to appeal. Even with the evidence, the mayor said, the Cardanos could easily buy the jury at any level. He didn't want to spend the city's time or money on another defeat. Instead, he wanted more evidence, even stronger evidence against the Cardanos before they went to trial again.

At the end of the trial, Cardano's organization ballooned. His distributors—and the justice system—realized that Salvatore was unstoppable and untouchable. If he could weasel his way out of a trial stacked with evidence proving his guilt, he could get out of anything.

Not only could Malloy have convinced a jury to release Salvatore Cardano, he could have arrested Leone Puglisi last year specifically to stop the Puglisis' advance in the corn sugar industry. When Puglisi's conviction and short jail sentence didn't stop the growth of the Puglisi's business, the Cardanos chose to shoot him instead.

Rollin sat down on the log again. "Malloy was the one who asked me to join the police force."

"Did he hire you to stop the Cardanos?"

"At the request of the mayor," he said, "Malloy was putting together a division to fight the different factions of bootleggers and distributors. Malloy knew some of my history with your family, and he assigned me to track what they were doing."

"I'm guessing he paid particularly close attention to your findings."

Rollin nodded. "I thought he was seeking vengeance after he lost his case against Salvatore."

She finished his thought. "When really he was making sure you didn't find out too much…"

He thumped the tops of his legs with his fists. How could he have been so stupid? "The entire time, he's been steering me the wrong direction."

"Don't feel bad, Rollin. Heyward Malloy played all of us."

Anger boiled inside him. "Malloy told the other cops that Lance and I are in Florida. Before we came here, Malloy steered us to a librarian to find out where Sugarcreek was located. Apparently he wanted us to come here so he could kill us."

"Which means you're close to finding something the Cardanos want to keep hidden."

He looked back toward the cornfield. He couldn't see the trees beyond the corn or the barn, but something big was happening back there. Something that would expose the Cardanos and perhaps even Malloy.

Standing again, he reached for her hand and helped her up. "I've got to go back to the barn."

"Not now, Rollin," she said, releasing his hand.

He thought of the men scouring the forest for him and he agreed. He would have to come back later. Tonight.

She motioned him toward the Yoders' farm, and he followed her.

He pushed aside a cornstalk. "I attended your funeral."

She stopped, turning back to him. "My funeral?"

"They said they found your body in the fire as well."

"My funeral..." she repeated. "What was it like?"

"They held it at Holy Rosary," he said. "Hundreds of people were there, crying for you and Liz, and there were so many flowers that it took four cars to deliver them to the funeral."

"I wonder what they put on my tombstone." Her eyes caught the sunlight again, but this time they were sad.

"I don't know. Your father only allowed immediate family to attend the burial."

"Even my father told people I was dead..."

"He probably did it to protect you, Katie. So Malloy and the others would stop searching for you."

"Or to protect himself," she said. "If they thought my father was willing to kill his own daughter for them, they would trust him to keep their secrets."

They emerged from the field, stepping into the Yoders' yard together. Chickens clucked in the coop beside them, and the sun dipped toward the horizon, cooling the air.

Katie deserved to have someone to protect her, someone willing to die for her. She believed her father was willing to sacrifice her in order to shore up his kingdom. The sad thing was, he couldn't protest it.

"The papers all said you were dead."

"Thank God for that."

"It's strange, though," he said as they walked toward Ruth's house. "I don't remember anyone ever mentioning Henry."

"Only my parents and Antonio knew about Henry."

He quickly did the math in his head. Katie would have been only about fifteen or sixteen when she left Cleveland. And Henry said he was about to turn nine.

"How old was Henry when you left?"

She brushed her hands together, and for a few seconds, he didn't think she would answer his question. Her voice was barely above a whisper when she spoke again. "He was three weeks old."

"Three weeks?"

She shook her head. "Don't ask me about Henry's father."

"You were so young…"

She stopped walking, turning back to him. A shield barricaded the soft blue of her eyes. "Yes, I was."

"Were you afraid?"

"Very," she said. "And I'm still afraid."

"What are you afraid of?"

"Not being the mother Henry deserves."

He lifted her chin, and he saw her fresh tears. "You are a good mother, Katie."

She broke away from his touch, her gaze sinking to the grass. "No, I'm not."

"Do you remember my mother?" he asked.

"I remember seeing her at parties."

"She was intent on rearing me well, but she focused most of her attention on making sure I said the right words to her guests and combating the dirt on my skin and under my nails."

He rubbed his hands together, in wonder for a moment that his skin was still intact after the hours upon hours of scrubbing with lye soap. If only his mother could have seen him in France. Days would go by without the opportunity to bathe. Weeks sometimes. He hadn't minded the dirt.

"You aren't so concerned about the words Henry says or the dirt he carries on his skin. You're focused on molding Henry's heart and mind, Katie." He wanted to reach out, take her hand again, but he willed himself to keep his hands at his sides. "Henry is one lucky boy to be your son."

She shook her head again. "I love him so much, but I don't know what to do with him. Salvatore was a terrible father, and my mother… She tried hard to love us, but she should have taken us far away from him."

He was proud of her and what she had done. She'd escaped from the clutches of the Cardano family and taken her son with her. She was brave and determined, and the enthusiasm that annoyed him as a young man endeared her to him now.

"You're not a Cardano anymore, Katie. You're a Lehman." He took a deep breath. "You will lead Henry into the right world for him, far away from your past."

"Thank you," she whispered.

When he looked into her eyes again, he didn't see Liz in them. Nor did he see Nicola Cardano. He saw Katie Lehman—a courageous and beautiful woman. And, for the briefest of moments, he wanted to kiss her.

His hands twitched and he stepped away from her, emotions stirring inside him. Anger at Malloy. Betrayal. And the passion that was drawing him to Katie.

"Is my mother still alive?"

"She is," he said simply. Celeste would have to decide if she wanted Nikki to know about her role in Rollin's life.

"And she's still with my father, isn't she?"

He nodded.

"I thought she would leave my father after what happened. I thought she would finally see what he was really like and get away."

"You don't think she knows what Salvatore is like?"

"I think she likes his money and even his power. And I think she's too afraid to break away from it."

"Maybe one day she'll surprise you."

Her shoulders sloped. "I'll never know if she does."

"Maybe I can take a message to her when I go back to Cleveland."

Because he would be going back to Cleveland.

Over Katie's shoulder, he saw Ruth Yoder in the kitchen window, waving at them. He waved back and then met Katie's eyes again. "Do you think the Lehmans will let me stay for one more night?"

"Erma said you are always welcome in our home."

"And Isaac?"

She shrugged. "I didn't ask him."

CHAPTER 23

After the boy climbed to the top of the bank, he wiped his muddy hands on his pants and held one out to her. Celeste shook his hand, and he looped his fingers over his suspenders.

"Are you lost?" he asked with a toothy grin.

In the car, she'd rehearsed over and over what she would say when she saw Nicola or Erma, trying to explain why she was here, but at the boy's simple question, the words tangled in her throat. Should she ask about his mother? His father?

"I'm looking for someone," she said.

He rocked back on his heels. "I know just about everyone around here."

"Oh, good," she said, sounding as relieved as she felt. "I'm looking for a family by the name of Lehman. Isaac and Erma Lehman."

She didn't think it was possible for his smile to grow any larger, but it did. "Isaac and Erma are my aunt and uncle."

Her lips trembled, and she pinched them together before speaking again. "I see."

He pointed up the treed hill. "They live up there."

"Are your parents home?"

He shook his head. "Mamm went to town to sell some eggs."

Her shoulders relaxed slightly. She had thought she was ready to see Nicola, but now she wasn't certain.

"What is your mother's name?"

"It's Katie. Katie Lehman."

The words rolled off her tongue. "Katie Lehman. That's a pretty name. Are you Henry?"

When he nodded, she reached up to her neck and fingered the pearls hanging around them. She was looking at her grandchild.

"How many children do you have?" Henry asked.

"Three. I used to have three," she said slowly. "Now I have one."

"What happened to your other two children?"

"They..." she started. "They grew up."

He pulled out his suspenders, creeping up on his toes. "Mamm tells me I'm not allowed to grow up."

She wanted to reach out and tousle his thick hair, but she clung to the seams of her dress instead. "Your mother is a wise woman."

"She tells me that *all* the time."

A quiet laugh escaped her lips, and the laughter felt good. Her little girl had grown up, and Henry obviously loved her. If Nicola were lucky, Henry's love would last even after he became a man.

"I knew your family a long time ago," Celeste said. "How are Laban and Josiah?"

The smile faded from Henry's face. "They're in heaven now."

Her heart clutched. "They died?"

"Laban caught the measles, and Josiah..." He shook his head. "There was an accident in the field before I was born, but they never told me what happened."

Celeste brushed her fingers over the goose bumps on her arms. Both she and her sister had lost children, but they hadn't been able to comfort each other. She should have been here to hug Erma when her boys passed on, but she was in Cleveland instead, wallowing in her own pain.

"Erma was always so good with medicine."

Henry nodded. "She's the best in the whole county."

"And yet she couldn't cure her own children."

"The Lord gives, and the Lord takes away," Henry started, and she finished the verse with him. "Blessed be the name of the Lord."

She cleared her throat. "Where is your father?"

His gaze fell to his bare toes. "I don't have a father."

She nodded, almost glad that Nicola hadn't married. Perhaps there was still a hint of her little girl left.

Celeste bent down, confiding in him. "I don't have a father either."

"You don't?"

"The Lord took him away a long time ago," she said.

Henry nodded, very adult-like. "I never had a father."

"Oh…"

"But I have the best mamm in the whole world."

She twisted her pearls in her fingers again, a smile back on her lips. For so many years she wondered, questioning her decision to send Nicola and Henry down here alone during those late-night hours, and she'd been angry at herself for letting them go. But Nicola was well and so was Henry. Perhaps she should leave well enough alone.

"What does Nicola—" Her daughter's name escaped from her mouth, and she stopped talking for a moment. Surely they hadn't told Henry his mother's real name or what happened when he was a baby.

She took a deep breath. "What does Katie say about her mother?"

Henry scratched his neck. "She doesn't talk about her parents very often."

She could hear the creek trickling in front of them, the geese honking again over her head as Henry reached for a stick in the tall grass. He shoved it into the ground, twisting it in the dirt.

"Mamm told me once that her mother was scarred," he said. "Something about the burdens of life."

"Indeed."

"Do you know my mother?" he asked.

"I do."

"She will want to see you then."

Celeste nodded. "When will she return?"

"I don't know, but my aunt is home. Do you want to visit her?"

She thought of going to Erma, catching up on all the years, but what if her sister asked her to leave before Nicola returned? She'd guarded her heart for so many years, pretending the pain was gone, but right now all she wanted to do was hug her daughter and her grandson. It would crush her to leave without seeing Nicola, even for the briefest of moments.

"Perhaps I could come and visit your mother in the morning."

Above the trees, she saw a blaze of green soaring through the puffs of clouds, and she squinted her eyes. Henry reeled around.

"It's the airplane," he shouted, leaping and waving his arms.

Her eyes focused in horror as the plane soared toward them. With a glance toward the road, she clutched Henry's shoulder and pushed him under the cover of the trees. Then she clung to his arm as the plane passed over them.

"I want to see it." His neck strained, struggling to watch the plane.

"You can't let those men see you!"

She released his arm, and he whirled toward her. "Why not?"

Why not? How was she supposed to answer that question...

"You don't know who they are."

"They've been coming around for days now," he said. "The pilot always waves to me."

Fear snaked up her spine, and she shivered. "When will your mother be back?"

He shrugged. "Could be after dark."

"I'll return, Henry," she said, moving toward her car.

She needed to speak with Nicola right away.

* * * * *

Antonio Cardano waited by the long field for the airplane to land. The last time he'd seen Uncle Ray was that autumn night in the basement of Mangiamo's when everyone went crazy. In his opinion, Uncle Ray was the smartest of the Cardano pack. He'd disappeared for a season to drum up business in Columbus and Cincinnati under a variety of names while the others battled the Puglisis in Cleveland.

While the other Cardanos thought Leone orchestrated the murders of John and Arthur Cardano, Uncle Ray knew Salvatore was the one who'd killed their two older brothers.

John had been picking up cigarettes at a local drugstore when he'd been shot through the head, right before noon. In spite of the daylight, no one stepped up as a witness, and the cops never solved the crime.

Arthur Cardano was taken out during a fishing trip on Lake Erie. He'd gotten soused, the police report said, and fell overboard. Everyone in the family knew Arthur had never gone fishing a day in his life. He was terrified of water. But the flatfoots didn't know that—nor did they need to know it.

There had been rumors over the years that blamed the Puglisi family for the deaths of both the Cardano brothers, but Leone and the others denied having anything to do with it.

Raymond Cardano disappeared from Cleveland soon after Arthur's body washed up on the shores of Lake Erie. For a long time, Antonio thought his favorite uncle had gone swimming with the fishes as well, but last year he received a letter from Raymond. Over the next few months Raymond's intentions became clear—his uncle was ready to return to the Cardano circuit. And he wanted to partner with Antonio to run it.

Salvatore didn't know about Raymond's return tonight or his desire to modify their current leadership, but his father was anxious about this meeting. In order to beat the Puglisi family, they had to expand their business dealings from Cleveland across the state of Ohio. Even though Salvatore worried about the risks of expansion, Antonio knew that his father's obsession with beating the Puglisis far outweighed his worry.

Antonio would deliver tomorrow night and this expansion would be the final nail in the Puglisi family coffin. He would earn the respect of the men who once thought Club Cardano was king, and they would follow him.

Antonio brushed his sweaty hands on his beige slacks.

He hated his father—everyone coming to this meeting hated him—but hating him didn't mean it would be easy to eliminate him. He would have to be strong if he were going to take over the organization. He would have to prove to the men that he was ready to lead them alongside his uncle.

Raymond Cardano hopped out of the biplane, tossing his goggles back onto the seat. His uncle's hair had grayed over the years, but his easy grin hadn't changed. Antonio wondered if the grin was still as deceptive as it had been a decade ago. Back then, Uncle Ray wasn't afraid to kill anyone.

"Junior, boy." Raymond clapped him on the back. "When did you become a man?"

He cringed. "I've been one for a long time."

"And you're finally acting like one too." Raymond glanced around the flat pasture in front of the house. "Who is here?"

Antonio rolled off their names.

"And when will the rest of them arrive?"

"Tomorrow. Late afternoon and evening," he said. "Everyone will come at a different time so we don't attract attention."

"Good thinking, Junior."

It had been his father's idea, but he didn't mention that to his uncle.

"Only Benito and Larenz know why they've been invited," Antonio said. "The rest will be surprised."

"It will be a good surprise to all of them."

"I hope so."

"And we'll be finished before daylight?"

"Long before," Antonio said.

"When does Club get here?"

"Around five tomorrow."

"I'm sure he'll make a splash."

"He's waiting until we have everything almost ready."

"We'll have everything ready, all right," Raymond said with a wink. "Get my bag, would ya?"

Antonio retrieved the luggage from a compartment in the back of the biplane and led his uncle toward the house. "We have some catching up to do."

"Plenty of time for that, boy. Plenty of time."

Antonio looked back at the men guarding the barn. His uncle had less time than he knew.

CHAPTER 24

The road back to the Lehmans' house was marred with holes and bumps. Even so, Rollin handled the cart and horse like he'd driven one his entire life. As she rode beside him, Katie didn't dare look over. If she did, he might see the admiration in her eyes, and she couldn't let him glimpse that.

She hadn't thought she would ever tell him about her family, but now he knew she'd once been Nicola Cardano, the ridiculous girl who kept pestering him and Liz. She couldn't imagine what he must have thought about her then. Or now.

She shook her head.

It didn't matter what Rollin thought about her. Even though he hadn't gone back to Cleveland last night, he would return to his life in the city soon. Once he figured out how to stop Heyward Malloy. Her heart would remain in Sugarcreek, completely intact without him.

Still, it was good to know Rollin was surprised when she told him that Heyward Malloy made a dark deal with her father years ago, a deal sealed with blood. She'd wondered for a long time if Rollin was part of her father's large network of supposedly good guys. And maybe even one of the men who'd help cover up the reason Liz died.

But Rollin hadn't known, and the thought lightened her heart.

"After I take you back to Isaac and Erma's," Rollin began. She kept her eyes focused on the gravel road in front of them. "Can I borrow Prince?"

She turned. "You're not going back…"

"I'm going to find a way into the barn."

"Into the barn?" Her voice was climbing, but she didn't care. "That's impossible."

He lifted the reins a few inches. "I have to find out what they are doing."

"You can't go inside there," she huffed. "Not without friends to back you up."

"Darkness is my friend."

She sighed at his set jaw. If something happened, no one would even know he was gone.

"I'm going with you, Rollin."

His eyes narrowed. "You most certainly are not."

"You need help…"

"No, I don't."

She crossed her arms, bracing herself for a fight. "What if they are speaking Italian?"

"They're always speaking Italian."

"I can translate for you."

He shook his head. "I know enough to figure out what they're saying."

She tapped her hands on the edge of the open cart, her kapp strings trailing in the breeze. "How do you plan to get inside?"

"I'll wait until someone leaves the back door unguarded and then sneak in."

"They'll see you."

He glanced over at her again, unswayed by her words. "It's not like I'm going to announce myself."

"What if the men don't leave?"

"They will."

She rubbed her hands together. She only had one more trick left in her bag. "I know another way into the barn."

"Through the front door?"

"Of course not," she said with a roll of her eyes. "An entrance where they won't see you."

He sighed. "So how else can I get inside?"

"I'll show you tonight."

"Oh, no..."

"Do you think you can climb with your injured arm?"

He put his hand over the bandage. "Climb what?"

She pinched the ribbon that threaded over her shoulder and fiddled with it. There had to be a way to convince him not to go back alone.

"Did you see my father at the barn?" she finally asked.

He hesitated. "No."

"My brother then?"

His response was a nod, ever so slight.

"I haven't seen Antonio since I left Cleveland."

"I wish I hadn't seen him since you left either."

"He's becoming just like my father, isn't he?" she asked.

"Unfortunately."

"Do you really think Antonio will leave the barn doors unguarded?"

"Maybe."

"You're a terrible liar, Rollin."

The sun faded over the forest beside them, its beams piercing through the leaves and branches. She shielded her eyes until the shimmering light surrendered to the night.

"When I was six, a boy named Ralph tied one of my braids to the back of my chair in school. Antonio talked another boy into beating

Ralph up for it, and no one in my class ever played a prank on me again. Even though he wasn't the strongest or the tallest kid in school, they were all afraid of what my big brother could do."

"He got another kid to fight for you?"

"He never did the bloody work himself."

Rollin turned the cart into their driveway. "Unlike your father."

"He wanted to be just like our father, except Antonio always took care of our family. With my father, it was optional."

When he looked at her, she saw pity in his eyes. Even though she didn't want him to feel sorry for her, she was grateful that he understood. Family was important to her father, but it was all about showmanship. How good his family looked and acted reflected on him. Power was what drove him. Power and respect. While her entire family thrived on the income made by their father's business dealings, Antonio was the only other one in their family who hungered for power and respect.

Antonio might not have the stomach to murder someone himself, but he had no problem getting someone else to do the dirty work for him. If they caught Rollin tonight, she had no doubt he was as good as dead. Antonio, though, might have compassion on her. If some of that big brother instinct remained, he would make sure the others wouldn't hurt her.

Crossing her arms, Katie looked at the outline of Isaac and Erma's home as they rolled up the hill. Lanterns brightened the front rooms, showering light onto the lawn and barn.

Henry shouted from the front porch, and Katie hopped out of the buggy before it stopped. She wrapped both arms around her son and squeezed him like she hadn't seen him for days instead of hours.

"I missed you," she said, kissing his hair.

Not for one second did she regret taking him with her when she left Cleveland. If they had stayed, her son would have followed the Cardanos' quest for power like Antonio, and neither Heyward Malloy nor her uncles would have let her live to watch Henry grow up, not after what she saw.

Rollin was right. She and Henry were no longer Cardanos. They were part of the Lehman family, and the past was behind them.

"Did you sell all your eggs?" Henry asked, looking down at the smeared egg yolk that coated the basket in her hands.

She hesitated. "I actually stopped at Ruth's on my way to town and left them there."

She didn't tell him she'd left most of them crushed on the Yoders' land.

He clapped his hands. "Did Ruth send me some cookies?"

Rollin joined them, patting Henry on the back. "She sent her love, champ."

"But I wanted cookies."

"Next time we visit, I'm sure she'll give you something good to eat."

Henry shoved the rocks on the driveway with his toes, making a circle. "Someone came to visit you today, Mamm."

She caught Rollin's eye in the dim light and saw his concern.

"You mean the men in the black cars?" Rollin asked.

"It was a woman," he said. "She drove a brown automobile."

"A woman?" She hadn't made a single English girlfriend since she moved here. "What was her name?"

He scratched his head like it would help him recall the woman's name. "I don't think she told me."

Rollin moved closer to Henry. "What exactly did she look like?"

"Her hair was short and real puffy and she talked low, like this," Henry said, dipping his voice to demonstrate. "There was a string of tiny balls around her neck that she kept playing with."

Rollin glanced at her. "Balls?"

"I think he means pearls."

Henry kept talking. "She asked me about you and Erma and even Josiah and Laban."

Perhaps it was an Amish woman who'd left their community and was returning for a visit, but it was strange that she would be asking about Erma's sons. "How did the woman know about Josiah and Laban?"

"She just knew." Henry shrugged. "She was really nice until we saw the airplane. Then she made me hide under the trees."

Rollin was watching her, and his eyes mirrored the anxiety in hers. Who was looking for her and why did this woman make her son hide from the airplane?

One of the dogs started barking, and then the others joined in their warning. Her back bristled, her eyes searching the darkness below the house. Then she heard a crunch of gravel, and a sharp light streaked up the driveway, blinded her. Instinctively she shielded her eyes against the head-lamps, and with her other hand, she pushed Henry toward the porch.

"Get inside the house," she whispered. "To your hiding place."

"Mamm…"

"And don't leave it until I come for you."

Her son started to protest again, but she shoved him even harder, imploring him, and he scrambled up the stairs. The door banged behind him and the sound rumbled across the hill.

Slowly, the car moved closer toward them, the wheels grating over the rocks.

She nudged Rollin's arm. "You better follow him."

"I'm not leaving you."

"If that's Nico, and he recognizes you, he'll kill all of us."

Even as the car drew closer, Rollin wavered. "But what if he tries to hurt you?"

"Bennett here will take care of me." She rubbed the dog behind the ears, her eyes on Rollin. "You take care of Henry."

He hesitated, and for a moment, she was afraid he wouldn't leave her. In the light of the car's beams, she could see the conflict in his eyes.

"I don't want to lose someone else..." He didn't finish, but the implication was there. He didn't want to lose someone else he cared about.

Her heart fluttered. He cared about her.

"Please, Rollin," she begged again.

When the car stopped about twenty feet from them, he stepped toward the porch. "I'll be standing inside the front door, with the fire poker in my hand."

The headlamps darkened, and the car's engine made a clunking sound before it silenced. She spread her feet apart, rolled her shoulders back, and glowered at the vehicle.

Erma and the others wouldn't condone her fighting, no matter what the reason, but for Henry's sake, she would stand up against whomever her brother or Heyward Malloy sent. She would fight until they put her in the grave, alongside Liz.

As she waited for the men to step out of the car, she prayed Henry was hiding in the attic as she'd taught him. And she prayed that Rollin would fight for all their lives, with the fire poker or whatever he could use to stop the men.

She didn't want to die, but it was a miracle that she'd lived for so many years after they took Liz. She'd enjoyed a rich life, one full of blessings. She wouldn't trade the last nine years with Henry for anything.

The front door of the automobile clicked open, and she held her breath as a shadow emerged.

* * * * *

"Nicola?" Celeste whispered as she stepped out in the darkness. "Is that you?"

Silence met her question. She squinted in an attempt to see the features of the woman before her, but all she saw was an outlined form of a dress against the few lights gleaming in the house. Someone had blown out the lanterns as her car drew closer to the house, and she watched Henry and a man rush into the house, leaving this woman to greet her alone.

She hoped the man wasn't a coward. She despised cowards.

"Nikki?" she said.

This time the woman responded.

"Who are you?"

Celeste stepped closer, eyeing the dogs beside the woman. She couldn't say her name, not until she knew for certain who was standing in front of her.

"I'm not here to hurt you or anyone," Celeste said. "I'm just looking for my daughter."

The girl's voice dropped to a whisper. "Mamma?"

Mamma. The word never sounded so beautiful to Celeste. It wasn't full of flattery or insult or anger. It was full of wonder and even love.

Celeste didn't run to her daughter, nor did she open her arms for a hug, but her steps quickened until she was at Nicola's side. Her hands weighted at her hips, she and Nicola studied each other. Her daughter had grown into a lovely woman with a simple and strong beauty. She'd never tell her daughter, she wouldn't want her getting proud. But Nicola, in her bonnet and purple dress, was even prettier than the sister Nicola had once envied for her glamour and style.

Celeste could see the shock in her daughter's eyes. And the fear. Celeste opened her mouth, wanting to tell her daughter there was nothing to fear, but her lips wouldn't seem to move.

Nicola examined her face, and Celeste wondered what she saw, looking at a mother who'd grown ugly and old. Could she see how tired her mamma had become?

"What are you doing here, Mamma?"

She glanced toward the trees, wondering if the leaves had ears. "We have to talk, Nicola, but not out here."

"Please don't call me that name."

"Katie..." she said, the name sounding strange. "I was going to wait until morning, but it's not safe to come in the light."

"Antonio is here," Nicola whispered.

Celeste brushed her hands over the ruffles on her dress. Her daughter knew. "Have you seen him?"

"Not yet."

"I'm afraid for you."

Katie's voice quieted again. "I'm afraid for Henry."

Celeste glanced up toward the porch and looked for her grandson's eyes peeking through the glass, but she didn't see him. "Where is our boy?"

"Henry is my child," Nicola whispered. "Not *our* boy."

Celeste swallowed hard. Not once did she remember Nicola ever talking back to her, not in the entire sixteen years she'd been at home. The anger ran deep in her daughter's veins, as it should, but there was something else there. Nicola wasn't just afraid of Antonio. She was afraid of her mother.

"Who should we say I am?"

Nicola hesitated. "A family friend."

"A friend," she repeated. She wanted to tell Henry she was his grandmother, tell him how much she loved him. Perhaps in time she could share her love with Henry. At least Nicola didn't insist she climb back into her car and leave. Her daughter was still talking to her.

"Erma will want to see you," Nicola said.

She nodded back to the car and the hill beyond. "I shouldn't stay long."

CHAPTER 25

Squeezing a fire poker in his hand, Rollin pressed his nose against the windowpane to watch for more visitors. The other two dogs were sleeping in the barn tonight, but Bennett lay at his feet, his ears alert. Everything seemed to be quiet outside the house. Isaac snored in the hickory rocker in the family room behind him while Celeste and her older sister Erma chattered like schoolgirls.

Back in Cleveland, he never would have guessed that Celeste Cardano had grown up an Amish woman, just as he never would have guessed Heyward Malloy had been dancing with the Cardanos and now wanted Rollin dead.

Rollin twisted the fire poker in his hands, rolling it back and forth.

Malloy probably knew what was going to happen in that barn. And perhaps some of the other men in his unit knew as well. Malloy's friends. Lance couldn't have been one of his men, could he? Was there another reason for them to kill his partner, or had Lance gotten in their way?

He heard a soft cry behind him, and he turned to see the two sisters holding each other's hands. He stepped closer to the sitting room.

"I wish I had a photograph of them to show you," Erma said. "Or a drawing."

"It's okay." Celeste pointed to her sister's chest. "You'll keep your boys there with you. Always."

"After Josiah died…" Erma began. "Some moments I was so angry at God. I didn't want to bless His name."

Rollin looked back out the window, pretending not to listen. But he understood what Erma was saying. Not once had he blessed God's name since He'd taken Liz away. Instead, he'd cursed God's name for years.

"I worked so hard to save them," Erma said. "But Josiah's leg was already gone when I got there and there was so much blood. I held him in my arms..."

As Erma cried, Rollin leaned back against the doorpost.

Two women from two different worlds, bound together by family and grief. One woman walked through the fire, and her life had been purified with grace and forgiveness and thankfulness for what she had. The other woman walked through fire and her soul was scarred for life.

Soft steps padded down the staircase, and Bennett perked up, watching Katie until she leaned down to pet him behind his ears. The dog lumbered his body close to her legs, as if he couldn't get enough of Katie Lehman.

Rollin nodded toward the stairs. "Is Henry still hiding?"

"He's in bed now," she said. "Fast asleep."

Tendrils of wavy hair fell around her face, and he wished he could reach out and tuck them behind her ears. And he wished he could make the worry lines around her eyes disappear.

"You look like you could sleep as well," he said.

"You're not talking me out of this."

His lips turned up into a smile. "I wouldn't dare."

Turning toward the family room, Katie stood alongside him as they watched the two sisters. "They seem glad to be together, don't they?"

"Very much."

"I never thought I would see my mother again," Katie whispered. "I thought I didn't want to see her."

He shifted the poker to his other hand. "And now?"

"I'm…" She hesitated. "I'm glad she came."

Rollin nodded toward the women. "You might want to tell her that before we leave."

Katie stepped toward the room, and when Erma saw her, she opened her arms and motioned for Katie to join them.

Rollin knelt down beside Bennett, lifting the dog's ear. "You don't think it will take very long, do you?"

The dog didn't even bother to look at him. Rollin leaned back against the doorpost and sighed. "Of course it will take a long time."

And it wasn't like he would rush Katie. It might be the last time she ever saw her mother.

"Thank you for caring so well for Nicola," he heard Celeste tell Erma.

"Don't call me that," Katie muttered.

Celeste kept talking. "And for helping take care of our… For taking care of Henry."

"I don't help one bit," Erma said with a light laugh. "No one takes better care of him than Katie."

"I always wanted to get my girls out of Cleveland, but I was never sure how to do it," Celeste said. "Until the night of the fire."

"The Lord gave us Katie and Henry for a season," Erma said. "And Isaac and I are both grateful."

"He gave them to you, but He took them away from me."

"You made the right decision, Mamma," Katie said. "Being here has been good for both of us."

"It's good that you and Henry have a family who loves you."

"Henry will always have a family who loves him," Katie told her.

"Perhaps—" Celeste began. "Family is good, Katie, but you have to let Henry find his own way."

"Henry's too young to find his own way."

"He'll find it soon enough.'"

There was a pause before Katie spoke again. "I'm glad you came to see us, Mamma."

Rollin eyed the front door. If he snuck out right now, he could get much closer to the barn in the darkness and circle. With enough persistence, he could find Katie's way inside without her.

Reaching for the doorknob, he tried to open it quietly, but the hinges betrayed him with their screech. It was loud enough for Bennett to sit up and Erma to call his name.

He closed the door and joined the ladies.

"Are you going out?" Erma asked.

He nodded at Celeste. "If you can't tell me what's happening, I'm going back to Bowmans' barn to listen."

"But what could these people possibly be doing this late at night?" Erma asked.

Celeste patted her sister's knee. "Everything they do happens at night."

Erma leaned back in her chair. "Irene told me she received a large order to cater an evening wedding at the Bowmans' barn. She said there are supposed to be fifty guests."

Rollin steadied his voice. "And when, exactly, is this ceremony supposed to happen?"

"Irene is supposed to deliver the food on Friday afternoon."

Rollin blinked, trying to remember what day it was.

"It's Thursday," Katie reminded him.

"Fifty people tomorrow."

Erma clucked her tongue. "Tomorrow night."

Celeste stood up, dangling a car key in front of her. "Do you want me to take you to this barn?"

He glanced at Katie, and she nodded.

"Partway to the barn," he replied. "We can't get too close in an automobile—and we can't let Antonio know you are here."

"Antonio wouldn't hurt his own mother..." she said, but her voice trailed off. None of them was certain what Antonio would or wouldn't do.

"Just a moment," Erma said before she shuffled out of the room.

He groaned to himself. The minutes were slipping by, and every interruption cost him another piece of dialogue that might be happening in or around the barn. A fleeting look at Katie told him that she was ready to go as well, probably so she could be home when Henry woke up.

Minutes later Erma came back into the room, the satchel with her medical supplies looped over her arm. Carefully, she placed it on the floor and started rummaging through it.

Instead of pulling out a vial of medication, she drew out a ball of cloth and began to unwind it. Inside, he caught a glimpse of ivory and then silver.

His gun.

"Erma!" Katie gasped, but Erma didn't respond.

His hands twitched, wanting to swipe the ball of cloth from her and unravel it, but he waited as Erma methodically unwound the layers. Finally, she pulled out the gun. Pointing the barrel toward the ground, she handed it to him.

"You might need this tonight."

He took the gun and slid it into the holster he'd kept hidden underneath his jacket. "I might."

Erma reached for his arm, patting it to get his attention. The look in her eyes was raw. Desperate. "You need to bring Katie back to us."

He nodded. "I won't let her get hurt."

Erma slid around them to open the door, but she clung to both Katie and Celeste before she let them go.

* * * * *

It was a bit like a dance, trying to follow Rollin through the forest. He told her when to step and which way. Then he'd hold out his arm and she'd freeze in place before he motioned her ahead once more. She wore her black bonnet and a black dress to blend into the night, and as long as they were quiet and stayed in the shadows, no one would see them.

She'd said good-bye to her mother on the road, and in her heart, Katie knew she would never see her again. It saddened her that her mother chose to empower the Cardano family's world of crime with her silence when she could always come home to a community who would forgive her and welcome her back. Her mother was secure in her prison. And enamored with worldly things—her home and her food and the bit of notoriety that came with being a Cardano in Cleveland.

Here she'd been one of many, everyone dressing the same, believing the same way. No one standing out. Her mother craved drama, and she loved to stand out, even if she was standing behind her husband or son.

Rollin held a branch up for her, and Katie ducked under it.

Ever since she moved to Sugarcreek, Katie stood out. A sixteen-year-old with a baby, even though she'd pretended to be eighteen. Those in their community didn't know much about her upbringing, but they knew she'd been raised by an English father and Erma's sister, a woman who'd deserted their community. They'd been curious from the beginning about her, but they didn't ask questions.

As Isaac and Erma's niece, the Amish people loved her, and the solidarity of the community had been refreshing for her. Over time she'd moved from being an outsider to becoming part of their community. Her mother had taught her bits of the language as a child, and she learned how to act and speak so she wouldn't stand apart from the others. It wasn't that different from her life in Cleveland except the people here followed the rules because of their faith instead of their fear.

Sometimes she longed for a place where she wasn't forced to fit into a mold. Where people's expectations weren't placed on her. A place she didn't have to be afraid.

Rollin stopped her, and as they waited in the darkness, she patted her apron pocket.

Inside was a roll of bills her mother insisted that she take. At first she refused, knowing almost every bit of money that came through her father's house was stained with blood. Her mother told her the money was legit, from the coffers at Mangiamo's. Whether or not it was true, her mother convinced her to keep it when she said Katie should use it for whatever Henry needed.

It felt ominous in a way, taking the money from her. The last time her mother had given her money, Katie used it for bus fare. She'd worked hard over the years to help Erma and Isaac, trying never to be a burden to them, and they provided well for her and Henry. But she'd never earned a penny of income in her life.

Maybe the money was what she needed to find a safe place for her and Henry to start over.

In the sliver of moonlight, she could see the barn in front of them.

Years ago, when she was about nineteen, she'd discovered several young people climbing up the tree beside the barn. Curious, she'd climbed it behind them and found a window at the top, opening into the hayloft. At the time, she'd been much like the other young people climbing the tree—except, of course, none of them was rearing a child on her own.

Rollin put out his arm, stopping her again, and she watched the dark outline of two men guarding the back door. She tugged on Rollin's arm, and he followed her to the north side of the barn.

No one was guarding the wide trunk of the sycamore tree.

Katie tied her long skirt in a knot, tucked it between her knees, and pointed toward the top of the tree. Rollin helped hoist her bare foot up to a limb about four feet off the ground, and she pulled herself up. Feeling for a branch above her, she balanced herself and then slowly climbed the tree, to the closed window above. When she reached the top, she opened the shutters and climbed inside.

There were small mounds of hay in the loft, but they stank of mold and decay. In front of her was a wooden railing and below it, the room glowed from lantern light. A ladder hung at the end of the railing, leading to the main floor below.

Rollin crawled into the loft behind her and sat on a bale of hay.

"Where's your jacket?" she whispered close to his ear.

"I couldn't climb with it."

Her gaze wandered back toward the opening. "Where did you leave it?"

"I stuffed it into a hole in the tree."

"No one's going to bother us out here," someone said below them, and neither she nor Rollin whispered again. He edged toward the railing while she backed away into the shadows of the loft. Something scampered in the hay next to her, and she scooted the other direction. She didn't mind most animals, but she was not fond of mice.

"Junior thinks that cop is on to us."

"The dead one?" the guy said with a laugh.

"No, the one who won't keep his nose out of our business."

"Junior's coming," another man said.

Silence invaded the barn until her brother walked through the door.

"Any sign of visitors?" he asked.

Katie rubbed her arms at the sharp tone in her brother's voice. She'd hoped he would find his own way in life instead of following their father's steps.

"No one but the owls."

And the mice.

"Wells is out there," Antonio said. "And we have to keep him away."

"He's not going to come alone." Katie remembered where she'd heard that man's voice before. It was Eligio Ricci, their driver and one of her father's bodyguards. If Eligio was here, her father must be coming soon.

"Detective Wells prefers to work alone."

Rollin looked back at her, catching her eye. Her brother was right, and they both knew it. She'd forced her way into joining him, even when he didn't want her here. If there were some way she could help stop her father and her brother and the others from hurting anyone else, she would do it.

"Our friends from Cincinnati will arrive before lunch," Antonio said.

"What about your uncle?"

"He's already here."

The voices were muffled for a moment, and then she heard Antonio speak again. "There will be no sleeping tonight, gentlemen."

The men swore to him that they would stay awake until morning.

Footsteps thudded across the wooden floor again as Antonio walked outside. Rollin motioned for her, and she snuck toward the railing and glanced over. Below were thirty or forty chairs set up in straight lines. At the far end of the barn was a long banquet table covered with a maroon tablecloth, ready for Irene's food.

A car pulled into the driveway outside, and a door slammed. She followed Rollin back into the shadows.

"Maybe they are having a wedding," she whispered.

"It will be some type of union," Rollin said, his cheek brushing her bonnet. "Just not between a man and his bride."

CHAPTER 26

A dozen men played poker and smoked cigarettes in the cramped dining room of the farmhouse like nothing major was about to happen. And Uncle Ray was dealing the cards.

Antonio stood in the doorway, watching the men for a moment. Except for his uncle, they were all Antonio's men, handpicked for their loyalty to his cause. They'd all done what was required to be part of the Cardano organization.

It was a good thing that he was in charge of this meeting. His uncle and the others would squander the opportunity.

Raymond called out to him as he stepped back, saying he should join them for a game, but Antonio shrugged him off. There was much more at stake tonight than a card game.

He marched through the sparsely decorated living room, and the screen door slammed behind him when he stepped outside. Emanuele watched him from the barn door, but as he turned toward the driveway, his cousin didn't ask where he was going.

There were five cars parked in the long drive now, but by tomorrow night there would be at least twenty. Men were coming from Columbus and Dayton and as far away as Cincinnati. They all knew what was expected of them and what they should expect.

When he was finished, the Cardano family would be the sole supplier of corn sugar to every major bootlegger across the state, and

Antonio would no longer be the underling, following in his father's shadow. His father's top men were on his side, and Heyward finally realized that Salvatore wouldn't be in this business much longer.

With the Puglisis still reeling from Leone's death, the Cardano family would swoop in and take everything. And Antonio would be at the helm.

He chewed his fingernails as he walked down the long lane, trying to remember if he'd forgotten anything.

If all went as planned tomorrow night, he and the key players on his team would take his main adversary down, and he would organize the rest of the men into a well-oiled machine to meet the supply and demand of their customers' unquenchable thirst.

He patted the new Smith & Wesson pistol at his side. His father personally taught him how to shoot a pistol before Antonio's seventh birthday, and not long after he turned fifteen, Salvatore assigned him the task of eliminating a man who'd betrayed their family. Instead of killing him, though, Antonio hired someone to do the job.

His father thought he was gutless, but it wasn't about guts. Antonio hated the sight of blood, and he couldn't understand his father's disdain when he refused to kill. It had been a smart move to hire a soldier who shot when asked. A man who didn't feel queasy when things got bloody. And it kept Antonio's hands clean.

He may not be fond of blood, but he had the brains in the family. No one had ever pinned a murder on him nor would they ever.

Tomorrow, for just a moment, his father would be proud of him. Salvatore Club Cardano would pay him some respect.

At the end of the lane, he saw Heyward's Cadillac parked under the low limbs of a tree. Antonio slid into the passenger seat, his eyes focused on the dashboard.

"When are the others coming?"

"In the morning." Heyward nodded toward the house. "Do you think Raymond knows what's about to happen?"

"He doesn't care about anything except his poker hand right now."

"And you're certain he'll pull the trigger?"

"Without a doubt. He wants Salvatore gone as much as I do."

"A lot could go wrong tomorrow."

Antonio slipped an envelope out of his jacket, filled with five thousand dollars in large bills. Half the payment up front. He wouldn't pay Heyward the other half until it was over. "But it won't."

Heyward took the envelope and tucked it into his coat. "It's a pleasure doing business with you, Junior."

"And with you," Antonio said before he climbed out of the car.

Not only would he be a free man after tomorrow. He would be in charge.

* * * * *

Rollin stepped over the windowsill and his foot searched for the branch underneath. The army taught him how to crawl, shoot, and run, but they'd never taught him how to climb trees. He supposed they assumed their troops learned to climb when they were boys, but Rollin never had.

His foot found a branch, and he reached out in the darkness for a branch to clutch with his hands. He'd made it up the tree without making a fool of himself. Surely he could make it down as well.

He didn't look down, didn't think about how high they'd had to climb to get up to the loft. All he needed to do was get down to solid ground. He and Katie would walk back to the Lehmans' house, sleep for the remaining hours of the night, and then he would figure out his next step.

Clinging to the curved tree limb, he slowly eased himself toward the trunk. His arm ached, but he ignored the pain. All he needed to do was maneuver both arms around the middle of the tree. Then he could inch himself down. He didn't care how manly he looked in the process. He just wanted to get down alive.

"Be careful," Katie whispered, like he wasn't trying.

With his fingers entwined around a big branch, he put his other foot onto the peeling bark and moved toward the center. If only he could see what he was doing, he could get down this tree.

Leaves brushed across his face. His hands pressed into the strength of the wood. He was so close to exposing the Cardanos, so close to finding out what they were doing. The only thing between him and his escape from them tonight was a lousy sycamore tree.

He should have gone behind his mother's back when he was a kid and climbed a few trees. Then he wouldn't be a thirty-one-year-old adult who couldn't get down from a barn.

Katie nudged his back. "You've got to move faster."

"I'm trying."

Swinging even closer to the center, he stepped down a notch and searched until he found another secure hold for his foot. Below him, in the dark web of branches, he looked for ground, but all he saw were sticks and leaves.

It was going to take him a lifetime to get down.

Katie said something else, something he didn't understand. When he glanced upwards, his hat slid toward the back of his head. He hesitated, leaning down again, but his hat still teetered. He tried to reposition his hands, to grab his hat before it fell, but it was too late. His hat slipped off his head, bumping down the branches below.

Katie sucked in her breath.

Someone moved around the barn, and he froze, both hands secured on the tree limbs. A flashlight illuminated the woods behind him and then the wide base of the tree.

He could see his hat now, perched on a branch about fifteen feet down from him. And he prayed the man below didn't look up.

Katie's hand tapped on his shoulder, and as quietly as he could, he tried to get back through the window. The flashlight scanned the woods again as he pulled his torso and then his legs back into the barn. He closed the shutters.

Reaching for his hip, he checked for his gun, and it was still there. If Mr. Hatchet down there decided to climb up the tree, Rollin would pick him off.

"What were you trying to say?" he asked.

"When?"

"When I was in the tree. You said something, and when I looked up, I lost my hat."

"Oh—" She paused. "I was telling you to be careful."

"Next time, you might want to just think it instead."

"It shouldn't take but three minutes to get down that tree."

He brushed off his arms. "It takes me a little longer."

"Haven't you ever climbed down a tree before?"

"You're one brilliant woman, Katie." He leaned back against the wall, bracing himself for her laugh. "How did you figure that out?"

But she didn't laugh at him. Instead the irritation in her eyes turned to sympathy.

"You never climbed a tree before?"

"We didn't have any good climbing trees in our neighborhood, and even if we did, my mother would never have allowed it."

"Your mother didn't want you to get hurt."

"She didn't want me to get dirty."

"Oh…"

He heard voices again downstairs, and he and Katie stopped whispering.

She yawned as she settled back into the hay, and he felt the weight of exhaustion bear heavily down on him as well. Neither of them had slept much the past few nights.

The men guarding the doors and probably the sycamore tree would be up all night, alert and waiting for him. His only hope was that he would rest well tonight, and the guards would go to sleep around dawn. Then he and Katie could escape.

Someone turned off one of the lanterns below, and he could see the shadows of the men posted at both doors. He moved back to Katie.

"Are we spending the night?" she asked.

"I'm afraid so."

The stench of moldy hay ballooned into the air as he pushed together a small lump beside Katie. How many people were coming for this meeting? Maybe he could catch more than the Cardanos tomorrow. Maybe he could catch a whole network of criminals and possibly even Malloy and some crooked cops.

He shifted in the hay.

Antonio was right about one thing. Rollin preferred to do things alone, but in order to catch these men, he'd need help.

Katie leaned her bonnet back against the hay. "I'm exhausted."

His focus shifted, from the men below to the beautiful woman next to him, and his heart seemed to skip a beat. He usually preferred to be alone, but tonight he wanted to be with her.

He cleared his throat. "You should be tired."

"You should be tired too."

He shifted in the hay, scooting away from her an inch or two, and then he felt silly. She would wonder why he was moving away.

"Let's go to sleep," he said.

"Uh-huh," she replied, her voice fading.

He rolled onto one shoulder, away from her. "Isaac and Erma will be worried."

"Ya. But Erma will continue to pray."

"We could use some help from above."

"God always listens, Rollin, but that doesn't mean He will choose to rescue us."

That was his problem. In his experience, God's hands seemed to be tied, like He was up there but unable to stop the bad from happening.

"Then what's the point of praying?"

"To ask God to guide us where He wants us to go," she said. "And ask that we are wise enough to follow in the direction He leads."

"Let's hope His direction leads us right out of this barn."

Katie shivered in the night air.

"Are you cold?" he whispered.

"A little."

Night air seeped through the cracks in the siding, and Katie shivered again. Sleep would be a long time in coming—for both of them—if she was cold. With his jacket hidden in the tree, all he had to offer her for warmth was himself, but what if he reached out now and she pushed him away? He would be here all night, beside her, humiliated by her rejection.

But he couldn't let her be cold either.

"My jacket—"

"Don't worry about me, Rollin."

He hesitated before he stretched out his right arm. "I could try and keep you warm tonight."

Silence lingered between them as the mice shuffled over the worn floor on the other side of the barn. He'd presented his offer as kindly as possible, one old friend helping another, but she didn't say a word. Not a thank you or an uncomfortable laugh or even a flat-out rejection. He would have preferred a rejection to the stone-cold silence.

He pulled his arm back to his side, and he was almost ready to slink back into the corner when she spoke.

"How are you planning to keep me warm?" He could hear the soft hint of teasing in her voice.

"I…" He started. "All I have are my arms."

"All right then," she said, edging toward him.

When he opened his arms again, they swallowed her. Her head on his chest, he could feel her body with every beat of his heart. With every swell of his breath. He only wished he could feel her hair against his face instead of the starched material on her bonnet.

Even as her headpiece scratched his chin, he didn't say anything to interrupt the sweet moment. It was bliss, being here with her tonight. He didn't care anymore about the Cardano brothers below or the fact that Malloy was probably close by. It was only he and Katie for these short hours. And she was resting in his arms.

Minutes later, she shifted again, and he was afraid she was moving away from him. Reluctantly, he released her, and she sat up.

"Are you comfortable?" he asked.

"Ya." Her fingers reached up to her bonnet, slipping pins from her hair, and she took the material off and laid it beside her. "Now I can rest."

He softly brushed her hair away from her face, back behind her ears and her neck. Tonight he wouldn't have to wake her up to go back to the house. He could hold her all night long.

He wanted to tell her that he didn't care if she was a Cardano or a Lehman. He didn't care that she was Liz's sister or the mother of Henry Lehman. He only wanted to be with her.

Her breathing slowed, and he could feel the weariness settling over his bones, but he couldn't sleep. How was he going to get any rest with Katie Lehman at his side?

CHAPTER 27

Celeste watched the sunrise from an intersection in Canton. Her hands on the steering wheel, she looked both directions, but she didn't know which way to go. Last night she'd started back to Cleveland and made it an hour north before she stopped. She didn't want to go back to her shell of a house when both her children were in Sugarcreek.

It hadn't been hard to find a speakeasy last night, and in her fine attire, the maître d' let her inside without an inquisition. She hadn't danced or drunk in a nightclub since long before the beginning of Prohibition. Salvatore could go to all the clubs he wanted, but his reputation would be bruised if his wife were caught drinking at one, so he kept her supplied at home instead.

But being at the speakeasy exhilarated her last night. The music and the dancing and the seemingly endless supply of fine wine. She hadn't tasted red wine on her lips for such a long time. It felt like a small piece of her was returning home, much more so than her trip back to Sugarcreek.

When they finally shut down the club for the night, she'd stumbled back to the hotel and flirted with the hotel manager as he escorted her to her room. Not that the manager reciprocated—he was aggravated that she'd awakened him from his sleep—but for the first time in a very long time, she felt alive.

She wanted to spend her nights dancing again. Wear finery the masses would admire. She wanted to dance her extra pounds away so she felt beautiful again. She wanted men like the hotel manager to flirt back with her instead of dumping her off in her room alone.

When she woke up this morning, in that lumpy hotel room bed, her heart was pounding. Not from the alcohol, but from the music of last night's jazz band still ringing in her ears. She'd only heard music like that on the radio, and even though it was loud, she adored it. Her headache would fade away this morning, but she hoped the memory of her night out never would.

A green airplane with yellow wings flew over the shops in Canton and breezed past her without acknowledging that she was below. The plane looked like the one Salvatore purchased last year so he could visit the places in the country that supplied him with the goods necessary for his business. He didn't tell her about the airplane, of course, but he'd described the machine to Antonio in detail. Never before had she heard him speak with such pride. It was like he'd given birth to a child who finally met his expectations.

The tail of the plane faded in the morning light.

Celeste looked right, at the road leading back to Cleveland, and then she looked left.

Starting the car, she didn't hesitate as she pulled forward.

There was nothing left for her in Cleveland.

She would follow the airplane back to Sugarcreek.

* * * * *

The airplane roared over the barn, startling Katie awake, but she lay still in Rollin's arms. When she was younger, she'd dreamt for hours about what it would be like to be close to Rollin, and now here she was, closer to him than she'd ever imagined possible. And it was better than she'd ever imagined.

Ruth had always been one of Katie's favorite women in the Bible, especially when she made the right choice to leave behind the evil in her past to follow God. Was this how Ruth felt when she woke up at Boaz's feet? Her heart filled with the richness of being near the one she loved.

Katie snuggled closer to Rollin, to the place where she was safe. Antonio and Salvatore and the others could do what they wanted.

Light streamed into the barn, and she heard a voice outside. She didn't want to move away from Rollin, but they had to get out of here. Once the men started arriving, they'd never be able to leave.

"Rollin," she whispered, gently prodding his arm. "It's time to get up."

He opened his eyes slowly, like he was savoring the memory as well, and he smiled at her.

"Good morning," he said quietly as he raked his fingers through his hair.

She scooted back from him and slid her bonnet over her head. She wanted to stay hours longer, before the world encroached on their solitude, but she tied the strings around her chin instead so she wouldn't lose it down the tree.

As Rollin opened the shutters, she moved to the side of the loft and glanced over the railing. Four men were asleep downstairs, spread out on blankets, and one man was asleep on a cot. Rollin motioned to her, and she tiptoed toward the window, praying her footsteps wouldn't wake the men below.

He started out the window, but she tapped his shoulder, whispering in his ear. "Follow me."

She thought he might protest, but he let her slide by him. Her hands and bare feet grasped the familiar knobs and branches as she hustled down the limbs. She swept Rollin's hat in one hand and carried it to the bottom. With a glance both ways under the tree, she hopped onto the ground and shuffled into the cover of the forest.

Holding her breath, she watched Rollin snake down through the limbs. It didn't matter that Erma had given Rollin his pistol. If they were caught, there weren't enough bullets in Rollin's gun to stop the men.

A squirrel scampered toward her hiding place, and she shooed it away before someone heard it. The seconds turned to minutes, crawling in her mind. Finally she saw his feet straddling the sides of the bottom limb. Hitting the ground.

His crumpled jacket strung over his good arm, Rollin ducked and rushed toward the trees.

The walk back to the Lehmans' house took forty-five minutes, and they talked about their early years, growing up in the city. She didn't want to talk about last night, and he didn't mention it either. They were two old acquaintances, thrown together for the night in a barn. It was nothing. Meant nothing.

But Isaac and Erma would know they hadn't come home last night, and she was mortified at what they might think.

Filled platters and bowls waited for them on the kitchen table, and she silently blessed her aunt for making them a feast. Rollin dug into the hotcakes and bacon at the table alongside her, and her mouth was filled with hotcakes when Isaac walked into the kitchen. He walked past them in silence, filling a cup with coffee.

He took a long sip before facing her. "Where were you last night?"

"At the Bowmans' barn."

"Henry asked why you weren't in your bed this morning, and I didn't know what to tell him."

"You don't have to tell him anything." She rested her fork on the plate. "I will tell him where I was."

Isaac circled the air with his cup. "I don't know what you two are doing, but I can no longer allow it in my home. You've come and gone as you pleased this week, Katie, with no thought to the rest of the family or your son."

No thought to her son. His words drilled through her chest, blasting her heart. All she did was for the best of her son. Or it usually was. This week she had been distracted by the appearance of Rollin Wells and her family.

Words poured out of her mouth, trying to say how sorry she was, but she wasn't making much sense. She never meant to do anything wrong. She'd been torn between what was right to do for Henry and Rollin and the people in her community.

Rollin shoved back his chair and stood. "She hasn't done anything wrong."

Isaac didn't move. "Your standard of what is right and what is wrong is very different from ours."

Katie's face burned under Isaac's scrutiny, her mind wandering back to her night in the barn. She'd rested her head on Rollin's chest. Not just for warmth, but for the pleasure of being wrapped in his arms. She never should have let herself be close to him. She should have moved to the other side of the barn and slept alone.

"I want to help Rollin." Her gaze traveled between Rollin and her uncle. "Help him stop the people who killed my sister...and the people who would kill Henry and me if they knew we were still alive."

Isaac shook his head. "Vengeance is the Lord's, Katie, not yours."

"There is a big difference between vengeance and justice," Rollin said.

"And which drives you, Rollin Wells? Vengeance or justice?"

Rollin leaned back against his seat, his lips silent. He might want vengeance, but vengeance no longer drove Katie—she'd forgiven her father and her brother and the others a long time ago. What she wanted was for them to stop using the justice system for their own good and stop hurting innocent people in their mad quest for power.

"I want to be free of the Cardano family," she tried to explain. "I don't want to hurt them. I just want them to be in jail where they belong."

Isaac started to say something, but Rollin stopped him.

"You ever have wolves on your property?" he asked.

"I've never seen one."

"How about a coyote?"

"Of course."

"What if a coyote attacked some of your cows or got in your chicken coop?"

Isaac's head fell a notch, but he kept his eyes on Rollin. "I'd make him leave."

"By talking him out of it?"

"No—"

"With your shotgun?"

"It is different."

"God gave us the ability to protect our women and children from men like the Cardanos, and I believe it's more important to keep them safe than to keep coyotes away from chickens or cows."

She heard Henry's feet pounding down the staircase. When he raced into the room, he sprang into Katie's arms and hugged her shoulders. "I was so worried about you, Mamm."

She tweaked his cheek. "You don't have to worry about me."

"I didn't know where you had gone."

Rollin looked back at Isaac. "Could you take me back to Sugarcreek this afternoon to use the telephone?"

"Are you calling another friend to come get you?" Isaac asked.

He shook his head. "I'm calling a friend to help me."

"I won't have anything to do with it," Isaac said before he turned to Henry. "I need your help in the field today."

Isaac stomped out, and the room quieted for a moment. Henry looked to her for an answer.

"Isaac is having a rough morning," she tried to explain.

He lowered his voice, like Rollin wasn't right next to him. "He doesn't like Rollin Wells, does he?"

"It's not that…"

"Henry's right." Rollin picked up his dishes and put them in the sink. "He doesn't like me."

"Why not?" Henry asked.

Rollin's eyes pleaded for her to answer.

"Isaac just doesn't understand," she said.

Like Erma, Isaac had grown up in a community that loved and served each other. He didn't know much about a world where people lived solely to please themselves. And where they made big plans to grow wealthy without working.

Work was the backbone of the Amish society. Work and respect for each other and for *Gott*.

"I'll take you to Sugarcreek," she volunteered. "I just have to get cleaned up first."

"Can I go too?" Henry asked.

When Rollin looked at her, she shook her head.

"Isaac needs you in the field," Rollin said. "But I was hoping to play a bit of softball before I went to town."

Henry hopped toward him. "I have a softball!"

"Oh, good," Rollin said, winking at her. "But we'd need a bat as well."

Henry clapped. "I have one of those too."

From her bedroom window, Katie watched them play. Rollin throwing the softball. Henry hitting it. And she couldn't tell who was having more fun. A week in the country had been good for Rollin. It was almost like no one was chasing him.

After she poured water into a basin, Katie washed the dirt from her skin, but she couldn't rid herself of the strength in Rollin's arms or how his tenderness made her feel. He treated her with respect last night. Like a little sister even. Liz's little sister.

Sighing, she brushed the remnants of hay from her hair. Outside the window she heard the crack of the ball against bat. Laughter. It warmed her heart, even more than the hours she spent sleeping on Rollin's chest.

She picked a light blue dress from a hook and began pinning it around her. Then she looked out the window again at her son and Rollin playing.

He was changing so quickly. It wouldn't be long before her son reached adolescence and would need to determine on his own whether or not he wanted to join the Amish church. As she watched Henry hit the softball, she knew what her son would decide. He would choose to leave their community.

No matter how much she wanted him to stay in their secure world, she wouldn't try to manipulate him into spending the rest of his life as an Amish man when his heart was full of passion and determination and a thirst for adventure and progress.

Her mother was right. She shouldn't hold Henry back from what he was meant to do.

CHAPTER 28

"They're inviting leaders from across Ohio." Rollin tried to whisper into the payphone, but he felt like he was shouting across the static. Even with the glass booth around him, it felt like everyone outside IGA and across half the town could hear him, but somehow he had to convey to his former partner what was happening near Sugarcreek without telling him all the details.

He slid another nickel into the phone and kept talking. "The big guy is here."

"Salvatore?"

"No…the other one."

Gilbert paused for a moment and then swore. "Where did they find him?"

"No idea, but it doesn't really matter. He's here, and the others will arrive tonight."

"I'm on my way," Gilbert said.

It was what he wanted to hear, but instead of picturing Gilbert fighting alongside him, he saw Lance grinning at him in his new coupe. Gilbert had four grandchildren and a wife of forty-plus years.

"I don't know, Gil."

"It doesn't matter what you think," his former partner replied. "I've been waiting my whole career for this."

Rollin leaned back against the wall. He'd been waiting his whole career for this as well. Isaac was right this morning. He didn't want justice alone for the Cardanos. He wanted vengeance. And once he got it, there was nothing left for him to chase.

"So you'll come?" he asked.

"If you'd let me hang up this darn telephone."

Rollin smiled, setting the earpiece back on the hook, and his gaze wandered back out to the parking lot, to the pretty woman in the buggy wearing blue. At least he had two people on his team.

Hopping up onto the bench of the buggy, he couldn't take his eyes off Katie.

"What?" she asked, a twinge of pink creeping up her cheeks.

"You are beautiful."

"I'm not."

"I'm not trying to flatter you, Katie. You are a beautiful woman."

She looked at her lap, twisting her fingers in her skirt. "Thank you."

They sat in awkward silence for a moment. He'd told her the truth—he thought she was beautiful. Still there was so much more he wanted to say.

But the words escaped him.

"I need to go to the police station," he said instead.

Music filled the street from the fair, and children squealed as they rode the large merry-go-round in the center of town. The air was filled with the smells of cotton candy and roasted hot dogs and buttery corn.

People roamed the streets as they visited the different booths. The police would be distracted this weekend, their focus on town instead of in the country at places like the Bowman farm.

Two blocks off the main street, Rollin parked the buggy in front of a tiny brick building that housed local law enforcement. When he began to tie Prince to the hitching post, Katie stopped him.

"I need to use the buggy while you're inside."

"Where are you going?"

She flicked the reins. "I have to pick up some pies."

* * * * *

On her drive back to Sugarcreek, Celeste stopped to phone Olivia. Her friend told her Salvatore was gone when she arrived at the house that morning, and Celeste could only assume he was joining Antonio and the others down here. Salvatore wouldn't want to do the dirty work preparing whatever they had planned, but he'd want to oversee the action.

She asked Olivia if Salvatore inquired about her yesterday. Olivia tried to sidestep her question, saying she'd only seen Salvatore once and it was brief. But any other husband would have hunted down their housekeeper right away, asked where his wife was.

A good husband wouldn't have even asked. He would have demanded she tell him what happened to his wife.

At one time, Salvatore would have cared if she left. Back when she was full of fire and passion for life. She'd been taught to turn the other cheek growing up no matter what happened, to take whatever was dealt to her and absorb the pain. Even when some Englishers threw rocks at her on her way home from school, bruising her arms, her parents didn't fight for her, and she'd despised them for it.

It wasn't about persecution. It was about passivity. The other children hurt her again and again, and her parents never stopped them. They told her to forgive them, but she couldn't forgive. She wanted revenge instead.

She rebelled against the passivity as a teenager and in her younger days in Cleveland. She was passionate and driven, determined never to let anyone throw rocks at her again. Her friends in the city would never even know about her past or accuse her of being passive. And perhaps that was what she admired most about Salvatore when she met him. He didn't let anyone speak against him or anyone in his family. People were afraid of him.

She'd been angry at her parents for ignoring those who'd hurt her as a child, but now she had done the same thing. Instead of standing for what was right, she'd turned the other cheek and allowed herself and her children to be battered. Instead of protecting her children, she watched the abuse as a bystander. And how they'd suffered because of her. Because of what she'd allowed. No matter what Salvatore did or said, she should have protected the children entrusted to her.

She drove past the driveway where she'd taken Rollin and Katie yesterday, and about a half-mile from the drive, she pulled off the road, shaded behind the tall stalks of a cornfield. Even though her belly was full of sausage and muffins from breakfast, her head still pounded. She couldn't falter tonight because she was tired or weak. Focus was what she needed, and in order to focus, she needed sleep.

After she cracked her window, she collapsed back in her seat and covered her face with her satin cloche. She could sleep all day if she wanted. No one except maybe an Amish farmer would bother her here, and all he would do was ask her to move on.

She'd wait until the bright sun set this evening to ensure Salvatore had arrived. Then, for a few minutes, all the living members of her family would be within a mile of each other. It would be the closest they'd ever come to having a reunion. For just today, she'd pretend that her husband loved her and her children delighted in seeing her.

She'd pretend her grandson adored her and her sister appreciated the woman she'd become. She'd even pretend that she respected herself as a woman and as a mother.

Her eyes closed, and as Celeste began to drift off, she shifted on the seat.

She was finished standing on the sidelines, allowing Salvatore Cardano to ruin her family. Tonight she would visit him and remind him of the fire that once burned within her.

* * * * *

Low clouds blocked the sun as Rollin stopped the buggy beside the forest that hid the Bowmans' farm and tried to hand Katie the reins. She stared at them for a moment but didn't take them, so he set them back in his lap. He and Katie were alone again, and he feared it would be their last time together.

Katie crossed her arms over her chest, her eyes focused on her lap. "I should have told you the truth."

He shook his head. "Katie—"

"When you first arrived, I should have told you who I was instead of hiding it from you."

"You didn't have a good reason to trust me."

"But I shouldn't have lied to you."

He brushed his fingers against her lips, gently hushing her. In her eyes, he saw her apology.

"You didn't do anything wrong," he said. "Not at the basement at Mangiamo's nor in the Yoders' barn."

"I said I didn't care what happened to you."

He smiled. "You did mention that."

"It was another lie."

He reached for her hand and drew her closer to him. "I know."

"I've cared about you for a long time."

He shook his head. "I don't deserve it."

"Back when I was a kid, I used to follow you and Liz around."

He squeezed her fingers. "Here I thought you really wanted me to eat your tea and cookies."

"A ruse," she laughed. "And a terrible one, at that."

"You were so young back then. I barely talked to you or even noticed you."

"You shouldn't have noticed me."

"But now…" This time she inched closer, and desire burned within him. "You are a strong woman, Katie. And brave."

"Not so brave."

"Did Henry's father love you like he should have?"

"Henry's father—" she started.

He reached up, sliding off her cap so he could feel the soft tendrils of her hair again in his fingers. "You don't have to tell me now."

Tears wet her eyes. Tonight he may go down with the Cardanos, fighting until the end. He didn't need to know who Henry's father was, but he couldn't leave until he told her what was in his mind.

"I spent most of my life following in Liz's footsteps," she said.

He cupped her face in his hands. "When I look at you, I don't see Elizabeth."

Her voice trembled when she spoke. "Who do you see?"

"I see Nicola Cardano, all grown up. And I see Katie Lehman, a woman full of love and beauty and grace."

"You will always love Liz."

"I was crazy about Liz," he said, weighing his words as he spoke. He wanted Katie to understand the difference between his past and who he was today. How much he had changed. "We were so young and made plenty of mistakes."

"You have regrets?" she asked.

"The regrets haunt me," he said. "I never got to tell your sister how sorry I was."

"Thank you, Rollin." She paused. "Thank you for telling me."

"I don't want to be with Liz," he said, his heart swelling with the truth of his words. "I want to be with you."

She leaned into him, and his lips touched hers, savoring the softness of them. Tasting the sweetness.

He pulled her closer to him, kissing her again, and she rested her head on his shoulder, her cheek touching his. He didn't want to let go. He wanted to stay here forever with Katie Lehman in his arms.

In the hills beyond, he heard the blasted motor of the airplane, poking its nose over the trees. The moment she pulled away from him, he knew she was right on one other matter. Progress wasn't always a good thing.

The plane flew low over the buggy top and landed in the field behind them.

"Another guest for the party," he said wryly. "Your brother will be busy entertaining today."

"Poor Antonio."

"Your brother isn't as poor as you think." He searched her eyes. "I want you to go home, Katie."

"I am going home."

He took her hand again, wanting her to understand. "I don't want you anywhere near this barn tonight."

"I'll pray for you tonight."

"Please pray hard."

He handed her the reins again, and this time she took them, but as he climbed out of the cart, she reached for him one last time. Stopping him.

"Henry's father is a good man."

His chest clenched. "He's still alive?"

"When you come back, I will tell you about him."

He squeezed her hand. "I will come back."

CHAPTER 29

Tremors shot through Katie's body, all the way down to her bare toes. Never had she imagined Rollin's kiss would feel like this—and she'd imagined often what it would be like to feel his lips on hers. She pressed her fingers to her mouth as she watched him vanish into the trees. Then she leaned back against the leather seat and giggled.

Her very first kiss.

She took a deep breath, trying to steady the lightness in her head as she lifted the reins and clicked her tongue. Prince trotted forward. She would go back home like she'd promised Rollin, long before dark, but first she had a job to do.

The drive up to the Bowmans' house was lined with pine trees and tall wildflowers. The propeller on the airplane had quieted, and if she didn't know for certain there were people on the grounds, she would think the property was still vacant.

The airplane was in the field to the left of the house, and she saw two large men in suits standing under the forebay along the barn. She prayed that Rollin was correct, that her father wasn't in Sugarcreek, but if he was, she prayed he wouldn't recognize her.

The men at the barn eyed her plain attire, but they didn't make any move to question or deter her. She walked to the back of the buggy and lifted a box off the floor. Holding it close to her chest, she walked toward the house.

Eligio Ricci, her father's driver and bodyguard, answered the door. She held her breath as he glowered at her and her brown box.

"I'm Katie," she said lightly. "Irene sent me."

"Who?"

"Irene Woodman. The woman catering your wedding."

Irritated, he nodded toward the barn. "She already delivered the food."

"I know." Katie opened the edge of the box, and the man sniffed the baked apples and cinnamon in the pie. "But you didn't order any pies or cakes, and Irene said she couldn't imagine a wedding without a few *schnitz* pies. She said you don't have to pay her a cent. Just enjoy your special day."

Eligio's eyes clouded, and it was obvious that didn't care a lick about weddings or cakes. But he pointed toward the barn. "It goes in there."

"Oh, good." She picked up her skirt, turning. "I'll put them with the rest of the food."

With the box in her hands, she breezed toward the men at the door.

"Don't you just love weddings," she said.

She didn't wait for their response. She walked right past them, into the dusty main floor of the barn.

To the left was a small platform with a podium. The buffet table was set up at the back of the chairs on her right. Irene had spread plates across the table for meats, cheese, and fruit. The bread was on the table, and she assumed the rest of the food was being cooled outside in the springhouse, waiting for all the men to arrive.

She set the pie on the table and edged one of the ceramic platters at an angle to match the others. And then she began situating another platter. There were two men hidden in the shadows of the loft, arguing, and her fingers froze on the platter. Her father was here.

MELANIE DOBSON

Dropping her hands to her sides, she backed toward the wide door. She'd wanted to see Antonio before tonight, but she never wanted to see her father again.

Turning, she could feel the sunshine on her face as it radiated through the open door. Rollin didn't want her here, and her father certainly wouldn't want her here. Prince would take her home to Henry, and she would spend the rest of the evening on her knees.

Footsteps pounded behind her as she moved forward, but before she stepped outside, she heard her father's voice.

"Stop," he ordered. And she stopped.

She didn't turn around nor did she take another step, but her heart trembled. What would her father do if he recognized her?

"Who are you?" he demanded. His hand was on her arm, turning her toward him. She felt the hiccup rising in her throat and she swallowed hard.

"Katie," she said with her head bowed. "Katie Lehman."

She didn't look up at him, but she could feel his rising fury without seeing his face. He poked her leg with his walking stick like she was some sort of animal.

"Why are you here?"

She kept her mouth closed for a moment to fight off another hiccup. Then she pointed at the buffet table. "I'm delivering the rest of the food."

"This is a private meeting."

"Wedding," Antonio mumbled. "It's a wedding."

At her brother's voice, she dared to look over and meet his eye. "I love weddings," she said.

Antonio stared at her, blinking as he recognized her face. A curse word ripped through his lips.

Her father's voice hardened. "What is it?"

Her brother looked away from her face, and she bowed her head again.

"I just remembered something," Antonio said.

"What did you remember?" he demanded, but her brother didn't respond.

She stepped forward, speaking quietly. "I was bringing the pies for dessert."

"The pies," Antonio said with a nod.

"Get her out of here."

Antonio gave her a small push out the barn door, toward her buggy.

In the fresh air, she could breathe again. Away from the oppression of her father's presence. She could smell the wildflowers out here and feel the warm breeze on her face. Her father had allowed his thirst for power to overtake him, and he was blinded by his own deception.

In the years away from the Cardano house, she'd forgotten how broken she'd been. How broken all of them had been. Without Liz and Antonio to protect her, she might never have survived her childhood.

Antonio followed her to the back of the buggy, hidden from the eyes in the barn, and her hiccups slowly subsided. Long ago, she'd glimpsed the seeds of kindness inside her brother's soul. Seeds that could sprout if he'd let them.

"What are you doing here?" he whispered.

"I live here," she replied. "And I live in peace, Antonio. Without the fear."

He nodded back toward the barn. "He can't know you're still alive."

"He doesn't even recognize me." It was an answer to her prayer, but it still hurt.

She reached for another box in the back of the buggy and tried to hand it to Antonio, but he didn't take it.

"How did you know I was here, Katie?"

Her face warmed as she tried to think of a truthful answer that wouldn't indict Rollin, but a lie tumbled out of her mouth instead. "I didn't know until I saw you in the barn."

Antonio paused as he seemed to contemplate her answer, and her gaze traveled to the forest beside them. Was Rollin near the barn yet? She couldn't tell Antonio what was going to happen tonight, but she could remind him that he had the option to leave. Today. Just like she had done. He could flee from this mess and become the man God created him to be instead of a man molded by Salvatore and the other members of their union.

"How's Henry?" he finally asked.

"He's well." She managed a smile as she tried to hand him the pie again. This time he took it. "He reminds me a bit of you."

"Poor kid."

She stepped out and glanced back at the men by the barn. They were facing the house, but she knew they were watching them. She moved back under the cover of the buggy.

"You don't have to stay here, Antonio," she whispered to him. "You can come with me right now."

His laugh was low. Gruff. "And become Amish?"

"You can become whatever it is that you want to be. You can help people instead of hurt them."

His arm swept toward the barn. "This is what I want to do with my life."

She ignored his words. He was a man now, able to choose for himself the vision for his life, but he was so much better than this. He'd always been determined, but when he was younger, Antonio stood up for others. As an adult, he could continue fighting for those who needed help.

"Tell your men you need to go to town." She was tugging on his arm now. "We will find you a car and you can drive far, far away."

"Nikki," he said slowly, like he was searching for his words. "It's been a long time since you left."

"You can leave too, Antonio. Right now."

"I can't."

"One day, you'll be the one found in a lake or shot in the head." She didn't care that she was begging. He had to understand. "And it won't be worth it."

He rested his hand on her shoulder, his face resigned, and she knew there was nothing else she could say. Only death could end this life he'd chosen.

"It's good to see you, Nikki."

She nodded. She'd never gotten to say good-bye to him when she ran all those years ago. Never got to thank him.

"You were the one who stopped them, weren't you?" she asked.

"Stopped them?"

"From killing me at Mangiamo's."

His gaze fell to the ground. "I'm not the same person anymore."

"But you are still my brother."

A black automobile drove up the driveway, and Antonio didn't speak again until it parked beside three other vehicles. The driver and one other man tipped their hats to Antonio as they walked toward the barn.

They must wonder what Antonio was doing, talking in the yard with an Amish woman, but they didn't comment on it. Her brother waited until the screen door slammed before he spoke again.

"I tried to stop them," he mumbled. "From hurting both of you."

For a moment, she caught the glimpse of sorrow in his eyes. The guilt. It was the same burden she'd carried with her for almost a decade. If she'd told her sister she wouldn't go with her to the restaurant, Liz wouldn't have gone alone. And if she hadn't run that night, she might have stopped them from killing her.

His voice was barely above a whisper when he spoke again. "There are some men inside that house who wouldn't hesitate to kill you if they realized who you are. I didn't help you back then so they could kill you today."

"Come with me," she offered one more time, but Antonio shook his head.

He kissed both of her cheeks, and she watched her brother walk away.

* * * * *

At the north side of the barn, Rollin threw a second rock toward the stone springhouse and the soldiers guarding the door finally noticed. His hand on his gun, one of the men moved away from the door to inspect the sound. Rollin threw one more rock for good measure and then ran toward the tree.

Swinging himself onto the first limb, he climbed the rest of the tree as quickly as he could. And carefully. The daylight blew his cover, and if the Cardano men found him now, the entire night would be ruined. In 1926 they'd had dozens of police officers trailing the Mafia elite through their city, but now it was just him. If

Antonio and the others discovered he was alone, he wouldn't be the one doing the chasing.

When he stepped through the window, he scanned the loft, and his gaze rested on where Katie spent the night beside him, asleep on his chest. He would never let Katie come with him tonight, but he wished she were here. He didn't want to be in this fight without her.

If he survived tonight, he would have to make a decision and so would she. A decision that could change the direction of both their lives.

Moving to the corner, he sat down in the pile of hay. Katie was so young when she became pregnant with Henry. If her boyfriend was such a good man, why did she leave him? It didn't make any sense. If Katie had been his, he never would have left her.

A pigeon flew across the loft and startled him. It flew to the other side of the gables and then back toward him again as his mind wandered to what it might be like to marry Katie Lehman. He'd never seriously considered marriage after he proposed to Liz, and especially not since he became a detective. But he'd never met a woman like Katie before.

Would she ever consider leaving the Amish community to be with him? And if she did, could they marry?

He tipped his head back against the hay and closed his eyes, thinking about what it would be like to wake up with Katie in his arms every morning. And go to bed with her every night.

She'd grown up with a father who'd manipulated and mistreated her, but if she'd have him, he would treat her with the kindness she deserved. He would love her with all his heart.

He shifted onto his side, trying to focus his mind back on his work tonight, but his mind wandered back to its dangerous dance of possibilities. He thought about Katie swinging on a porch alongside him.

Their porch. They were holding hands and laughing together as they watched Henry chase fireflies in the front yard.

If he ever married Katie, he wouldn't just become a husband overnight. He would be a father as well. The thought of rearing a boy like Henry should overwhelm him, but it didn't. Instead, it exhilarated him. The responsibilities of fatherhood aside, he would revel in the role. He could fish with Henry and play softball with him and perhaps even climb trees. He could even find someone who could take him and Henry flying.

He shook his head. He was fooling himself to think it would work.

First of all, Katie hated any idea of aggression or progress, and he represented both. She would never allow him to take Henry flying or talk to him about his work. Second, he couldn't risk having a wife or a child with his line of work. Even though some of the detectives had wives and children, they were forever afraid of what could happen to their loved ones.

A hay straw poked his face when he moved again, and he pushed it away.

Even if Katie were willing to allow him in her and Henry's life and even if he ignored the risks of marrying her, he could never take her back to Cleveland with him. He might put both Club Cardano and his son in jail tonight along with Malloy. But there were plenty of others who would seek revenge on their behalf.

As long as he was a detective in Cleveland, he had to remain a single man.

CHAPTER 30

Henry rested his head on her shoulder, and Katie savored the moment. It was their nightly ritual to sit on the ottoman and read from the Bible, but the past few days had been anything but normal for them.

This afternoon she'd known it would take a miracle for Antonio to ride away with her, but she believed in miracles. She also believed God gave second chances to people who were willing to forsake their sins and ask forgiveness.

Her brother wasn't willing to accept this gift, but tonight she prayed silently that Rollin would take it. And that as God's forgiveness poured over him, he also would forgive others, because vengeance against those who'd wronged him could never be satisfied, no matter how long or hard he fought. Only forgiveness would satisfy.

Henry picked the Bible off the coffee table in front of them and handed it to her.

"Can you read about David?" he asked. "David and Goliath."

She flipped through the pages. "I'd rather read the story of Ruth and Boaz."

"Please, Mamm," he persisted.

"Boaz was a strong man too."

"But I like King David."

Sighing, she turned to the book of 1 Samuel. It was Henry's favorite story in the Bible, and she couldn't tell him she wouldn't read it. After all, it was God's story about a warrior who'd served him. A man who'd failed God in terrible ways and yet he was still called a man after God's own heart.

Even as she began to read the story of David flinging his stone at Goliath, her mind wandered. Long before she came to live with the Lehmans, she abhorred violence. So many men had been killed at her father's hands, and even as a girl, she hated the rare times that her father patted her head or her shoulder. It was like the blood that contaminated his hands contaminated her as well.

Jesus said the peacemakers would be blessed, not the warriors, but as she read the story of David again to her son, she wondered if some people had to make peace by going to war. David had to kill Goliath so the Philistines would flee instead of conquering the rest of the Israelites.

Did Rollin have to defeat the Cardano family to keep thousands of others on the east side of Cleveland safe from harm? To keep the peace?

As Goliath fell under David's solitary stone in the story, she thought of Rollin alone at the barn tonight. Fighting the mighty Cardanos with the equivalent of a stone. He could never defeat them with his own power, but with God's strength behind him, perhaps he could defeat them alone.

After she finished the story, she led Henry upstairs to the mat beside her bed again and scratched his back until he fell asleep.

Rollin told Isaac that he was keeping the predators away, like Isaac did when one attacked his animals. If God could use a warrior like David to protect those He loved, why couldn't he use a man like Rollin Wells?

If only he would let go of his anger and surrender his pain—and his life—to the God who loved him. The God who could offer him peace and forgiveness and take away the guilt that crippled his heart.

Rollin might fight his battle with pistols and shotguns, but she had a different weapon.

In the darkness she knelt beside her bed.

She didn't pray for protection for Rollin Wells. She prayed he would surrender.

* * * * *

The men were gathered in the barn across the driveway to hear his father's proposal. Some of them had been waiting for hours, but his father still didn't bother to come down the stairs. Everyone knew how much Salvatore liked to make people wait. Time was power, and he believed no one's time was as valuable as his.

Antonio didn't want the men to wait. He wanted them to work.

He paced across the living room floor again and glanced up at the mantel clock. It was almost eleven, and all the pieces were in place. Raymond was waiting in a separate bedroom upstairs and Heyward Malloy was hidden in one of the automobiles. His henchmen were by the doors, watching for trouble. All the guests had agreed to leave their weapons in their vehicles for the meeting, but most of them would probably try to sneak in a pistol...or two. His guards agreed to search everyone except Raymond...and Salvatore.

His father would have a weapon, but he wouldn't be prepared to use it on his brother.

After Raymond got rid of Salvatore, Antonio was ready to explain the new vision for their union. A vision that would take them through the next decade. As long as he was alive.

Salvatore didn't know Raymond and Heyward were here, nor did he know all that encompassed this new direction for the union. It would be good for him to be surprised. And once he found out what was happening, it would be too late for Club Cardano to do anything except run.

The clock chimed, and Antonio stopped walking. He sat down on the piano bench and pounded a few notes on the keys.

Nothing had prepared him for the surprise he received today when Nikki walked back into his life. He'd never expected to see his sister again, and then she was there in front of him, wearing the garb of an Amish woman.

He shook off the fear that it was a bad omen to have Nikki near. The last time he'd seen her, everything went amuck. He couldn't risk failure tonight.

But at least, after all these years, he knew Nikki was all right. And Henry. Almost every day, he'd thought about her and wondered where she had gone. And whether she'd taken Henry with her or if Salvatore had taken the boy's life.

His parents had never spoken of Nikki or Liz again, at least he didn't hear them mention their names. After the funeral, they all pretended both Cardano girls were dead.

That night at Mangiamo's, he'd told Heyward and his uncles to stop, but no one listened to him. He wasn't the one who saved Nikki's life. It was Liz who stepped in front of her and told her to run.

In the confusion, they'd shot Liz and started to chase Nikki, but he blocked the entrance to the storm door so they could make a plan before they went blazing through Murray Hill, waking up the neighbors. Heyward was so desperate to stop Nikki from telling anyone she'd seen him with the Cardanos, he'd almost shot Antonio, but even as Liz lay dying on the ground before them, Heyward finally listened to reason.

Heyward said he would catch Nikki by himself and convince her not to talk, but none of them believed he would let her live. Not after what she'd seen. And his father didn't do a thing to stop Heyward.

In those short minutes that they'd talked about what to do with Nikki, his sister disappeared, and somehow she'd managed to take Henry with her. After the fire, he'd searched Murray Hill alongside the rest of the men, but even as he tramped through the trees looking for her, he secretly celebrated Nikki's escape. Somehow she'd broken free from the clutches of their silence and disappeared into a different kind of order.

He played a few notes of a jazz tune and then spun around on the seat.

This afternoon Nikki had come to him with the offer that he could break free as well. He'd thought about running before, but he was too close to the top to walk away. Tonight the entire organization would be under his control, and he'd put the fear of God into anyone who dared question his authority.

He stood up, and with a glance out the window, he saw more than a dozen black automobiles lined up beside the barn. These men would be leaving long before daylight, with a new direction for the future. And new leadership.

Most of the men hated Salvatore, but they'd had no choice but to work with him on some level. Tonight all of that would change. Tonight they would organize like his father suggested, but not on his father's terms.

He would cement in their minds that he wasn't going to mess around in this new union. His father would be gone after tonight, and so would Uncle Ray. He'd be the only one left standing, and after the fall-out, he would be in charge of the corn sugar racket in Cleveland.

Footsteps pounded down the stairs, and his father's presence overpowered the living area. "You can't play a lick of piano," Salvatore clipped.

"I wasn't playing for you."

His father stepped toward the door. "Is everyone here?"

"They are."

"Then why are you standing there like an idiot?"

Antonio opened the front door and his father bumped him as he pushed by.

The door slammed behind them, and Antonio smiled. The lion was leading himself to the slaughter.

* * * * *

Cigar smoke tickled Rollin's nose, and the barn was an eerie quiet as he stretched his arms. The black of night jelled into the cracks above him and light glowed below, but there was no sound of voices or shuffling of chairs or even the clearing of a throat. Gilbert and the Sugarcreek police were someplace in the blackness outside. Or at least he hoped they were. Without them, he would be dead.

Rollin snuck to the side of the loft. Below him about thirty men sat in stony silence, a cloud of smoke hovering above their heads. At the far end of the barn was a platform and podium, and directly under him, Rollin could see part of a table overflowing with food. None of the men moved toward the food.

He moved away from the edge, back into the shadows. These men weren't friends. They were competitors, forced together under the leadership of a floundering union that pitted one man against another. An eye for an eye. Each of them was probably packing at least one gun under his suit, and if someone started shooting, the aftermath would be devastating.

He fingered his gun. Maybe he should be the one to start the shooting.

Isaac Lehman had questioned Rollin's motives for capturing the Cardanos, and the man was right to ask. He wasn't seeking only justice for the Cardanos. He wanted revenge.

Something clicked—not in the barn below but in his mind. Something he'd heard as a boy, seated between his parents on the rare Sunday they went to church. The preacher had said that in God's eyes, there was no difference between someone hating his brother and killing them. Both hatred and murder were sins, and the reverend said they were all sinners.

All of them were sinners.

How he'd hated the Cardanos over the years, enough to kill them if he hadn't been a cop seeking his revenge for Liz's death instead. He wanted to do more than see one or two of them die. He wanted to see the entire Cardano kingdom destroyed and their racketeering networks ripped apart.

What if the reverend was right? Salvatore and Antonio and the others had cheated, killed, and thumbed their noses at the laws of their land, but they weren't the only ones who needed God's forgiveness. All the anger that burned within him needed to be forgiven as well.

But who was he apart from this anger? Apart from the man who'd spent his life intent on crushing the Cardano family?

Below him, several of the men looked toward the door, and Rollin caught his breath as Club Cardano strode into the room with Antonio in his shadow. The barn doors closed.

Rollin hadn't seen Salvatore since his appearance in the courtroom.

His shoulders were high, the notorious walking stick secure in his hands. He commanded the attention of everyone in the room without saying a word.

Still, he'd aged since Rollin saw him last, like he'd spent the last three years doing hard labor instead of running his organization.

Salvatore shook the hands of the men on the front row as he walked toward the platform with Antonio close behind him. On the stage, Salvatore handed his walking stick to his son and put both hands on the podium.

"We meet tonight as men of honor who know the power of an alliance."

The men of honor sat in silence as Salvatore presented his plan to organize the loose ties of their organization. Several men nodded as he talked about increasing each of their businesses, but others leaned back, crossing their arms. If they organized, there would be much discussion about who would take charge of the entire state. Rollin had no doubt Salvatore would nominate himself as boss.

The barn doors shook at the side of the room, and Rollin's eyes shifted to the left along with the rest of the men. When the elusive Raymond Cardano stepped into the room, the men gasped. But Uncle Ray didn't look the least bit afraid of his big brother.

CHAPTER 31

"Glad to hear you're finally going to organize." Uncle Ray's voice was an eerie calm as he walked toward the platform.

Salvatore laughed. "I thought you'd gotten yourself killed by now," he said to his brother. "Are you planning to join up with us?"

"More than that." Raymond paused. "I'm planning to run the organization."

"The devil you are." Salvatore pushed the podium, and the men in the front row scattered like ants as the wood splintered on the floor.

Antonio stood like a sentry beside his angry father. Any moment now, his uncle was supposed to tell the entire group that he and Antonio were partnering to run this organization together, but Uncle Ray didn't look at him. His eyes were focused on Salvatore.

"You did fine running the rackets in Cleveland, Salvatore, but everyone knows the Puglisis have been cutting into your business. These men need to be confident that their leader knows the business, not just in Cleveland, but across the state. A leader who won't allow some small-time operators like the Puglisis to steal away the profits."

Salvatore reached for the podium and almost stumbled when he realized it was gone. It didn't stop him from commanding the attention of his audience. "I hope none of you are listening to this nonsense. Raymond doesn't know a thing about running a successful racket."

"Oh, I don't know about that." Raymond stepped even closer to the platform. "Why don't you ask the boys from Cincinnati and Columbus about how I helped them?"

Salvatore's gaze traveled over the crowd, narrowing in on Tom Sandrelli. "Have you been working with Raymond?"

Tom stood up. "He helped us increase our distribution."

Salvatore swore.

Antonio stepped to the edge of platform. If Uncle Ray wouldn't tell them about their partnership, he would. "My uncle is right. We need new blood at the top of the organization."

Salvatore looked over at Antonio and stole the walking stick back out of his hands. He pointed it at his son. "You can't possibly think you are ready for this."

"I do, and Uncle Ray does as well." He nodded at his uncle, the signal for him to pull his gun on Salvatore.

But Uncle Ray didn't draw his pistol. Instead his lips twisted into a smirk.

The realization sickened Antonio. His uncle was double crossing him? He was supposed to be the one—

"You think Junior can run this organization?" Raymond asked the crowd.

Antonio glanced over at his father as voices rose in front of them. Salvatore's face had gone white.

He and Uncle Ray had a plan. Tom Sandrelli and many others said they supported Antonio as their new leader, but he didn't hear any voices of support in the audience. Instead there was confusion and dissent.

His uncle wouldn't meet his eye and neither would Tom. He looked for Emanuele, but he'd told his cousin to guard the door. He had no inkling that he would need a guard for himself.

Antonio stepped closer to his father. Suddenly, he feared for his life as well.

* * * * *

A bat buzzed by Celeste's head, and she waved her hands in front of her face. Her head swam, but she felt better tonight than she'd felt in a very long time.

She might be in Amish country, but she thanked her stars that the good folks about two miles down the road weren't the least bit Amish. Nor were they teetotalers. It didn't take much convincing when she opened her handbag and pulled out a roll of cash. They offered her the top pick from their collection of moonshine and a full meal along with it. She hadn't eaten much of the food, but she'd helped herself to the hooch. Yes, they were good folk, and their bitter drink even tasted half-good after she'd drained the second glass.

Her beaded purse hugged close to her side, Celeste swung around a tree that lined the driveway and then continued toward Nicola's Place.

The kids told her the real name of the farm when she dropped them off last night, but she'd forgotten who owned it. So she would tell everyone it was Nicola's Place. No one remembered the name of her daughter anyway. They'd all forgotten about what happened in the past.

Well, tonight they would never forget.

She wrapped her fingers over her mouth, trying to choke back her laugh, but she couldn't stop the giggle. It was too funny.

There were cars parked along the drive. Stupid men who thought they ruled the world, like no one could ever knock them off their thrones.

"One. Two. Three." She counted as she thumped her fists on the trunks of their fancy Lincolns and Cadillacs. Then she lost count.

Ahead of her, Nicola's Barn looked like a giant firefly in the woods, its belly glowing against the dark. Stumbling up to the door, she saw her nephew guarding the door, a gun at his side.

He jumped when he saw her. "What in the—"

She kissed his cheek. "Don't you dare try to stop me, Emanuele."

Then she twirled around and flitted around her nephew like the dancer she once was. No one could catch her if she flew.

The men had set up a stage in front of the room. Like they were politicians or something. Salvatore was on the stage next to their son, and a giggle escaped her lips at the walking stick shaking in his hands. Everyone thought the name Club came from the stick he liked to threaten people with, but really he was named after his greatest weakness. The nightclubs he loved.

"Hello, Sally," she hiccupped. "Whatcha doin'?"

The man in front of her husband turned around, and she realized it was Raymond Cardano. Just in time for the show.

She giggled again as she opened her purse.

Oh, this was funny. Too, too funny.

* * * * *

Rollin heard a giggle followed by the sharp pop of a pistol. The room exploded in chaos as men launched from their seats and began scrambling around the room and across the platform. His own gun was clutched in his hands, his focus riveted to both sides of the room as he waited for the onslaught of gunfire.

No one else fired his gun.

He strained his neck over the railing, trying to see who started the shooting. There was a woman below, but he couldn't see her face.

Her pistol in front of her, the woman's voice was clear when she spoke again. "Someone needs to head up this ridiculous organization, and it won't be Salvatore or Raymond."

The men backed away from Celeste and her gun.

"I want you to nominate my son to be in charge."

No one spoke.

"So," Celeste said, her voice cracking. "Are you fools going to nominate my son or do I have to shoot someone else?"

Rollin froze along with the rest of the crowd, thinking. For the past six months, Celeste had been feeding him information, saying she wanted to put an end to the Cardano organization. But maybe she didn't want to stop the organization. It could be that she was giving Rollin information so he could get rid of Salvatore. And Antonio would take over.

Celeste was the one who'd told him to be there the night Antonio's men took down Leone Puglisi, but Antonio hadn't done the killing. He could easily have blamed the murders on Salvatore's men.

Every bit of information she'd given him was meant to criminalize her husband so Antonio could take over. And he'd been a willing participant.

Rollin shook his head, frustrated by his foolishness, and then he looked at the stage again. Salvatore was still standing up, looking over something...or someone.

If Salvatore wasn't dead, who had Celeste?

CHAPTER 32

Never again would Salvatore harass Antonio and neither would any of his men. After tonight they would respect her, and they would respect her son.

"Antonio," she called out, the pistol steady in her hands. Antonio would love her now, after she'd taken such good care of him. And he would take care of her for the rest of her life.

She squinted toward the platform, but she couldn't see Antonio with all the men running around like chicks searching for their mother hen.

It looked like Raymond wanted to say something. She fixed the pistol on his head. Salvatore was dead, and she'd kill Raymond too if the men wouldn't listen to her.

"Antonio?" she said again.

Where was he? She'd done her part, now all Antonio needed to do was what he'd been born to do. Take charge. He needed to stand up and tell these men what they were supposed to do.

In front of her, the crowd seemed to part, and the dark hulk of a man plodded toward her.

It couldn't be.

She'd hit him. She was certain of it. The moonshine was making her see things. Nightmarish things.

"Sally?" she slurred. Then she pulled the trigger, but nothing happened. She stared down at her fingers and realized her gun was gone.

Who had taken her gun?

"You idiot," Salvatore said, towering over her. "You can't even shoot the right person."

She was on her tiptoes, desperately searching over his shoulder.

"Who—" she muttered.

"Now you've killed all of your children."

For a moment she couldn't breathe. Then her scream ripped through the barn.

She collapsed to her knees, calling Antonio's name over and over. Her son didn't answer. She begged Salvatore to shoot her, but her husband lowered the gun. Sorrow ballooned inside her, and she thought she would explode.

"Please," she begged Salvatore again.

A blast pounded her ears and something ricocheted through her body like lightning. As she fell to the ground, she welcomed the darkness. And the pain.

＊＊＊＊＊

Antonio tried to push himself off the floor, but he couldn't move his arms or his legs. People moved around him in a blur, but no one stopped to help him. When he cried out, no one seemed to hear him either.

Malloy was supposed to be in the barn, arresting Raymond for killing Salvatore. The men were supposed to see his authority with the police and his willingness to kill anyone for their organization, including his father. They were supposed to be listening to him right now, to the speech he'd prepared to lay out the future of their organization.

Except Raymond never pulled the trigger.

And his mother had come into the barn.

He saw the flash of silver in her hands. He heard her slurred words.

His own mother had tried to murder him.

* * * * *

Captain Malloy stood behind the body of Celeste, a smoking pistol in his hands. The barn doors flew open, and on the left, a half-dozen corrupt Cleveland police raided the building, guns in hand. On the right, Gilbert led the police troop from Sugarcreek.

Rollin bolted down the ladder from the loft and sprang onto the barn floor. For once, he was glad he wasn't alone.

The Mafia leaders looked back and forth at the police, not knowing who was playing on their team, and several began slipping their hands into the air. Malloy looked almost as confused as the rest of the crowd until his eyes rested on Rollin. He began to lift one hand, like he was going to greet Rollin, but instead of waving, his boss spun around and ran.

Rollin chased Malloy out the door.

If the captain made it back to Cleveland alone, he could make up any story he wanted about what happened to Celeste Cardano and to Antonio. It wasn't like any of the men here would testify against Malloy. It would be Rollin's word against the word of a popular police captain.

Malloy jumped into a Cadillac and the door slammed behind him. Rollin raced toward him with his gun ready. He would blow out the tires if he had to. Not that it would stop Malloy, but he couldn't go far.

The engine choked and sputtered when Malloy tried to start it. And then Rollin heard other cars sputtering around him.

Rollin chuckled. Gilbert had always been good at making sure the bad guys couldn't run.

He pointed his gun at Malloy's car as the man climbed out the passenger door. Malloy positioned his gun over the roof of the car, and Rollin ducked behind another one.

"You want me?" Malloy shouted.

"I want you to put down your gun so I can take you back to Cleveland without making a bloody mess in the car."

"I'll go back to Cleveland on my own, thank you. Without the blood." Malloy laughed. "It's too bad about you though."

"Don't worry about me, Malloy. I'll be returning home on my own as well."

Two of Cleveland's finest raced by them, headed toward the forest. Malloy yelled for the men to stop and help him, but they didn't even turn around. Apparently they were done taking orders from him.

"Was everyone on the force working for you?"

"Enough," Malloy said from behind the car. "And they are still working for me."

"Those men were quite devoted," Rollin said. "Did you hire Lance Dawson to keep tabs on me?"

Another man jumped out of a car and began running down the driveway.

"Lance wasn't smart enough to hide a needle in a haystack," Malloy smirked. "I just figured he was too green to find anything out."

Another gangster ran by the car, and in the moonlight Rollin recognized the great Club Cardano, fleeing like the common criminal that he was. Leaving his dead wife and his son and the loyal men in his organization behind.

"You played me for a fool, Malloy."

The man laughed. "It wasn't hard."

"I know you killed Liz."

"It was a darn shame to see her go too," Malloy said. "She was the prettiest of all the Cardanos."

Heat rose to Rollin's face even though he knew Malloy was trying to anger him.

Malloy ducked behind the car, and Rollin took a deep breath. "Why did you hire me to be a detective?"

"Because you were so intent on getting the Cardanos that you were blind to everything else."

Malloy was right. With his entire life focused on stopping the Cardanos, Rollin had missed the fact that his own boss was collaborating with them. Not only had he neglected to see the truth, he'd traded the past nine years of his life for this quest. He'd given up getting married, having a family of his own. He'd given up everything to get revenge.

Gravel crunched near the cars, but with other people running nearby, it was impossible to know if it was Malloy moving. Slowly, Rollin crept around the trunk of the car until he reached the back of Malloy's Ford.

Malloy called his name, and Rollin stole a glance around the car, searching where he'd last seen Malloy. The man wasn't there, so Rollin crawled toward the front of the car. As he rounded the hood, he saw the back of the police captain, searching for him.

Rollin thrust his gun out farther in front of him. He could pop Malloy off right now, for killing Liz and for ratting out Lance and for collaborating with the Mafioso. His finger pressed against the trigger, he wanted to pull it. Killing Malloy might get him his revenge, but perhaps that was for God to give. He would allow Malloy to face the justice system.

Behind him, the airplane engine started, and Malloy jumped at the sound. When he glanced over his shoulder at Rollin, his eyes grew wide.

"Drop the gun," Rollin said. He didn't want to shoot Malloy, but he would if the man didn't surrender.

Malloy slowly placed the gun on the ground and with hands up, he turned toward Rollin. The police chief from Sugarcreek and two deputies rushed from behind Rollin and started to secure Malloy's hands behind his back.

Malloy struggled against them. "Get your hands off me."

"Not until you're behind bars," the chief said.

"Do you know who I am?" Malloy asked the men.

The chief picked Malloy's gun up off the ground. "A criminal."

"I'm a police captain in Cleveland," he said, and then he nodded toward Rollin. "Rollin Wells is the criminal. He's been out here for a week, supporting the Cardanos."

The police chief looked from one man to the other.

"You know I'm not," Rollin told the chief. "I've been trying to find out what the Cardanos were planning."

"What they were planning?" Malloy said. "You helped them put together their plan and were probably paid quite handsomely for it."

Rollin kept his gun pointed on Malloy. "You are the one who's been collaborating with them for a decade now. They couldn't operate their business without you covering for them."

"Did you tell him what happened to your partner?" Malloy said. "How you shot him and left him to die?"

"That's not—"

The chief homed in on Rollin. "What happened to your partner?"

"Cardano's men murdered him when we got too close to the Bowman property, and they tried to kill me as well. Malloy told them we were coming."

"Ease off him," the chief told his two deputies behind Malloy.

Then one of the deputies stepped closer to Rollin, his eyes focused on Rollin's gun.

"You don't know what you're dealing with here," Rollin said.

"Come on," the chief said, motioning to him. "We'll sort it out back at the station."

An explosion knocked Rollin to the ground, the sound deafening. He'd been trained not to react in the toughest of situations, but he'd never been blown off his feet before. He turned for an instant, in time to see flames engulf the biplane.

The chief swore, and Rollin turned back. The moment he did, Malloy stepped backward. With the officers focused on the fire, Malloy ran into the trees.

The police chief looked stunned for a moment, by both the explosion and the disappearance of the captain from Cleveland.

"Stop him," Rollin yelled. And then he raced into the woods.

CHAPTER 33

Katie rolled over on the narrow bed, but she couldn't sleep. Rollin was still at the barn, and Henry was asleep in the room across the hallway. She edged her feet over the side of the cot and lit a match. The lantern illuminated her bedroom, and she moved around the bed, to a large chest.

From the top of the chest, she removed her winter coat and several dresses and quilts. Under the quilts, she found the small satchel that she'd packed when she ran away from Cleveland.

Dumping the satchel on the bed, she rifled through the things she'd tossed inside that fateful night. There were the baby clothes she'd taken for Henry—clothes he'd never worn in Sugarcreek. A mismatched skirt and blouse. Three pairs of fancy shoes. And the clothes she'd run away in—her navy blue skirt and silk blouse and the strapped shoes her mother gave her the night she ran out the back door. They would probably look almost as old-fashioned in the world now as her Amish garb, but it was all she had.

She took off her nightgown and began to dress in the skirt and blouse. She tossed the envelope with her mother's money into the satchel, and then her fingers fumbled with the buttons on the back of her satin blouse and blue skirt. She felt naked without her long skirt and her toes ached in her pointed shoes, but she couldn't go barefoot in an English outfit.

I don't want to be with Liz, I want to be with you.

She'd longed for those words most of her life, but she and Rollin could never be together. She couldn't return to Cleveland, and it wasn't fair to ask him to leave.

Her fingers shook as she brushed her hair over her shoulders. If only Rollin would steal her and Henry away from here, to a safe place where she could introduce her son to the good in the world instead of the bad.

She could never ask Rollin to run away with them. He'd spent his life trying to fight for justice, and he had to finish the job, but she'd be ready when he returned tonight. Ready to take Henry out into the world on her own.

She placed her brush in her satchel.

She'd promised to tell Rollin about Henry's father when he returned. Part of her prayed he would ask her again, but part of her was terrified for him to ask.

It would change everything between them.

She closed the lid of the trunk. Maybe she should wake Henry and leave now, before Rollin returned. It would save them both the agony of the truth, and the pain of having to say good-bye. She could wake Isaac and ask him to take her and Henry to Sugarcreek before daylight. She'd hire someone to take her to the train station in Dover for a ticket to the East Coast.

Or maybe they could go west.

One of the dogs barked below, and then she heard footsteps. The lantern in her hand, she slid out into the hallway. She hadn't expected Rollin to return until morning.

She walked across the hallway, and at the top of the staircase, she stopped. She expected to see Rollin, but there were two shadows below.

Her mind flashed back to the last time she'd been confronted by the shadows at Mangiamo's. The time she ran away.

But her son was upstairs now. And her aunt and uncle.

She took a deep breath and took another step forward.

These men hadn't come for Henry or the others. They'd come for her, and this time she wasn't running.

* * * * *

A woman walked down the steps toward them, holding a lantern in her hands. Her long hair was brushed straight over her shoulders, and she wore an outdated outfit, but it fit her so well that no man in his right mind would care about the style.

Recognition came slowly to him. He could hardly believe it was Katie.

"Where do you think you're going?" he asked, his voice husky.

"Rollin?"

She hung the lantern at the foot of the steps and walked toward him. Wrapping her in his arms, he didn't want to let go.

"You're all right?" she asked.

He held her out, staring at her again in the dim light. As he and Gil drove back from the Bowmans', he'd prepared himself to convince Katie that she and Henry needed to leave Sugarcreek until they found Malloy, but it didn't seem like she needed convincing after all.

Was she planning to leave without saying good-bye? Or maybe she figured he wouldn't come back alive.

"Were you leaving?" he asked.

Her voice shook. "I—"

Gilbert cleared his throat beside him, and he let her go.

"Katie, this is my former partner, Gilbert Simmons, and Gilbert, this is the old friend I told you about." Neither Gilbert nor anyone else needed to know Katie's relationship to the frayed family they'd left behind minutes ago.

"I don't recall you using the word 'friend,'" Gilbert said.

"Did you—" she started again, flustered. "How did it go?"

"Let's talk in the morning." He took her hand, gently squeezing it. "You will be here in the morning?"

She nodded.

"I hope you don't mind." He let go of her hand. "But I offered Gilbert a place to stay for the night as well."

"I'll move Henry," she said. "One of you can sleep on the floor."

"Actually, we'd prefer to sleep by the doors down here."

She didn't ask questions, but she insisted on feeding them sliced ham and bread before she brought enough pillows and quilts to pad the wood floor. Gilbert went through the sitting room to guard the back entrance. Rollin spread a quilt beside the front door.

Bennett lay down beside him, and when Rollin closed his eyes, all he could see was the ball of flames on the field. Gilbert said he hadn't touched Salvatore's airplane, so Raymond or one of the other men must have fixed it so there was no way that Salvatore could escape if he ran.

Salvatore was gone, and the Sugarcreek police took Raymond to the local jail along with dozens of others they arrested trying to run away. Antonio was barely alive when they lifted him up on a cot to take him to the town doctor. The bodies of Celeste and several others they would leave until morning, and hopefully they would find Malloy in the morning as well.

Orange and red flames blazed through Rollin's mind as he fell asleep on the floor, and then he was awake again, the morning rays heating the front door. The dog was gone, and Rollin's entire body ached.

If only the police hadn't listened to Malloy last night. His boss would be in prison, and Rollin and Gilbert would be getting ready to escort him back to Cleveland.

Henry shouted a good morning from the top of the steps, and then he bounded down the stairs and jumped on Rollin's back.

"Giddy up," Henry said, smacking Rollin's side.

Rollin stood up, lifting Henry to his shoulders, and he twirled the boy around. The sound of Henry's laughter drained away some of Rollin's weariness and frustration.

"I'm going to find a bed upstairs," Gilbert said as he dragged himself into the sitting room. A pillow was tucked under one arm and a quilt trailed behind him like a blue and white tail. The lines around his ex-partner's eyes looked as wrinkled as the quilt.

Henry tugged on Rollin's ear to steer him left.

"Where's your mother?" Rollin asked as he slowed his spin.

"Isaac—" Henry started, and Rollin stopped.

"What about Isaac?"

"He wasn't feeling real well again this morning so Katie went to the barn for him."

"Went out?" Rollin turned toward Gilbert. "You let her go outside alone?"

His old partner shrugged. "She said she had to milk the cows."

"You could have helped her."

Gilbert clutched the pillow tighter to his chest. "I don't know the first thing about milking cows."

"But Malloy—"

"Malloy doesn't know what my car looks like."

"But it's a car, Gil. In the driveway of an Amish home."

"We hid it behind the barn."

"He could still find it."

"You got the Cardanos," Gilbert said with a yawn. "And Malloy is on the run. He's miles from here by now."

Rollin looked out the front window. He couldn't see Gilbert's car, but Malloy was a smart guy and could be charming if he wanted. One of the neighbors might tell him about the visitor staying at the Lehmans' house.

Malloy wouldn't run until he found Rollin. Once he eliminated his former detective, Malloy could smooth things over with the Sugarcreek police and convince the chief back in Cleveland that he'd only been doing his job at the Bowmans' farm.

Henry on his shoulders, Rollin galloped to the back door. "Let's go check on your mother, champ."

"Maybe she'll let us help with the milking."

"Maybe."

Bennett was at his heels as Rollin stepped out into the yard. And as he walked, he glanced down at Henry's bare foot. At his toes.

Rollin blinked hard, and then he stopped.

"What's wrong?" Henry asked.

Rollin couldn't tear his gaze away from Henry's foot. At the smaller toe curved outward, like it was dancing away from the others. Just like Liz's toes.

Rollin shook his head and stepped forward again. "I have a few questions for your mother."

* * * * *

A pail of milk in each hand, Katie felt silly traipsing through the barn in her navy skirt and blouse. Now that she'd decided to leave Sugarcreek, it didn't seem right for her to continue hiding behind her kapp and dress. She wasn't an Amish woman nor would she ever be one. This place had been a safe harbor for her for years, and she was grateful for it, but she could no longer hide.

Through the barn door, Katie watched Rollin hurry across the driveway with Henry on his shoulders. It warmed her heart to see them together. And it tore it apart.

She opened her lips to call out to them, but before she shouted their names, she heard Bennett's growl. Outside the barn, someone stepped between her and the men she loved.

The man was lean, with a white shirt that had been wrinkled and stained with green, and his blond hair stuck up across his head like bent pieces of straw. She looked up at Henry, and every feature on his sweet face was paralyzed with fear.

The milk pails shook in her hands as she quietly set them down. The stranger's hands were in front of him, and she knew what he held.

She wouldn't let this wolf of a man threaten her son.

Removing a shovel from the wall, Katie tiptoed out the door. Rollin met her eye and picked Henry off his shoulders and put him on the ground. Her son was still focused on the stranger.

"Get behind me, Henry," Rollin said calmly, and her son obeyed.

"It won't help him a bit," the stranger said.

Rollin stepped forward. Henry was behind him, clinging to Bennett's neck. "You're not going to hurt a boy."

"I don't leave behind any witnesses, Rollin. No matter how old or how Amish."

The shovel was over her head, trembling in her hands as she crept out of the barn, into the sunshine. Her very breath a prayer. She wanted to startle the stranger, but not so much that he pulled the trigger. Just so he faced her.

When she was about four feet behind him, Katie whistled. The man turned around.

"No—" he started, but before he finished, the shovel hit his gun.

The pistol blast rang in her ears, and she raised the shovel again, prepared to do whatever she had to do to protect her son. But she saw Rollin at that moment, twisting the stranger's arms behind his back. The gun was on the ground, and one of the man's brown shoes was soaked with blood.

"Do you remember Heyward Malloy?" Rollin quipped.

She threw the shovel on the ground, and for an instant, she was back in the basement at Mangiamo's, watching Heyward pull his gun out of his jacket.

She glanced down at his bloody shoe. Heyward had tried to shoot at her again, but this time he'd shot himself.

Henry rushed into her arms and she hugged him close to her. Isaac and Gilbert dashed out the door behind them. Isaac in his nightclothes. Gilbert with handcuffs clanging at his side. Heyward moaned in pain as Gilbert clicked the cuffs around his wrists.

"What happened?" Isaac asked.

"There was a wolf," she said, flustered. "And he was going to kill my son."

Isaac paused, looking at the gun on the ground and the shovel by her feet. She wondered if he was going to berate her in front of Heyward for her violence, but he didn't. Instead, he simply said, "Well done."

She felt Heyward's glare on her, and when she turned toward him, his face turned white.

"You…" he stuttered. "I thought you were dead."

Instead of responding, she looked at Rollin. "Can you take him away from here?"

Rollin nodded. "We'll take him to the jail in Sugarcreek until we can escort him to Cleveland."

"I'm not going to jail," Heyward said, but they all ignored him.

Rollin was still looking in her eyes, searching for something. "You want to drive to Sugarcreek with me?"

She stepped back from him. She didn't want to leave Henry, and she shouldn't spend another moment alone with Rollin, but then Isaac put a protective arm around Henry. And she did want to find out what happened last night.

"I'll stay with the family," Gilbert said.

"Then I'll go."

Rollin yanked on Heyward's arm, but before they stepped toward Gilbert's automobile, Erma came rushing out of the house with her medicine bag in her hands.

"You're not leaving until I look at his foot."

Rollin hesitated, but Erma was right beside him. "The man may be following the wrong master, but he's still a child of God."

Rollin shoved Heyward toward a log and he sat down. Erma tapped a vial of feverfew over a spoon and told Heyward it was for his pain. At first, Heyward refused to take the medicine, but when Erma began to shake the powder back into the vial, he changed his mind.

Erma removed Heyward's shoe and sock, and he moaned as she cleaned the blood around his wound and wrapped it. Then she told

Rollin to find a doctor after he took Heyward to the jail.

Rollin hooked his fingers under Heyward's arm. As he directed his former captain to the backseat, Katie kissed Henry and climbed into the passenger seat.

CHAPTER 34

Rollin sat across from Katie on the picnic table, across from the Sweet Shoppe. She licked the strawberry ice cream on the cone, savoring its coolness. On one side of them dozens of children with dolls and toys and wagons paraded through the street fair, and on the other side of the park, weeping willows drooped over a slow-moving stream.

The Sugarcreek police had taken custody of Heyward without question this morning, and Rollin told the chief he would escort Heyward back to Cleveland later today. But in their last hours together, Rollin didn't talk to her. Instead he just stared.

She held out the ice cream cone. "You want a lick?"

"I don't like ice cream."

She laughed. "How is that possible?"

"I'm an oddity."

"I figured that out a long time ago."

He didn't even smile.

The ice cream dripped on her hand, and she licked it. "It might help if you told me what happened last night."

"I'm not ready yet."

"Okay." She fidgeted on the bench. "Why do you keep staring at me?"

"It's strange to see you in ordinary clothes."

"You think I look ordinary?"

"No—" he said. "I think you look beautiful."

The heat from her blush traveled up her neck, and she turned her head away from his gaze. Not that he couldn't still see the red, but maybe he wouldn't be able to see the pleasure in her eyes.

An Amish couple walked toward the park, laughing together as they enjoyed ice cream cones, and she realized it was Jonas Miller alongside Greta Hershberger. Both of them were smiling.

"Look at that," she whispered, and Rollin turned his head.

"Katie?" Jonas asked as they got closer, his eyes wide with surprise at her attire.

"Hello, Jonas," she said with a curt nod. "Greta."

She wasn't angry at either of them, but still she felt uncomfortable. Just days ago Jonas had asked her to marry him.

"You look—" Greta started, but struggled to finish the statement.

"Different," she said.

"Ya. Different."

She looked at Jonas. "I'm leaving Sugarcreek."

Something flickered in his eyes. Relief, maybe. "Isaac and Erma will miss you."

"And I will miss them."

Greta leaned closer to her. "Did you hear what happened at the Bowmans' place last night?"

"Not yet." She glanced at Rollin. "But I was about to."

Jonas stepped away from her. "You will be safer if you leave."

"I pray so."

Greta took one of her hands and squeezed it. "You come back and visit us, Katie Lehman."

She smiled. "I will visit one day."

And when she did, she guessed she would meet a few of Jonas and Greta's children.

As they walked away, Rollin leaned forward. "Are you all right?"

"I am," she said, and she meant it. Jonas deserved a woman devoted to him, and Greta was the perfect one.

Rollin studied her face again, so intently that she rubbed away the goose bumps on her arm. "You won't be able to visit Erma and Isaac after you leave."

She leaned forward. "Why not?"

"It's too dangerous for you to come back."

The thought sobered her. She'd hoped she could come visit, but he was right. Now that Heyward knew where she'd lived, he or some of his men would find her.

"What happened last night?" she asked.

He shook his head. "I want to talk about this morning first."

The ice cream dripped on her hand again, and she looked down. She'd forgotten she was holding it. "What happened this morning?"

"I gave Henry a ride on my shoulders."

She took another lick. He was trying to tell her something, but she didn't understand. "He loves shoulder rides."

"Katie—"

When he hesitated, she lowered her cone close to the table. "What happened, Rollin?"

He took a deep breath. "I saw Henry's toes."

"His toes?" she said with a laugh, and then her laughter crumbled.

Henry's adorable, curved toes. Just like the woman who'd birthed him.

Her strawberry ice cream splattered across the picnic table.

She tried to breathe, but her very breath had been stolen away. Rollin knew her secret.

She stood from her bench, and Rollin stood up on the other side, both of his hands on the table.

"Henry's not your son, is he?"

Her back stiffened. "I didn't birth him, Rollin, but he's my son."

"Is Liz the mother?"

Katie cringed. "She birthed him, but she never wanted to be his mother."

Confusion washed through Rollin's eyes. Questions. She didn't want to answer any of them. All she'd wanted to do was leave the past alone.

"Liz birthed him…" His voice trailed off. "Who is Henry's father?"

She didn't reply.

"Katie?"

All she could do was shake her head.

Rollin collapsed back on the bench. "Dear God—"

Her fingers swiped across her skirt. Up and down like she was whitewashing a fence. She didn't know what to say or do.

"Why didn't she tell me?" he implored

"When I left Cleveland, I thought you knew." She sat down across from him. "I thought you didn't want the baby."

"I wanted to marry her." His gaze wandered over to the trees. "I would have taken care of her and Henry."

"I know that now."

"She should have told me."

"Liz didn't want a baby."

"That's no excuse."

"And our father didn't want anyone to know Henry existed. That's why you didn't see Liz for so long. He sequestered her for most of her pregnancy and then wouldn't let her out of the house after Henry was born."

"That night at Mangiamo's," Rollin said. "You never told me why you and Liz were there."

"Liz wanted something from the locked room downstairs, and she asked me to play guard."

"Was she looking for money?" he asked.

"Probably."

"She was going to run away from home," he said, his voice trailing off.

As Katie had replayed that night over and over again through the years, she remembered how focused her sister had been on retrieving that metal box. And elated. Looking back, she assumed Liz was preparing to break free of their father's grip.

"Was she going to take Henry away with her?"

Katie wiped the sweat off her forehead. "I don't know."

"And yet you took him." Rollin's eyes were steady on her again. "You brought him to a safe place."

"I was afraid my father would get rid of him."

"Kill him?"

She paused. "I hope he would have given him to someone who couldn't have a child."

"And I would never have known I have a son," Rollin whispered.

Tears sprang to her eyes. This was the moment she'd dreaded since she left Cleveland. The moment Rollin Wells would want Henry back. How could she keep the boy from his father?

She met Rollin's gaze again and saw tears clouding the strength in his eyes. "You did all of this for Liz?"

She shook her head. "I did it for Henry."

And she did it for the man standing in front of her.

* * * * *

Rollin paced down to the stream as memories accosted him, all of them battling for his attention in a confused jumble of pictures and words. For so long, he'd fought off the desire to have a family, but he had a son. A smart, passionate, funny boy.

He fell down on the bank, beside one of the willows, and stared at the water. He knew Henry was his. Almost ten years ago, he'd come back from the war, and Liz snuck in through the back door of his house while his parents were sleeping to welcome him home. At the time, it was exactly what he wanted.

As the weeks passed, Liz stopped coming to his home, and she sent him a letter asking that he stop visiting her as well. He went to the Cardanos, demanding to see her, but Salvatore refused to let him inside. He kept trying over the next few months, even sending her a letter asking her to marry him, but after his proposal, all his letters to her were returned.

His shoulders slumped as the memories became even clearer. For years, he'd thrown his fist in the air at God, angry at him for taking Liz away. He'd blamed God when he should have blamed the woman who planned to leave their son behind when she ran.

And, even more, he should have blamed himself.

He raked his hands through his hair. The reverend was right. He was just as much of a sinner as the Cardanos. He'd impregnated his girlfriend, but he hadn't been there to take care of their child.

If only he hadn't touched Liz. Or if he'd known about the child. Perhaps Liz would still be here.

Heyward Malloy hadn't killed Liz. He had.

He buried his head in his hands, and with Katie's hands on his shoulders, he begged God to forgive him of his terrible sins.

* * * * *

Rollin's shoulders bobbed under his jacket, and Katie wasn't quite sure what to do. She'd never seen a man cry before, and she wasn't even certain Rollin was crying right now, but God had broken Rollin into tiny pieces today. As she waited, she prayed silently that God would now rebuild him into a mighty servant of His.

Minutes passed, and Rollin turned to her. His eyes were red, but his voice was clear. "I'm so sorry, Katie."

She let go of his shoulder. "I forgave you a long time ago."

"Does Henry know about Liz?"

She shook her head. "The truth is too dangerous."

Taking her hand, he stood up beside her. "Thank you for what you've done with him."

She released his hand. "I won't let him go, Rollin."

He eyed her for a moment, and she was prepared if he challenged her. There were a hundred reasons why she should keep Henry with her.

"You don't have to."

She released the air imprisoned in her lungs.

"I don't want Henry to know about me," he said. "Not yet."

She rubbed her arms, watching his face to see if he was hiding something from her. "All right."

"After what happened this morning…" Rollin hesitated. "Too much is happening right now."

Even as she nodded her head, disappointment pricked her heart.

Her sister had been planning to run away from her responsibilities, and now… She didn't want Rollin to take Henry away from her, but was he going to run away from his son too?

"Malloy is in jail," he continued, "but they didn't catch all of his men. If they found out about you—"

"I'm ready to leave." She stepped back and then hesitated. She couldn't take Henry to the coast yet. "You need me to testify at the trial."

He shook his head. "You won't be safe in Cleveland either."

"But I'm the only one who can talk about what happened at Mangiamo's."

"You and your uncle Ray."

"He won't say anything."

"We'll give him an offer he can't refuse."

She stood up a little straighter. "Where is my father?"

"Your father." He hesitated. "A lot of people got hurt last night."

"Is he dead?"

When he nodded, she wished she felt sadness, but all she could feel was relief.

"And my brother?"

"Antonio was shot, but the police chief wasn't certain of his condition."

There was no relief with those words. "Who shot him?"

He shook his head, his gaze wandering back to the creek.

"Rollin?"

"She didn't mean to shoot him."

Her knees wobbled under her skirt. "She?"

"Your mother," he finally said. "She was drunk, and she had a gun."

Her father was dead. Her brother injured by their mother's gun.

Her entire body felt like the Jell-O Erma liked to make. Those who were supposed to love her failed her a long time ago, and they continued to fail her.

She was glad she had taken the Lehman name for her and Henry. Never again would she consider herself part of the Cardano family.

She reached for Rollin's arm and turned him toward her.

"What—?" She swallowed hard. "What happened to my mother?"

"Malloy..." he started. "He killed her."

"Did she suffer?"

He met her gaze and held it. "I think she was relieved."

Katie fell into Rollin's arms, and he kissed the top of her head as he cradled her. He murmured apologies into her ear, like somehow he could have stopped the Cardano massacre, but she hushed him. The demise of her family wasn't his fault.

Gently he held her away from him, looking back into her eyes. "You are Henry's mother, and you always will be."

Tears filled her eyes.

"And if you'll have me, I want to be part of your and Henry's life."

She started to talk, but he put his fingers on her lips.

"But before we talk about the future, I have to get Malloy and the others behind bars."

She moved back from his touch. "And you have to stop the Cardano rackets."

"There won't be much left to stop," he said. "Last night they crushed their own organization without help from anyone."

"Pride goes before destruction..." she quoted from Proverbs.

"Katie." He nudged her chin up to meet his eyes again. "Where do you want to go from here?"

"As far away from Cleveland as possible."

"Like California?"

Her mind wandered to the pictures she'd seen of the Pacific Coast. The ocean lapping up against the rocks. The miles of sandy beach. The small towns where no one would know who she was or where she came from.

"California sounds really nice."

A smile came slowly to his lips. "And what do you think about airplanes?"

She groaned.

"Henry will want to take an airplane."

She leaned down and tossed a rock into the creek. "Can you fly an airplane all the way to California?"

He nodded. "You'll have to make a few stops along the way."

She picked up a second rock and threw it into the water before she turned to him. "Then I suppose Henry should ride in one."

He took her hand and escorted her back to the car.

EPILOGUE

Six months later

Salt water sprayed Katie's skirt, and Rollin heard her squeal as she raced back toward Henry on the beach. The cold air didn't seem to bother Henry. His long pants were soaked from the wet sand, but his focus was on the cupful of sand he was adding to one of his castle towers.

The breeze rattled the palm trees along the coastline, and a rich purple colored the horizon. From the edge of the cliff, he watched Katie wrap her arms over her sweater. She'd cut her hair since he'd said good-bye to her, and it twirled around her shoulders. She was full of life, like she'd been when she was a girl.

He'd meant to surprise her and Henry at their cottage in Morro Bay, but as he watched them leave the house, his resolve withered. So much could have happened in six months. Now that Katie had found a new life, perhaps she had found a new love as well. Or maybe he reminded her too much of the old life she was trying to leave behind.

What if she changed her mind like Liz had done and turned him away?

He patted the ring in his coat pocket. He no longer wanted to pursue the entire Cardano family. He only wanted to pursue Katie.

As the tide edged closer to the castle, Katie lifted her skirt above her knees and knelt down. She took one of the cups and helped Henry finish the turrets before the water washed them away.

His heart warmed as he watched them.

In the past six months, he'd worked with the district attorney to put Heyward Malloy behind bars along with Raymond Cardano and a number of other men in their organization. He'd discovered that Raymond had been working with the Puglisi family for a long time, and in his supposed leadership of the Cardanos, he was planning to bring them under the umbrella of the Puglisis.

Because of Raymond's testimony, he received a shorter sentence than the rest of them, but he would still be behind bars for at least a year. Antonio probably wouldn't end up in the slammer, but the doctors said he would never be able to walk again. His body would serve as his own personal prison for his remaining years.

He and Katie had been writing letters, two or three every week, and he'd told her about the sentence for Malloy. He also told her that the police found the body of Lance Dawson buried near the barn, and Lance's family gave him a proper burial in Cleveland.

In her letters, Katie told him how much Henry enjoyed the long journey west by airplane. So much so that he continued to talk about their flight almost every day. She told him Isaac and Erma moved to Pennsylvania to be closer to Isaac's family, and while she didn't say it, he assumed they wanted to get lost in the sea of other Amish couples living in Lancaster County in case one of Malloy's friends came looking for them.

Rollin sent her money each month for Henry, but she still found work in Morro Bay, helping care for twin girls while Henry was in school.

On the beach below him, he watched the waves swoop through Henry's castle, collapsing the towers. And then Katie picked up their towel.

Rollin scooted back from the edge of the cliff and waited in the tall grass for Katie and Henry to climb the rocks. Either Katie didn't see him at first or she didn't recognize him. Her hair blowing in the wind, she mounted her bicycle. Henry got on his bicycle behind her, and they began riding toward him.

And then Katie saw him.

"Rollin?" she gasped.

Leaving her bike on the grass, she took Henry's hand and they ran to him. He pulled both of them close. Katie's soft hair against his cheek and Henry hanging on to his waist.

She stepped away. "You're supposed to be at the trial."

"It finished over a week ago," he said. "Malloy will spend the rest of his days in the pen."

Relief washed through her eyes as quickly as the tide had washed through their sand castle.

"We've missed you, Rollin." Her voice softened. "I've missed you."

He smiled. It was exactly what he needed to hear.

"How is your arm?" she asked.

He held it out. "All better."

"I'm so glad."

An awkward pause followed her words. It was his turn to talk, but the words seemed to catch in his throat.

Finally, he put his hand on Henry's shoulder. "I was hoping to talk to Henry alone for a moment."

Fear crept back into her eyes. "Why?"

"I wanted to share a small bit of my story with him."

Henry stepped toward Katie. "Please, Mamm."

She hesitated at first, and then she nudged him forward.

He and Henry walked through the grass until they found two black rocks overlooking the sea and sat down. Waves crashed into the rocks below, shooting water into the air.

"You are one lucky fellow, Henry, to have a mother who loves you so much."

"I know, but don't tell her. I hate it when she cries."

"Women," Rollin said with a roll of his eyes.

The boy sighed, shaking his head. "Women."

"Did you know I was friends with your mother's sister and her brother a long time ago?"

The boy's eyes grew wide. "I didn't know she had a brother...or a sister."

"I'll have to tell you about them sometime."

Henry wiped his hands over his gray pants coated in sand, and Rollin looked out at the purple haze rolling toward them. One day Rollin would tell him the entire story.

"I've never been married before," Rollin said.

"Ya, Mamm told me."

"But I've always wanted to have a wife and children, especially a son."

Henry smiled at him. "You'd make a good daed."

"The thing is, I'd really like it if I could be a daed. If I could be a father to you."

"To me?" Henry asked, excitement building in his voice. Then he paused. "But I can't leave Mamm."

"Of course not," Rollin said, drumming his hands on the rock. He was terrible at this. "I was sort of hoping your mother would become my wife."

"Really?"

"But I'm afraid she might say no."

Henry hopped up from the rock. "I'll help you ask her."

"You will?"

Henry tugged on Rollin's jacket until he stood. "She can't say no to both of us."

Together they walked toward Katie, Rollin's hand on his son's back. He prayed Henry was right.

There were questions in Katie's eyes as they stood in front of her, both for him and for Henry, but instead of answering them, he pulled a small velvet box from his pocket. And he kneeled on one knee in the sandy grass.

Henry kneeled beside him.

Katie's lips trembled as she watched him. He cleared his throat.

"I'd like to ask you a question."

Henry elbowed him, and Rollin smiled.

"We would like to ask you a question."

Katie glanced back and forth between the two of them kneeling before her. Rollin popped open the lid on the velvet box, and the sun's reflection made the diamond sparkle with color.

Her hands rushed to her throat.

"We've spent so much time talking about the past, Katie, but I don't want to talk about our past any longer. I want to talk about our future."

"Our future?"

Henry sighed. "He wants to marry us, Mamm."

"Technically, I want to marry you," he told her with a quiet laugh. "But I would be honored if you would allow Henry to be my son."

Henry stood up. "I already said 'yes.'"

Katie clapped her hands together and held them tight. "It looks like you two gentleman already have it figured out."

Rollin rose to his feet and stepped closer to her. And he whispered, "I love you with all my heart, Katie Lehman."

There were tears in her eyes when she looked up at him. "And I love you."

"Will you be my wife?"

"Ya." She laughed. "I've wanted to marry you for a very long time."

He removed the ring and slid it on her finger. Then he cradled her head in his hands and fire danced between them.

Henry elbowed his way into the center of them, his hands on his hips. "No one said anything about kissing!"

Katie leaned over and kissed Henry on the forehead. Rollin laughed when his son wiped it off.

He rested his arms around Henry's shoulders again as they walked toward the bikes. The Cardano family was behind him. And the path before him was better than he ever imagined.

"I don't want to lose you again," he whispered.

Katie kissed him softly on the ear and entwined her fingers around his.

"Then don't let go."

AUTHOR'S NOTE

Two very different worlds collided in *The Silent Order*, and I knew very little about either one when I began working on this novel. To research the story, I visited Cleveland first and explored the historic (and mysterious) Lake View Cemetery and the quaint streets and cafes along Mayfield Road in Little Italy. Then I drove south to Sugarcreek and spent several days touring the hills and farmland. My hosts were a delightful Old Order Amish couple who shared their lives and stories with me. I am extremely grateful for their insight and their hospitality.

Many people and resources helped me understand the culture of the Mafia in the 1920s and the Amish. Any errors are entirely my fault.

A special thank you to Rick Porrello, author of *The Rise and Fall of the Cleveland Mafia*, founder of the Web site americanmafia.com, and Cleveland-area police chief. Not only did the extensive information in Rick's book persuade me to set this novel in Cleveland, but his generosity in sharing original research material and stories passed down from his ancestors (seven of whom were Cleveland Mafia leaders during Prohibition) helped add authenticity to my fictional take on Cleveland's gangs.

Monk and Marijane Troyer from Sugarcreek helped me understand Amish culture and what it was like to live in an Amish family in the 1930s. Thank you for answering my many questions, no matter how odd (and some of them were very odd!). And thank you, Connie Troyer, for all your guidance and for helping me get the resources and information I needed.

Thank you, Pinn Crawford, for obtaining stacks and stacks of research books for me, and thank you to my friend and favorite fire marshal Kate Stoller for brainstorming with me about how Celeste would have set the kitchen fire and how the smoky smell would linger in her house along with her memories. One day I want to write an entire novel with you.

Thank you to my wonderful agent, Sandra Bishop, whose constant support and friendship have been a gift from God. She helped brainstorm the idea of setting this novel during Prohibition and encouraged me to pursue it. I'm so grateful for you, my friend.

Another huge thank you to the team at Summerside. You ladies and gentlemen are a gift as well. Thank you to Carlton Garborg, whose ideas and vision sparked the writing of *The Silent Order*. Thank you to Susan Downs for all of your insight and help in brainstorming the plot. And thank you to Jason Rovenstine, Rachel Meisel, Suzanne McDonough, and to Ellen Tarver, who did a tremendous job editing the manuscript.

Several girlfriends blessed me by reading a rough version of this novel and giving me their feedback. Thank you, Kelly Chang, Rebecca Fechter, Kimberly Felton, Leslie Gould, and Michele Heath for your insight, suggestions, and most of all, for your friendship. I love you ladies!

I'm so grateful to my friends and family who have encouraged and prayed me through my writing journey—Jim and Lyn Beroth, Christina Nunn, Carolyn Dobson, Tosha Williams, Earl Weirich, Jodi Stilp, Laurie Timberlake, and Miralee Ferrell. And I'm grateful to my friends at my favorite coffee shop—Dorie, Mary, and Jake. Thanks for taking such good care of me while I'm on deadline.

I couldn't have written this book without the support of my

husband Jon and my two precious girls, Karly and Kiki, who make sure Mommy works hard to make her deadlines. I love you all so much.

And, most of all, I'm thankful to the greatest storyteller of all for His love, His justice, and for His grace.

To God be the glory!
Melanie Dobson
www.melaniedobson.com

P.S. Not long after I began writing this book, one of our best friends was lost in the Haiti earthquake. Like King David in the Bible, David Hames was a man who followed after God's heart. Workers searched for four weeks before they discovered David had gone home to be with the Savior. This book is dedicated to our dear friend who is now playing his ukulele and (according to my daughter) singing "God Loves You So Much!" down the streets of gold. We miss you, David!

summerside
PRESS™

Soul-stirring romance...set against a historical backdrop readers will love!

Summerside Press™ is pleased to present our fresh new line of historical romance fiction—including stories set amid the action-packed eras of the twentieth century.

Watch for a number of new Summerside Press™ historical romance titles to release in 2011.

NOW AVAILABLE IN STORES

Sons of Thunder
BY SUSAN MAY WARREN
ISBN 978-1-935416-67-8

The Crimson Cipher
BY SUSAN PAGE DAVIS
ISBN 978-1-60936-012-2

Songbird Under a German Moon
BY TRICIA GOYER
ISBN 978-1-935416-68-5

Stars in the Night
BY CARA PUTMAN
ISBN 978-1-60936-011-5

Nightingale
BY SUSAN MAY WARREN
ISBN 978-1-60936-025-2

COMING SOON

Exciting New Historical Romance Stories by These Great Authors—
Margaret Daley...DiAnn Mills...Lisa Harris...and MORE!